The Subtle Psychopath

*Who can you trust when your
world falls apart?*

Pippa Barnes

To Doug & Nelly Chatburn

When the world says,
"Give up",
Hope whispers,
"Try it one more time".

UNKNOWN

Contents

Prologue

The girl was in control. By the tender age of five she had twisted her parents, like play dough, tightly round her little finger. Fiercely self-sufficient, she shunned her parent's protection, shying away from physical contact and spurning their cuddles. Her parents felt abandoned by their daughter's rejection. They tried to be tactile but she withdrew behind an invisible barrier she only crossed when it suited her. On those occasions she crawled onto her father's lap or flung her arms around her mother's neck in rare displays of warmth. Her parents basked in these glimpses of affection and always gave in to her desires.

Outwitting her mother and father came easily to the girl; their weaknesses as glaring as the bright gold buttons on her teddy bear's coat. Power over them was central to her sense of security and well-being. If she thought she was losing grip on the reins she had a number of weapons in her armoury. One was to scare the wits out of them by seeming to stop breathing with a dramatic gasping for air. Another was to throw an almighty tantrum and fling herself around in a frightening show of angry aggression. Ultimately, she always maintained her position in the driving seat.

In other times her parents would not have tolerated their daughter's outlandish and uncooperative behaviour. They would have taken draconian measures with the approval of friends, relatives and society in general. But this was the 1980s and precocious behaviour was considered to be a sign of intelligence. People were expected to use clever ways to discipline their children. The hapless couple agonised over how to influence the child into becoming more civil and less demanding.

They consulted books and health professionals but eventually concluded no advice was pertinent to their daughter. They tried every route they could think of to win authority over the girl but she wore them down to servility. So, they lived from day to day trying to keep the child stimulated and happy; grateful for the good days and struggling through the bad. They loved their daughter and consoled themselves her behaviour was due to her high intellect and would improve with age. They took the easy way forward and conceded to her every demand; responding with apology to her complaints. That kept her calm and allowed them to live in a fragile kind of peace and harmony. The girl hated visitors. Outsiders were less tolerant of her truculent manner and often voiced their disapproval. Some tried to influence her through reasoning, shaming and even threats. The girl resented their unsolicited comments. She answered their endeavours with a contemptuous stare; her striking steel blue eyes shooting icy chills straight through them. Her parents defended their daughter's behaviour, frustrating and nullifying any alien intervention.

As far as the girl was concerned all outsiders were a nuisance and an intrusion. She just wanted to be left alone and not have her life interrupted by finger-wagging busy-bodies. She was always pleased to see them leave and in gratitude rewarded her parents with several hours of exemplary conduct, giving them a taste of what life could be like with an appreciative good-natured daughter.

The family had thus developed into an isolated unit of three presided over by the child. That's what made it so shocking and devastating for the girl when one morning her parents approached her, together as a united front, and told her they had a *secret* they wanted to share. She was irritated by the interruption of her game but became wary when they asked her to sit between them on the sofa. They seemed different; an air of excitement hung about them. She saw straight through the *secret* ruse, guessing it was a ploy to distract her from the actual thrust of their news. She reluctantly sauntered to the sofa and perched on the edge between them.

She shrugged off her mother's attempt to put an arm round her shoulder whilst her father, exchanging a raised eyebrow with his wife, handed her a book entitled "New Baby to Love". The girl looked at the book and was momentarily puzzled, but her father soon revealed the horror. Her mother was pregnant! A new member of the family was going to join them in about five months!

The girl was distraught. Her life had instantly been turned upside down. The blow was devastating, an outrage. Her parents tried to tell her how nice it was going to be to have a little brother or sister. How could they say such a thing!? She didn't even like visitors, why would they imagine she'd want another person permanently living with them!?

Over the following months her parents doggedly tried to convince her it would be lovely to have a younger sibling. She was NOT impressed. She showed them her contempt but that just made them try harder. She tired of hearing their continual assurances that she would be pleased when the baby arrived. Meanwhile, with each inch her mother's midriff grew, the little girl's measure of the situation became more disturbed. Her mother grew physically unable to pander to the girl's demands and her father was increasingly indulging his wife and paying less attention to his daughter. She had lost control and there was nothing she could do but witness her world falling apart.

When Annie was born the little girl felt nothing but resentment and loathing for her crying, writhing little sister. She hadn't wanted to share one iota of her parent's attention but now she found they hardly had any time for her; they only had eyes for Annie. The girl folded in on herself, silently watching her parents and Annie as though from a distant planet.

As Annie grew into a toddler it became apparent she had a naturally amiable character, always ready with a smile and charming her parents and outsiders alike. For the parents Annie was a breath of fresh air and a vindication of their parenting skills. The girl's bitterness deepened, her jealousy intensified.

At any opportunity she avenged her sister, giving sly shoves or punches, snatching toys and even putting dirt in her sister's food. Her mother was exasperated by her older daughter's envious antics and, unable to reason with her, had to keep constant watch over baby Annie. That intensified the girl's sense of rejection.

Each day the girl's loathing for her sister deepened, she became increasingly consumed with hate. Her parents gave up trying to foster any sisterly love in their older child, just as previously they had given up on disciplining her. The family teetered on, the parents ignoring their first child's jealousy and pretending everything was fine, even though they never left Annie alone with her sister.

There was one particular summer's day that would remain in the girl's memory forever. She was about seven years old and it was a hot and sultry day, rare in England. The family had gone on a day trip to Weston-super-Mare to enjoy the sand and sea breeze. When the heat became too fierce they left the beach and found a small restaurant for lunch. There was a bit of fuss whilst the waiter went to find a highchair for Annie and the girl noted yet again that everything revolved around her sister. They were eventually shown to an oblong, gingham covered table. The parents sat one side and the children opposite, Annie having been lifted into the high chair and placed next to her sister.

The girl had suffered more than enough of Annie that day. Her parents had been fussing over her all morning; applying sun screen, getting her in the shade, giving her drinks, giving her snacks, applying more sun screen; it went on and on. In contrast the girl was constantly nagged; "don't run near Annie, sand might go in her eyes"; "don't throw the ball to Annie, she could get hurt". Her parents showed no concern for the girl's needs, telling her to help herself to drinks and snacks but making no effort to check she did. Worse was their constant badgering to play with other children; "That little girl looks nice; why don't you go and make friends with her?" or "Those children are building a sandcastle over there; why don't you go and help?" It was clear they didn't want her around. They also expected her to join them in protecting Annie, as though *she* should be looking after her sister; she was only a child herself! She wanted to be the one that was cosseted. She had no interest in caring for Annie.

In the restaurant she looked across the table to her parents who had their heads together behind a menu. She turned to Annie who was contentedly sucking on her well-favoured pink teddy. She felt estranged from the rest of the family and angry at their happiness. She brooded for a few minutes then she slipped off her chair and sidled over to Annie in the high chair. Aping the actions of adults, she pushed her face towards her sister in a peek-a-boo game.

Annie giggled at her sister's looming and receding face. Her parents looked up from the menu to watch. They hoped they were at last witnessing a change of conduct in their daughter but at the same time they were distrustful. The girl continued, with her left hand on the table she pivoted forwards and backwards causing her sister to chuckle endearingly. Then, still under the gaze of her parents, she slipped her right hand under the table and reached for the fresh, soft, velvety skin of Annie's thigh. She took as much of it as she could between her thumb and fingers and squeezed it viciously, digging her nails into the flesh and twisting her wrist. Annie's giggle instantly turned to an ear-piercing scream, her bottom lip quivering with shock. The girl was thrilled, gratified to have wiped that irritating, happy smile off Annie's face. She momentarily relished her sister's pain then turned to her parents with a bewildered expression, shrugging her shoulders and raising her hands out flat as if to say "what did I do?"

The parents suspected their seven-year-old but not having seen what she'd done just told her to sit back in her seat and leave Annie alone; Annie had stopped crying as soon as the pain subsided. The girl sidled back to her seat with satisfaction. She'd hurt Annie right in front of them and got away with it! It made her feel good. It was the best she'd felt since Annie had been born. She resolved to carry on attacking Annie but ensure she didn't get caught. It was an obsession that deepened over the ensuing years. She spent hours conjuring up ways to surreptitiously hurt her sister. She learnt that having Annie's trust was paramount to the success of her schemes so she always ensured she appeared to be a friend to her little sister.

The mother was not fooled by her daughter's outwardly amiable attitude to Annie. However, she never caught her red handed and felt powerless to influence any change. As the girl reached her tenth birthday any hopes her parents had that she would mature and stop abusing her little sister were gone; she was more artful and malicious than ever. Her mother grew exhausted trying to protect Annie and could hardly sleep at night for fear of what the girl might do to her sister in cover of darkness. The father became concerned for his wife's health and for his older daughter's sanity; surely it was not normal for a child to want to physically hurt her younger sister? He was reluctant to seek medical help for fear of what may happen to his elder daughter. He didn't want her labelled as mentally ill at such a tender age. He was desperate to find a way of changing the situation.

He confided his problems to a work colleague and it was this person that came up with what seemed like a brilliant idea. He suggested they look for a boarding school for their daughter. Both parents jumped at this suggestion. They were sure the stricter culture of such an institution would benefit the girl and they welcomed the thought of life without the stress of worrying about Annie. They told their older daughter the decision was taken to ensure she received an education befitting her high intellect.

The girl was not fooled; her malevolence intensified. She would spend many future hours over the coming years sitting alone in her dormitory plotting her revenge. She would conjure up several ways in which retribution would be sweet; it was just a matter of choosing the nastiest.

Part 1

Making the Vows

Chapter 1

To Love and to Cherish

It was a cold, winter Sunday morning; sleety rain lashed against the windows. Mia listened to the grainy tapping and felt grateful for the sanctuary of the warm cosy bed. She lay on her side with her slim, bony shoulder snuggled into the soft accommodating space under Ralph's arm pit, her head on his chest and her free arm and leg wrapped round him like a blanket. It was heaven and she wanted to stay like this for ever.

Ralph rested his chin on Mia's head. He had a contented look on his face, pleased with his sexual prowess and excellent timing. It had been a fantastic session.

They lay without speaking; their clammy flesh stuck together, a smell of sweat, semen and pheromones pervading the bedroom. Ralph gently ran his fingers through her long dark hair. He could feel her soft breast against his chest and her heart beating strongly. She drew slow circles round the hairs on his chest, her ear pressed to his side.

Eventually Ralph's arm had gone dead and he volunteered to make tea. He disentangled himself from Mia, put on his dressing gown and padded off to the kitchen, humming contentedly. When he got back Mia was stretched out naked on top of the bed, her back propped against the pillows, studying a mirror she was holding between her legs.

"What *are* you doing?" he asked as he put his tea down and carried hers to her bedside cabinet.

She didn't look up but continued to study her reflection "They were talking about "Designer Vaginas" at work the other day" she told him as she changed the angle of the mirror "apparently it's the latest thing in cosmetic surgery."

Ralph looked at her in disbelief "What's wrong with your office lot?" he asked rhetorically "they were going on about breast implants not that long ago!"

With incredible deftness for a large man he slipped off his dressing gown, stepped round to the bottom of the bed and gently taking the mirror from her hands, leaned in to where the mirror had been.

"Hmm, let me see" he said studying her like a work of art. "Perfect!"

He moved closer and ran his nose gently over her pubic hair, along the firm, soft skin of her stomach and up between her breasts until he was face-to-face with her.

"Perfect!" he repeated looking into her half-closed eyes.

***

For the second time that morning Ralph pulled his arm from under Mia's back. She roused and looked at him; a contented smile across her face.

"I think we'd better get up Angel" he said stroking her hair back from her face. "What do you fancy doing for the rest of the day?"

She thought for a while, savouring his attention rather than rushing with an answer.

"There's a wild life photographic exhibition at the Natural History Museum" she mused "or we could pay a visit to the Imperial War Museum, there'll be stuff about World War 1 as it's the 100th anniversary."

Ralph so loved his wife, she always had good ideas. He reflected again how lucky he was to be married to her. He had spotted her in the hospital canteen shortly after she came to work in the physiotherapy department and had immediately been attracted to her slim, tall physique, friendly face and beautiful thick, long, dark brown hair. He'd had previous relationships but none of those had made him feel this good; nowhere near. Not only was Mia beautiful, intelligent and sunny natured but they had completely compatible interests. And she was very, VERY sexy.

He moved on to fumbling with her small, perfectly formed ear. "My vote goes with the exhibition at the Natural History Museum, if that's good with you." he said "Stay in bed Angel-cake while I make us some brunch. We can go after that."

He swung out of the bed, stepped round to her side and kissed her on the forehead. Then he picked up her mug of cold tea, collected his own full mug and humming disappeared once again down the hall of their flat to the kitchen.

A warm glow raced through Mia's body and settled in her stomach. She felt so happy she thought she may burst. They had been married for nearly two years and she felt just as excited being around Ralph as she had felt the first time they met; in fact, their love seemed to get stronger by the week. She had noticed him soon after she came to work at Brentfield Hospital and was immediately attracted to this giant, friendly looking man with unruly dark hair and barrel chest. He was like a tall, cuddly bear and she had an immediate desire to snuggle up to him. She was delighted when he came to talk to her colleague in the canteen. They were introduced, got talking and had so much in common, well the rest was history.

***

They got back from the Natural History Museum, Chinese takeaway in hand, and sat at their kitchen table to eat. Mia made a grimace. "Monday tomorrow" she said with an exaggerated downturned mouth.

"What's that face for?" Ralph countered "you love your job."

"I know" she admitted "and I've got an interesting new referral this week; a girl who was in a car accident and has spinal damage. I really must do everything I can to get her walking again, she's only 16."

"Sounds nasty but if anyone can help her, you can" he said as he chewed on a prawn ball. "Oh, don't forget I'll be late home on

Wednesday. I'm going to that "Electronics in Health" exhibition in Birmingham. I'm hoping to look at hand-held computer pads for ward rounds. We shouldn't be hand writing notes when they could be tapped onto an electronic notebook and transferred to the computer. I'm sure it's worth the cost, it's just convincing those dinosaurs holding the purse strings."

"You are so clever with technological things!" she said indulgently. "I think it would be great, save time and there'd be less room for error."

"Can you tell management?!" he asked with a grin, soaking up her adulation.

They sat quietly eating for a while then Ralph raised a subject he'd had on his mind for some time.

"Mia" he said slowly "I know we've discussed this before but I really do think we need to start planning for having a family."

He caught what he thought was an agitated twitch run across her shoulders but she didn't say anything so he continued.

"It's just that we ought to start saving money. We're broke at the moment and we'll need some funding to support us when you go on maternity leave. Also, the flat isn't ideal for raising a child so we should look into the price of houses further out of London and consider whether we can manage to move to something larger with a garden."

"What made you think of that?" she answered evasively.

"Well you're thirty-two this year; we need to think about it."

"I'm actually only thirty-one at the moment!" she pointed out indignantly.

"You know what I mean" he said. "If we leave it too much longer there's a risk we'll be less fertile and there's more chance of something going wrong."

"Hmm I do worry about something going wrong" Mia confessed. "Vicky tells me all sorts of stor...."

Ralph cut her short.

"You can't take too much notice of what Vicky says!" he bristled "she runs the Genetics Diagnostic Department for God's sake! She sees every genetic defect in South West London; of course she has tales of what can go wrong! You mustn't get things out of proportion, Mia. If everyone worried about what might go wrong, nobody would have any children!"

Mia felt chastised but accepted Ralph's point.

"No, you're right" she conceded "I am getting too bogged down with what Vicky tells me."

They were quiet for a while, both contemplating the issue.

"You *do* want children, don't you?" Ralph finally ventured "We *did* agree we'd both like to have a family. You *do* know how important it is to me. I haven't had a proper family, no brothers or sisters, I don't even have any cousins."

"Yes, I know and of course I want children" she reassured him but added "eventually."

She saw the concern on his face and reached across the table to hold his hand. "It's just that, well I wouldn't mind enjoying our life together for a few more years" she explained "I like living here and I like my job. Our lives will change completely if we have kids and I don't feel ready to let go just yet."

He didn't make any response but had a sinking feeling in the pit of his stomach. They finished their meal in quiet reflection.

"I'm going for lunch with Vicky on Wednesday" Mia said as they started clearing up. "We haven't had a proper chat since she got her promotion. It'll be interesting to hear how she's getting on, especially as there were other people expecting to get that job. I can imagine she'll have some difficulty exerting her authority."

"Knowing Vicky, I'm sure she'll cope" smiled Ralph allowing Mia to move on from the subject of starting a family.

"Hmm, even Vicky must find some things challenging!" answered Mia. "Anyway" she added "if you can get a proper meal on Wednesday when you go to the exhibition it'll save us having to cook dinner that night."

Ralph inwardly sighed. Mia was always quick to seize the opportunity not to prepare a meal. He understood after a long day at work she lacked enthusiasm for getting out the pots and pans, but unless he did the cooking they ate out or got take-aways and he was putting on weight. Still, he would be late home on Wednesday. "OK" he said "I'm sure I'll find somewhere to eat whilst on my travels even if it's on the train."

***

The next day they rushed about the flat getting ready for work and as they were both due in at the same time headed to the tube station together. The train was typically packed with London commuters so standing room only. They found a space and Ralph used his bulk to protect Mia from being squashed. There were directions from the driver to "move down the carriage please" and everyone shuffled down reluctantly, wary of the wall of bodies building up between them and the doors.

A lady, determined to find some space, started to make her way to the centre of the carriage. She was short, middle-aged and clad in a heavy black overcoat and Cossack style black hat generously trimmed with fur. The hat was too large and would have fallen over her eyes but for her brown, thick-rimmed glasses. She barged into a woman who lost her balance and trod on the foot of a neighbouring passenger. He made a brief acknowledgement of the contact with a nod and outwardly maintained composure though inside he screamed at the thought of the damage that may have been inflicted on the shoes he had only just purchased that week-end.

Ralph and Mia watched as the lady, oblivious to this minor disaster, continued to make her way between the standing and seated commuters. The train rattled and swerved along the track and she lunged from one passenger to the next, holding on to whatever she could; coats, cases, arms and even one man's leg. It looked like she might fall onto somebody's lap but she managed to remain upright. Her shoulder-bag swung towards the faces of the seated passengers who bobbed out of the way in a strange type of horizontal Mexican wave. Her hat somehow managed to stay in place. Eventually she found a space, recovered her composure, reached into her bag for a newspaper and proceeded to read it. The only sign of her struggle was a slight pinking to her cheeks. The disrupted passengers settled back to whatever they'd been doing to distract themselves from the discomfort of the train. Peace resumed.

Mia and Ralph smiled at each other, amused by the episode. They didn't need to discuss it when they got off the train; they just shared the comedy with a chuckle and made their way to the hospital where they pecked each other farewell and headed their separate ways.

***

Later that day Mia went to the canteen for lunch with a couple of colleagues, Bina her manager and Pete, another physiotherapist. They decided to sit near the window meaning one of them had to squeeze into a seat behind a pillar. Mia volunteered being the slimmest of the trio by a fair percent. They had been happily chatting and eating for a while when Mia became aware of a group sitting on the adjacent table that evidently worked in the laboratory where her friend Vicky had just been appointed manager. They were loudly exchanging gossip and she couldn't help but hear that Vicky was the subject. They evidently hadn't noticed Mia behind the pillar; some of them were aware of her friendship with their boss.

Mia tried to ignore them, hoping the subject would change, but they grew louder as they vied to add to the tittle-tattle. She started to feel a hot sensation creeping up her neck and into her head. Beads of sweat formed on her brow. She knew she should stick up for Vicky but feared challenging the group in public. She carried on distractedly talking to Bina and Pete but her attention was continually drawn to the neighbouring conversation. Her heart thumped at the thought of having to speak out in the busy canteen. However, her reticence for public exhibition was outweighed by her loyalty to her friend, and the need to defend her.

"That Victoria would stop at nothing to get promoted" a middle-aged colleague called Alan stated with authority. "She was all fluttering eyelashes and sucking up to Ken before the interview; I wouldn't be surprised if she'd shagged him."

"Well I heard she deleted Roy's application form from his computer before he had the chance to submit it" added Leora. "Of course nobody could prove anything but Roy didn't have time to re-write it."

"How do you know Vicky deleted it?" a young new recruit called James asked.

"Who else would?" Leora snapped back so harshly that James blushed and tried to recover with "Ooo 'scuse me for asking". The others clearly didn't want anyone spoiling their entertainment by defending the accused and ignored James' interruption.

"I heard" continued a lady called Debra "that when she worked at Barts she sent an e-mail to the Manager from someone else's computer, so it looked like they'd sent it. Don't know what she put in it but it must have been bad as the person got sacked!"

"What a cow!" Leora exclaimed with relish.

"Sell her own mother that one!" added Alan. "And for a five-foot three midget she sure can throw her weight around."

By now Mia and her two colleagues had fallen silent, unable to continue their conversation above the noisy rhetoric. Mia, feeling dizzy with nerves, stood up and squeezed back past the pillar straight into view of the group, staring at Alan who she felt had been the centre of the character assassination. A hush descended over the table as those recognising Mia gaped and those that didn't soon got the idea it was better to keep quiet.

Alan faced Mia and for a few seconds neither spoke. Then Alan took the initiative and in a loud, clear, voice, he looked straight into her eyes and with a tone of exaggerated kindness said "You're a nice kid Mia, what are you doing hanging around with a vixen like Vicky?"

"I'm not a kid." Mia replied sharply, her heart beating violently "You've no need to worry about me! I know how bitter people can get when they don't get the promotion they thought they were due. You just can't accept that a younger person, female too, could possibly be more talented than you! You were just waiting in line for your management post, weren't you? Well maybe you should have the guts to look elsewhere for promotion instead of just sitting here bad-mouthing her!"

"You'll find out" Alan countered, unfazed by Mia's words. "That woman can't be trusted and isn't capable of having friends! Just look out Mia, just look out for yourself!"

The condescending way he spoke was humiliating, as though she were a child. She wanted to defend Vicky but her mind had gone blank. There was a hushed silence in the canteen; everyone was watching. She couldn't find the witty and cutting comments she so easily came up with when she relived this scene later. Instead she flushed hot red with embarrassment and stood there speechless. She glanced back towards Bina and Pete who were looking uncomfortable and undecided about what they should or could do to support her. She gave them a look of apology and walked out of the cafeteria, just about managing to hold back the tears. She raced to the toilets where she gratefully found the welcome privacy of a cubicle. There she was able to compose herself and didn't emerge until she felt ready to face whoever may come in.

Bina and Pete, conscious of the vacuum in Mia's wake and that several pairs of eyes had turned to them, and not wanting to get involved, simultaneously stood up and followed Mia out of the canteen, Pete picking up the remainder of his sausage roll as he went.

***

"Like a gang of wolves" Mia said to Bina and Pete when she joined them back at their office, her voice still a little shaky. "I'm going to report them!"

"It was disgusting I agree. They're supposed to be professionals and know better than to behave like school children" answered Bina carefully choosing her words and tone. She could see Mia had been unnerved by the spat and noticed her face had gone all blotchy so she didn't want to cause further upset. "But what could you report them for?" she reasoned "Insubordination? Being unkind? People can't be disciplined for having an opinion."

"I was thinking of libel or false accusation" Mia said persistently. "They were spreading lies about Vicky."

"With all the rumour and gossip that goes around here management aren't going to be concerned that you overheard some regarding your friend, true or not" Pete countered maintaining the soft tone to avoid agitating Mia.

Their sympathetic tones and realistic comments dispelled Mia's angst and her shoulders dropped with resignation.

"Do you think I should tell Vicky what they were saying?" she asked.

Bina looked at Pete; he shrugged his shoulders, unprepared to comment.

"Well it's your call Mia" Bina answered "I don't know what to advise but I'm sure Vicky can look after herself. Now, I'll make some tea then we've got ward rounds to do. You feel OK Mia?"

"Yes, I'll survive though I feel a right fool. Sorry to have embarrassed you both."

"We weren't embarrassed" said Bina for both of them. "They deserved to be torn off a strip."

"I wish I'd managed to do that" replied Mia. "But I didn't; I was pathetic."

"You made them stop and they may think before they start openly talking like that again" said Pete trying to make Mia feel better.

"Oh well, I can't dwell on it" Mia stated. "I'm seeing that new case this afternoon. The best therapy for me is absorbing myself in work!"

***

It took all of Monday night for Ralph to placate Mia. Outwardly he remained calm and conciliatory though inwardly he was raging with resentment towards the people that had upset his wife; he wished he had been there to protect her. He suggested she brave the canteen the next day to prove she hadn't been intimidated by the exchange. She needed to face up to seeing Vicky's work colleagues as soon as possible. Mia was anxious at the prospect of any further confrontation so Ralph agreed to have lunch with her.

The next day they met at the canteen and Mia soon spotted Alan who fortunately only had James for company. She walked past their table and looked Alan straight in the eye. He looked back and nodded but said nothing; he showed no sign of malice. It was enough to ease Mia and with some relief Ralph saw her relax. Inwardly he would have loved to punch Alan hard on the nose and he allowed himself a few moments to relish the idea.

Having got over that hurdle Ralph spent much of Tuesday night trying to alleviate Mia's anxieties over what she should tell Vicky when they met for lunch the next day.

Now it was Wednesday morning and Mia was getting ready to leave the train.

"You don't need to tell Vicky everything" Ralph advised. "I know you want to be honest but she may not thank you for it. Sometimes it's kinder not to tell the whole truth."

He knew his words were futile and that Vicky would soon extract all the details from Mia, who was never going to be the best candidate for the poker table.

"Just relax and enjoy your lunch" he told her.

She frowned slightly and leaned towards him to receive his kiss. Her scent filled him with a warm pleasant sensation. He would hold on to that feeling all day until he returned home tonight and took her in his arms again. She then left him, making her way through the jungle of passengers to the door. She sprung off the train regaining her usual optimistic gait, and waved goodbye from the crowded platform as the tube disappeared down the tunnel.

***

"You're late!" were Vicky's opening words as Mia joined her in the Black Cat cafe. "I'd almost given up on you."

Mia saw with a twang of guilt that Vicky had already started tucking in to her ham, egg and chips.

"Sorry, the last case took longer than I expected" she explained.

"You're entitled to a lunch hour you know" Vicky continued clearly irritated "you're always working extra hours. Your lot take advantage of your good will."

"I can't just walk out on a patient or leave them without being sure they understand the exercises" Mia replied in justification "and I don't mind covering emergencies, they aren't that common. Bina's a good manager and she has children to worry about, as does Katrina. Eddie and Pete don't cope very well with emergencies."

"So, you cover for other peoples' child care issues and incompetence!"

"It's not like that, can we drop this please else we really won't have any lunch hour left!"

Mia looked at the menu board and made her way to the service counter to order omelette, chips and cappuccino.

Vicky stalked Mia, her steel blue eyes drilling into her friend with such feline intensity she lost all awareness of anything else in the cafe. How attractive Mia looked in her knee-high, black boots, her thick, dark brown hair tumbling over the back of her navy coat. How readily the lady smiled as she took Mia's order. A familiar sensation welled in the pit of Vicky's stomach.

She snapped out of her trance as Mia came back to the table, cappuccino in hand. Mia looked anxious and Vicky realised she may have been too sharp about her friend's lateness.

"Like the boots" she said as a means of peace offering.

"Thanks" answered Mia "I got them in a sale; I only paid £45 for them."

They sat quietly for a short while. Vicky went back to her lunch whilst Mia ate the froth from the top of her coffee trying to think of how she was going to tell Vicky about the incident on

Monday.

"What's up?" asked Vicky, "I didn't mean to bite your head off."

"No, it's not that" answered Mia.

"Well?" pursued Vicky, lifting her prominent chin towards Mia.

"It's just that ..." Mia took a deep breath. "Well I was in the canteen on Monday and had a bit of a set-to with Alan Harper. He was talking to Leora and some other people from your Department and they weren't being very nice about you, so I told them what I thought of them."

"Really!" exclaimed Vicky "Good for you! Thanks for sticking up for me!"

Mia was surprised to see a big grin spread over Vicky's face.

The waitress came over with the omelette.

"Aren't you worried about your staff talking about you?" she asked as she spread ketchup over the chips.

"I'd be staggered if they didn't" Vicky explained. "Alan expected to get my job; he's just bitter that neither he nor his old crony Roy got the promotion. Let them get on with it, I don't care. If they're talking about me at least they aren't moaning about the work!"

"But they were saying some awful things" Mia found herself volunteering. Her friend's cavalier attitude made her feel even more embarrassed over her intervention.

"Yes, I can well imagine" Vicky stated. "No doubt they accused me of getting off with Ken and I believe I was apparently responsible for that twit Roy deleting his application form!"

Mia's mouth dropped open.

"Please don't worry Mia. My advice to you is to never go in for a management post; you're just too nice!"

The comment signified that Vicky was finished with that topic of conversation. She sat back in the flimsy plastic chair, still smiling. "Let's talk about something else" she said. "What have you been up to lately?"

As Mia ate her lunch they spoke about what they had done over the week-end, exchanged bits of gossip and discussed Vicky's latest date. She had met him at a friend's party. He was good

looking and owned a sporty BMW. But he'd got "the most disgusting habit of snorting into his handkerchief after finishing
each course of their meal". Vicky wrinkled her nose in an expression of disgust and they both laughed. "No wonder he was
single" she declared "being with him you'd have to wear ear de-
fenders and a blindfold every time you went out for dinner!"
They both laughed again.

"Poor you" Mia said with a little more seriousness in her tone.
"I'm sure you'll find your match soon, there's someone out there
with your name in his heart!"

"You're such a romantic, Mia. But maybe I'm meant to stay single. You're so easy going and attractive you don't realise how
difficult it is for us more physically challenged women to get
hitched."

She sat back and basked in Mia's reassurances that there was
more to being attractive than being tall, and Vicky should remember what great eyes she had and that her big boobs were
a definite asset. Eventually she interrupted Mia. "OK that's
enough about me" she declared. "What about you and Ralph,
what's new in the love nest? I keep wondering when you're
going to tell me you're pregnant."

Mia was taken aback. They didn't usually discuss anything remotely to do with children. Mia had a nagging concern that
their friendship might not survive such a life-changing episode
as her having a baby. Vicky was career minded and go-getting.
Mia was sure she'd have no interest in anything so domestic.

"Actually, you've hit on a bit of a sore subject there" Mia admitted as she finished her last chip. "Ralph's dead keen to get started
but I'm not too bothered. I'm so happy with just the two of us.
We have a great life together and I don't want to let go. Because
he's always wanted a family I think he's panicking that if we
wait it could get too late. He keeps telling me I'm getting old,
being a *whole thirty-two* next birthday" she raised her brows to
show her exasperation "and he constantly reminds me once I'm
in my late thirties it'll be harder to get pregnant and if something goes wrong there'll be less time to sort it out."

She sat back in her chair, surprised at her own outpouring.

"Well" Vicky responded with some hesitance "he does have a point. Lots of women do leave it too late."

"I don't think I fall into that category yet, do I?" Mia snapped.

"No, not really" Vicky answered hesitantly.

A short silence followed and Mia regretted she'd opened up to her friend who clearly agreed with Ralph's point of view. She sat sulkily staring into space.

Vicky recognised Mia was in one of her strops. They sat in silence for a few minutes. Then Vicky gave a little jump in her chair and made a eureka-type exclamation.

"I know!" she cried. "Why don't I run a DNA check on you and Ralph?! That way you'll know there are no complications and be able to relax and enjoy a kid-free life for the next few years!"

Mia was caught out by this unexpected suggestion and didn't share Vicky's apparent enthusiasm.

"I don't think that would be necessary" she said. "It's not that much of an issue. I'm sure we'll resolve it without going to all that trouble."

"What trouble?" asked Vicky. "It's only a blood test!"

"It's not that" Mia ventured. "I just don't think we need to go down that path."

Mia didn't really know why she wasn't keen on her friend's offer but instinctively it didn't seem right.

"Look" Vicky answered showing offence at Mia's reticence "I'm only trying to be helpful. Loads of couples would be jumping at the chance I'm giving you! Surely any information you can get before you start is useful? I'm your best friend; I just want to do something for you!"

"I know and I do appreciate that" Mia replied apologetically "but I'd have to discuss it with Ralph, I'm not sure he'll want us to have any tests."

"So *that's* what's bothering you!" Vicky smiled. "You needn't worry about Ralph, I'll soon convince him!"

"No, no!" Mia said quickly, knowing Ralph would be upset by Vicky approaching him about something so personal. "I'll talk to him."

The more Mia digested the idea the less enthusiastic she felt, especially as she didn't think Ralph would be keen.

"You know it's against the hospital rules to carry out private work" she pointed out. "If anyone finds out you've done a test for us you could face instant dismissal!"

Vicky threw her head back and laughed.

"You are such a goody-two-shoes always sticking to the rules!" she said dismissively. "Who's going to find out?"

"What about Alan? Say he snoops around and finds out, he'd be delighted to get you the sack!"

"Look I'm the Manager, there's no way I'd let him get the remotest inkling of anything I'm doing. It'll be fine, really. Wouldn't you like to have confidence before you throw away the pills? I know I would. Anyway, it wouldn't be private work because I won't be charging you."

"Even using hospital equipment for private use is a dismissible offence" Mia persisted.

"Listen to yourself Mia! Honestly, do you really think everybody in the hospital sticks to the rules? You're the only person I know that declares using the photocopier for personal use. I'll do the testing in my own time. The only cost to the NHS will be the needles. Have a chat with Ralph and let me know." Vicky looked at her watch. "God, look at the time! We'd better get going."

They chatted on their way back to the hospital.

"Don't forget to ask Ralph about what we discussed" Vicky said in a conspiratorial tone as they waved good-bye and went their separate ways.

***

Ralph was grateful to finally get home that evening. He wore the exhausted face typical of long-distance commuters; the train had been late and very crowded. He plonked himself on the sofa and was pleased to hear Mia had spoken to Vicky about the canteen episode and it hadn't amounted to the problem his wife had imagined. However now there seemed to be something else on her mind. It wasn't long before Mia had told him about Vicky's offer and her concerns over Vicky compromising her position.

"Let's just say we don't want the test" he said simply. "We don't need it."

"No, I know we don't *need* it" Mia answered contemplatively, "but I suppose it would be good to know whether there were any problems lurking. I know we wouldn't choose to pay for the test and have no reason to ask for it under the NHS but it would give us the opportunity to check everything's fine before we start."

"You realise we could get into trouble as well as Vicky" Ralph pointed out.

"Only if someone finds out they are our samples. This is unofficial so nothing has to be put on computer. Vicky will come and collect samples from us at home then work on them after hours when she has the place to herself."

"You two seem to have it all worked out!" Ralph said tetchily.

This was exactly what Mia was trying to avoid, it appearing she'd conspired behind his back.

"Look" she implored him "I told Vicky I wasn't bothered about the test and that I'd need to talk to you about it. It's just that, well, she is so keen to do this as a favour for us. I feel that I'd be snubbing her by saying no!"

Ralph was too tired to argue. He was also cheered and reassured that at last Mia was actively contemplating having children.

"I suppose it would be an opportunity to get something out of working for the NHS" he conceded "there aren't many perks. Why not? May as well find out what may be *lurking*" he mimicked gently. He watched Mia's shoulders relax. That was that, he thought. Now he could unwind in front of the TV.

Chapter 2

To Have and to Hold

Vicky didn't waste any time and came the following Wednesday to take blood samples. She had a business-like air about her, displaying a professional side they didn't normally experience in their social association. She spoke enthusiastically about her job, explaining the advancements that had been made in the field of genetics. She told them about genomic technology that was already used to aid the diagnosis, treatment and therapies for some diseases. She believed that very soon everyone would be offered testing for their genetic profile and that these would be held on databases so that when a person became ill they could be given the correct treatment. She told them about a project called "The Human Genome Project" that set about mapping a mass of genetic information and that this enabled doctors like herself to compare sets of genetic or genomic data against known patterns.

"What if a test reveals somebody carries a family weakness such as heart disease" Ralph asked. "Hasn't it been suggested insurance companies will use the information to increase premiums?"

"Well what would you prefer?" Vicky answered, pulling her shoulders back and pushing her chin forward assertively, "to know you have a potential weakness and have it checked or pay lower premiums and drop dead?! Besides" she added "most insurance companies will take account of the fact you're having treatment."

"I don't know" Ralph continued doggedly, ignoring Vicky's intense defence of her work, "I'm not sure I like the idea of us all having our very innermost building blocks on record. Who knows what may be done with them!?"

"I'm surprised at you, Ralph" countered Vicky. "I thought computer nerds were the least concerned about feely touchy things! You're the lot that would replace humans with robots!"

"That's completely different!" he exclaimed.

"Can we get on with this and stop arguing!" Mia interrupted.

"Well are you sure you want me to go ahead with the test?" Vicky addressed Ralph. "If you're not comfortable with it I'm happy to leave."

"We're fine!" Mia stepped in. "We know this is unofficial so it's only you, Vicky, that's going to see the results."

"Yes, and you'll destroy them afterwards, won't you?" Ralph added much to Mia's irritation.

"What else could I do with them?!" answered Vicky dismissively.

"OK" he said. "Let's get on with it."

Vicky sneaked a raised eyebrow towards Mia who returned a weak smile. Why was Ralph being awkward? He knew Vicky needed to get back to work with the samples that night so why was he delaying her?

"Thanks for doing this" Mia said as Vicky was leaving.

"Yeah thanks Vicky" added Ralph politely but insincerely.

"No probs" answered Vicky. "It'll take me a few days to do the testing but I should have the results by next week."

They walked down the communal stairway and Ralph put his arm around Mia's shoulder as they waved good-bye to Vicky from the front door. Vicky strode off down the road purposefully, heels click-clacking against the pavement, as she went to find her car. She disappeared around the corner without looking back. She was clearly on a mission. Mia watched after Vicky in admiration; she was so focused. Mia's Mother had often criticised Mia for having a lack of drive and now she understood what her Mother meant. Mia worked hard and looked for good outcomes but she never pursued work with the gusto Vicky displayed just now.

"I hope we don't regret having these tests" said Ralph as they went back into their flat. "What will we do if there is something wrong?"

"I'm sure there won't be anything wrong" Mia answered with her usual optimism.

She hadn't satisfied Ralph.

"No but say we did find a genetic problem; would you still want to get pregnant?"

Mia recognised the levity of Ralph's question.

"Yes" she said pensively "because I would be tested and if there was a serious problem we would do something about it." Her words were vague.

"So, would you be prepared to terminate the pregnancy?" he persisted.

"Well that would depend on what was wrong" she answered, "but in principle, yes, I guess I would. Would you want to?"

"Yes" he answered more positively than she had been.

They held each other's gaze for several seconds. A pact had been wordlessly agreed.

"I'm sure it won't come to that" Mia said trying to lighten the mood. "As you said before, we can't go thinking the worst! I'm sure it will all be fine!"

***

The next week Mia was particularly busy at work. There were more referrals than usual and she was hard pressed to complete the ward rounds and keep the paperwork straight. A new member of staff, Analyn, joined the team on Monday and added to Mia's work load by constantly asking Mia to check on cases. The interruptions caused Mia to lose concentration and have to start again when she got back to her own patients. It was Wednesday and she would be late finishing again, she had worked late on both Monday and Tuesday.

Analyn was a quiet, Filipino lady whose slight physique belied her chosen profession. It was incredible how she coped with manoeuvring and massaging the larger patients so capably. Her shyness and accent meant Mia couldn't easily hear what she was saying and the strain of trying to understand added to the stress of dealing with her all day. In spite of that Analyn seemed to be a pleasant person and Mia was mindful that she was a long way from home and in a new workplace, so didn't refuse help.

However, Mia noticed Analyn wasn't approaching anyone else with her queries. Pete, Katrina and Eddie kept their heads down whenever Analyn approached and were always "in the middle of something" Mia was getting exasperated by Analyn's continual neediness and irritated at being landed with the new girl whilst the others just got on with their own work uninterrupted, especially when they all went home on time whilst she had to stay late to catch up.

In spite of Katrina's minimal association with Analyn, she caught Mia in the tea-making area and told her how much she disliked the poor girl. According to Katrina, Analyn had been bitchy about her clothes. Mia thought that strange. Katrina wore the most outlandish outfits; Mia had often wondered where she bought the multicoloured skirts and blouses, there was nothing like them in the ordinary high street shops. Surely choosing to dress so unconventionally should make her immune to comments about her clothes? Mia also couldn't imagine Analyn being bitchy.

"I'm sure she didn't mean to offend you or be critical" Mia told Katrina. "She was probably just trying to make conversation. She's only just qualified and it's hard for everyone when they start at a new job. I don't think the team have been very welcoming. I'm the only person willing to help her and I'm just as busy as everyone else. I wouldn't mind other people getting involved."

"I know, Mia, you are very good" was Katrina's response. "You always see the best in people. Trouble is she makes my flesh creep and I don't want anything to do with her!"

"For goodness sake!" thought Mia but said nothing.

By Friday things were not much better and the workload and

Analyn were getting Mia down. She had even been snapping at Ralph who had told her she should take the matter up with her manager. She took his advice, sought out Bina and complained about the lack of co-operation from her colleagues. Bina however was more interested in the reorganisation currently being discussed and although apparently sympathetic to Mia's point of view thought Analyn would soon get less demanding. She intimated that Mia should be more patient! That made Mia angry and she pondered on Vicky's assertion that her colleagues were treating her as a soft touch and taking advantage of her kind nature.

At lunchtime she bought a sandwich and resentfully took it to eat at her desk. Another lunch break spent working and no colleagues in sight! She opened her e-mail where there were fifteen new messages. She groaned and started to wade through them when a new mail popped up; it was from Vicky. She opened it straight away and was surprised by its tone. Vicky referred to their "recent meeting" and suggested a "further meeting as soon as possible". Mia knew Vicky couldn't refer to the test directly but she felt she could have worded it less formally; it was as though she was a patient, not a close friend.

She sent back a friendly, casual mail jibing Vicky for her starchiness and suggesting she come over that night for a take-away.

Vicky mailed to say she would like to come tonight but couldn't stay to dinner; her excuse being something vague about a date with a friend.

Mia mailed to suggest they make it another night so that they *could* have dinner.

Vicky responded that she didn't want to leave it as she thought they should be given the results "as soon as possible".

This frightened Mia. She spent the rest of the day distractedly answering Analyn's questions, dealing with her own patients and brooding over Vicky's guardedness. She was already stressed with work but now her stomach knotted and a pain spread across her chest. She would have liked to phone Vicky but knew they couldn't discuss anything in the office for fear of

Alan ear-wigging. She wanted a reassuring word; she just knew something was wrong.

That evening Ralph tried to comfort her whilst waiting for Vicky to arrive.

"She's probably just being professional and wanting to convey the results as she would to any other client" he suggested.

"But why didn't she just give some sort of indication that everything is fine?" Mia asked as she paced the living room. "She is a friend after all."

"Maybe there is something" conceded Ralph "and she didn't want to start going into it by mail."

That didn't please Mia and she wrung her hands together nervously.

"Look" said Ralph consolingly, "if there is something wrong with one of us we'll just have to cope. The worst case would be us not being able to have children, although that's not something she'd find in that sort of test, is it?"

"I don't think so" answered Mia "though I'm not sure, but you're right we can cope with whatever she has to say!"

"That's more like my Mia" he said putting his arms around her shoulders and pulling her into his chest. "Whatever she says it won't be the end of the world; we'll always have each other."

"Yes, you're right" Mia agreed as she slipped her arms around his waist and buried her head in his chest. "That's all that matters."

Vicky arrived looking chilled from the icy late January evening. "It's lovely and warm in here!" she said as she took off her coat, scarf, hat and gloves.

"Would you like a glass of wine?" offered Mia.

"Oh no thanks, can I have a cup of tea?" she answered.

Mia went to get the tea leaving Ralph to make inane conversation with Vicky. They sat either side of the coffee table and he watched her take a slim folder from her briefcase and sort through the papers in it. She put these on the coffee table and sat back in the armchair. Mia came through with the teas and set them on the table, then sat close up to Ralph on the sofa. She was feeling nervous again and kept telling herself not to be so silly. She had never felt like this before. She'd experienced nerves when she'd had interviews or sat exams but this was a different feeling altogether. It was a feeling of dread as opposed to anticipation.

"Right" said Vicky "are you ready for me to start?"

They nodded.

"First I must explain how I have arrived at the results of my tests."

Mia shuffled in the chair, Ralph chewed his lip impatiently.

"The blood test enabled me to get a genetic profile for both of you showing the pattern of your chromosomes. I was then able to see whether there were any possible genetic problems individually and carry out testing to see if there were any problems with compatibility of your two sets of genes."

Ralph inwardly groaned at Vicky's preamble. He knew she was just being professional but his calm display for Mia was hiding his own desperate anxieties. Were they going to be unable to have a family? Something he had yearned for since childhood. He fought to contain his impatience and sat, gripping Mia's hand, looking at Vicky but not really listening. He could sense Mia getting increasingly more anxious; he thought she would explode if Vicky went on much longer.

"So, to tell you about the other part of the test" Vicky was continuing.

"Please, Vicky" Ralph cut in tetchily. "I'm sorry to interrupt, but do you think you could just get to the results?"

Vicky looked offended and Ralph realised he may have sounded boorish. He added more placidly, "sorry Vicky, I didn't mean to sound rude or ungrateful but the testing details are of limited interest to us non-geneticists and obviously Mia and I are anxious to know what you've found!"

"Yes, of course, I understand, sorry, I'll keep it as brief as I can" she answered.

Ralph and Mia shared an inner sigh and both sat forward expectantly.

Vicky took a breath then brightened. "It's good news as far as genetic problems are concerned" she told them. "I did not find any of the known defects such as down's syndrome, cystic fibrosis and a multitude of other possible conditions. There are a number but I won't bore you with that, suffice it to say there were no problems with either of you. Of course, that doesn't guarantee the health of any future baby."

Ralph and Mia slumped back in the sofa, relief chasing the wrinkles from their brows. Ralph felt a wave of anger follow on the tail of his relief. "Why the hell did she put us through all that worry for nothing!?" he thought. "Just to feed her own self-importance" he surmised.

Mia being less judgemental was just grateful to hear there were no problems.

"That's good!" she exclaimed getting up from the sofa. "Let's celebrate! Would you like a glass of wine now Vicky?"

"You weren't listening!" Vicky answered reproachfully. "I'm not finished! There was the other test I just told you about."

Mia froze looking like the TV on pause. Then she slowly sat back down next to Ralph.

"What else could there be?" Ralph thought. He was getting pissed off with Vicky. What was the matter with her? Did she get some perverse enjoyment out of watching them fret?

"So" he sighed as he gave Mia's hand a squeeze "tell us Vicky, what else have you found?"

Vicky settled herself and took a breath before resuming.

"I don't suppose you've heard of a sibship index, have you?" she asked.

They both shook their heads. "Now what's she on about?" thought Ralph.

"Well a sibship index determines the likelihood of two people being related. If the index is less than 1.00 the two people are not related. If it's greater than 1.00, the two tested individuals are likely to be biological siblings."

Ralph immediately saw where this was going and his patience was running out. What was Vicky about to come out with now? She could see him getting twitchy.

"Look" she said looking straight into Ralph's eyes "I can only tell you what I found in the laboratory. But I have to tell you that your results are staggering! Unbelievable! You scored well over the one. That means, it seems mad, I know, but that means, very positively, that you two are related; paternally!"

Ralph and Mia just stared at Vicky.

"I know what the results show is quite extraordinary" she continued into their silence "and difficult to believe" she sounded breathless, it was clear she could hardly contain her excitement "and to be one hundred percent accurate in sibship testing it is best to take samples from the birth mother or father, but from a scientific point of view, the test showed conclusively that you are related!"

The pair still said nothing but just stared at her.

She took a deep gasp of air as though she had been under water; her cheeks were flushed, her eyes wide.

"It's actually more specific than that" she continued. "It's incredible! Well I mean it's MOST strange! I don't know how to explain it, but genetically you are half brother and sister! You have the same father!"

Chapter 3

For Richer or Poorer

They were pleased to see Vicky go. They stood at their entrance door and watched her descend the stairs to the main exit where she turned to wave good-bye and left. They moved back into their flat and heaved a sigh of relief as Ralph shut the door.

They looked at each other and burst out laughing.

"What on earth was that all about?!" Ralph exclaimed. "She knows us, knows our families, how on earth can she come out with something like that?!"

"It's a question of believing the science without looking at the friggin' obvious!" agreed Mia. "Honestly I didn't know how to keep a straight face. How embarrassing was that? I'm beginning to wonder how well qualified she is! I've always thought of her as so brainy!"

"I ran the test three times" Ralph said impersonating Vicky, "but the results came out the same" then in his own voice "well you made the same mistake three times!"

"We shouldn't make fun of her" said Mia, "but it is extraordinary that even after we pointed out that our parents had never met until we got together, and that they came from completely different parts of the Country, she still stuck to her stupid results!"

"I suppose she couldn't ask anyone else to check her findings as she did the work unofficially" Ralph pointed out in defence of Vicky. "We all know how easy it is to keep making the same error, that's why we always get a fresh eye to double check things that don't look right."

"True" agreed Mia, then after a pause added "at least we know we don't have any of the other genetic defects."

"Assuming she got that right!" answered Ralph.

"I like to think we can trust that bit."

"Yes then at least it wasn't all a complete waste of time."

"Strange" pondered Mia. "Vicky has always told me we're like two peas in a pod and could have been brother and sister, maybe she's got a thing about it."

"Well, that's that then" concluded Ralph.

"Do you fancy a curry?" Mia asked. "We could wander down to Tooting."

"Yes Ok" he answered.

"I'm starving" she added "after all that anticipation and the strain of how to react to her results. Imagine one of our Dads having had an affair with one of our Mums! I can't picture it, can you?"

"No!" agreed Ralph. "Nor can I imagine the chance of both our Mums having an affair with the same man!"

"Well I'm meeting Mum next Friday" stated Mia. "I'll ask her!"

"That'll give her something to think about" Ralph commented.

As Mia put on her scarf and coat she looked at Ralph pensively.

"It's going to be awkward the next time I see Vicky" she said with her head down.

Ralph stepped in front of her and lifted her chin so that their eyes met. He could see her concern. He kissed her gently on the lips.

"Just act as though nothing has happened" he advised. "Carry on as though she didn't do the test. It's week-end, by next week it won't seem so raw."

"I suppose so" she pouted. "I'm on shift tomorrow but Vicky never works week-ends. I'll have time to think up what I'm going to say when I see her."

"Don't worry" Ralph said. "Remember she can't talk openly about it and anyway it really isn't any of her business! Now come on, Madras awaits!"

***

Mia liked working Saturdays because it was quiet and she was able to get up to date with her paperwork uninterrupted, there was enough of it this week. She did a short hospital round to check there were no problems and returned to the office to work in peace with a nice hot cup of coffee. The office took on an eerie feeling in the absence of its occupants and their idiosyncrasies; the personalities pervading the desks like ghosts. She mused that the others probably felt the same about her empty desk when they worked the Saturday or Sunday shift. Her presence would be at her desk, as theirs were here today, in a spiritual way. She kept thinking, irrationally she knew, that Vicky was going to appear. She feared the prospect of facing her friend in the empty office where Vicky would be able to talk openly. She still hadn't thought of what she was going to say and felt jumpy even though she knew Vicky didn't work on Saturdays.

In the early afternoon she rang Ralph to see what he was up to and was pleased to hear he was going to make them a "special" dinner. He'd bought the ingredients that morning and would start cooking after watching the rugby on TV with his friend James who was coming over. Mia felt obliged to suggest James might like to stay for dinner but was relieved to hear he had a prior date. She usually didn't feel like entertaining on a Saturday after working all day and was happy to spend the evening just with Ralph.

It was half past five. Only half an hour to the end of her shift and home was a welcoming prospect. With her work up to date she had time for a little quiet contemplation. She wondered whether she should work part time if she had a child and imagined Ralph playing with a toddler boy who looked just like him. Momentarily she was transported from the cramped and austere office in winter to a blossom filled park in the spring sunshine; picnic laid out over lush grass and perfect baby boy giggling contentedly. She held on to the image for a few seconds before an unexpected shiver ran down her spine and returned her to the reality of the empty office.

She warily turned towards the semi-open door. She was sure she'd seen somebody in the periphery of her vision. She became acutely aware of her complete isolation in this part of the building. There was only one door to the office and the corridor beyond had fallen into darkness. A small seed of panic planted itself in her stomach. She looked towards the large expanse of window but could only see reflections of empty desks sharply contrasted against the deep, deep blackness of the January night. She felt exposed by the fluorescent lighting, like being in a shop window display. Was anyone out there looking in?

She considered calling the security desk but felt embarrassed by her fears. She slowly crept towards the door "Is anyone there!" she called making herself sound bolder than she felt. The corridor was silent and dark. She stepped out and felt along the wall to find the light switch, her senses on the alert for any sound or movement. Finally, her fingers came up against the large, protruding round button and she thumped it hard, giving vent to her panic and chasing the shadows away from the passage in a flood of illumination.

She looked down the long, empty corridor but still felt uneasy. There were several half-opened doors to black unlit offices in which someone could have hidden. She turned back into her own office. Only twenty minutes to go. She was keener than ever to get away. She started to collect her bag and coat keeping one eye on the door, alert for any sound from the creepy silent corridor. Suddenly a noise made her jump. It was her pager! "Damn!" she thought "A&E at this time; typical!" She grabbed her things and fled out of the office, down the corridor towards the A&E Department. She didn't look back; she kept her eyes and mind on the way out and the emergency in front of her.

***

In A&E she found two nurses fitting up heart monitors to an elderly gentleman who was struggling for breath. He had a block in his respiratory system and it needed to be manipulated away before they could administer oxygen. Mia immediately set to work and, as they could not be of any assistance, the nurses left her alone in the side ward and went to deal with other patients. Mia was well trained to deal with this particular scenario and she manipulated the man confidently, working away at the obstruction. Just as she was beginning to succeed the heart monitor started to scream; the patient's heart was fading. She looked into the patient's grey, watery eyes and realised he was not fully conscious. Mia had never had a patient die in her hands before. She pressed the emergency button and stepped up her manipulation. In her head she prayed "Wake up! Please wake up!"

She was having no effect and could see the man fading before her very eyes. Without thinking, she stopped and for no reason, it certainly wasn't in any reference books, she frantically waved her hands in front of his face and yelled at him "Wake up!" It was a moment she would never dare share with anyone else at work but that she would never forget. Her unorthodox method succeeded. The old man rallied round as though he had heard her and decided to obey. By the time support arrived he was out of immediate danger, the blockage removed.

It was seven thirty by the time Mia left the hospital. She wrote up her notes on the ward computer rather than go back to her creepy office. On leaving the hospital she bumped into Sid, head of security, and told him she thought there had been somebody in her office block. She confessed to being concerned by her isolation when she worked alone in the building at week-ends. He assured her that nobody could get into that part of the building without their security cards but agreed to take a walk around later to check everything was secure. She accepted there was nothing else she could expect him to do.

It was well past eight by the time she got home. Ralph listened intently when she related how she had thought her patient was going to die and congratulated her on her unconventional remedy. He made her feel proud and clever, like a heroine. She had realised since living with Ralph that during her childhood she was given very little praise for anything. She was sure her mother and brothers believed she was stupid. She didn't have their quick wittedness and had been reticent about speaking out at home for fear of ridicule. Thankfully her father had been less judgemental and she had been successful at school, so her self-esteem had remained mostly intact. There were times however when her childhood fears came back to haunt her, exposing insecurities she wished she could overcome, such as her nervousness at speaking out in the canteen the other week. She hoped Ralph's encouragement may one day chase away these old ghosts altogether.

It was obvious Ralph's parents had raised him with a completely different approach. He was an only child and she could imagine him being nurtured. Yes, that was the word; nurtured. He would have been encouraged and congratulated all the time. She didn't resent her family, she just identified how beneficial it would have been for her to have grown up in a less competitive and harsh environment. She decided she would behave more like Ralph's parents with any children she may have. She was pleased however to have two brothers; she couldn't imagine what Ralph's life was like without siblings. In spite of all the arguing and mockery she appreciated that outside of home they were supportive and they were good companions, especially her closer brother Tony.

Ralph knew Mia must be tired and made her put her feet up on a footrest and gave her a large glass of red wine. The dinner he had prepared smelled wonderful and she was very hungry. He sat next to her with his wine whilst waiting for the vegetables to cook.

"I thought I saw somebody lurking around my office door this evening" Mia told him.

"Were you there on your own?" he asked.

"Yes and it gave me the creeps!" she said shivering at the memory.

"What did you do?"

"I went to the door and called out but there was no answer. When I turned the hall lights on there was nobody there."

"Did you tell anyone?"

"I mentioned it to Sid as I was leaving and he agreed to go and check it out. I don't expect he'll find anything; it was probably just my imagination. I felt jumpy today because I kept thinking Vicky was going to come in."

"You mustn't keep worrying about Vicky; you know what we've agreed to say. Anyway" he added "if anything like that happens again and you don't feel safe call security straight away, that's what they're there for."

"I did think of that but felt I was being a baby!" she explained.

"Better to swallow your pride than be attacked!" he countered, then added "I worry about you there on your own in the dark. Promise me you'll call security in future if you have any concerns, however small."

"Yes OK, you're right, better safe than sorry."

They were quiet for a moment and Mia took another sip of wine contemplatively.

"What's up?" Ralph asked.

"I wish I'd never agreed to that stupid test" whined Mia "I can see I may lose a good friend over it."

"That's a bit dramatic, isn't it? As I said before, tell her it's our business and just refuse to talk about it."

"But that sounds rude and offish and if I don't talk about it, it will be like, well, the elephant in the corner! I like seeing her for lunch and just having her as a friend at work, I'm scared that's all been ruined."

Ralph didn't respond because he suspected Mia may be right. He suddenly remembered the vegetables were cooking and ran to take them off the heat before they turned into a mushy pulp. Whilst he dished up their meals Mia found some candles and set them up on the small kitchen table. They finished the wine with their late dinner, the candlelight transforming their kitchen into their own little bistro. It was cramped, crude and basic but oh so very, very romantic. Afterwards they fell into bed and gently but passionately made love before falling asleep, their bodies entwined so that they looked like one.

***

Ralph didn't know whether his dead left arm or his freezing right arm woke him up on Sunday morning. He was laid on his left side curled around Mia, his right arm outside of the quilt over her shoulder. He understood why his left arm was numb, his weight would be more than enough to stop the flow of blood, but the chill on his right arm was puzzling. He could see daylight creeping through the gaps in the drawn curtains and knew it must be at least seven so the heating should have been on for over an hour. He gently pulled away from Mia and tucked his exposed right arm under the quilt whilst waiting for the blood to start flowing into the left. His nose was cold and he could see his breath so he nestled further under the bedclothes. "Damn" he thought "the heating's broken down, that's all we need."

Eventually he mustered up the courage to get out of bed. He quickly put a tracksuit on and padded into the kitchen where the boiler was. He looked through the sight glass into the boiler. He had no idea what he was looking for but hoped there'd be something obvious. There wasn't. He put the kettle on and went to the hall cupboard where he rummaged through the top shelf to find an old electric convector heater his mum had always said may come in handy. He took it to the kitchen where it immediately started to take effect.

Mia soon joined him, in leggings and jumper, scurrying to stand in front of the small source of heat.

"Any idea what's wrong?" she asked.

"None whatsoever!" he admitted.

"We'll have to get someone out to look at it" she declared.

"Not today" he answered with some resignation "we can't afford emergency call-out charges. In fact, we can't afford getting it done at all! We're still up to our neck in Christmas debt. All our cards are at their limit and there's nothing in the bank."

Mia felt a flush of guilt when she recalled Ralph's reaction to her new boots; but they were a bargain.

"We can't go without heating!" she exclaimed outraged.

"We'll have to until next week" stated Ralph "after pay day. At least we have the emersion heater for hot water and the gas fire in the lounge." He paused then added irritably "I told you we were too tight for money, you shouldn't have bought those boots!"

"You still pay for the gym!" Mia retaliated "You haven't been since Christmas. At least I'm getting wear out of my boots."

"You have two other perfectly good pairs in the wardrobe!" he exclaimed his voice rising "and" he added clearly on a roll "you never want to cook anything; we live on take-away and pub grub. No wonder I need to belong to the gym!"

In a fit of déjà vu Mia was back in her childhood arguing with one of her brothers. Just as then she felt inadequate to stand her ground. Her cheeks pinked with fury and frustration. It wasn't ALL her fault that they had run out of money, though she did concede she had some responsibility for it, but Ralph could just as easily refuse when she suggested eating out. Besides, he DID spend money on gym membership and he'd had an expensive "January Christmas" night out with his mates a couple of weeks ago. These thoughts whirled round in her head but they were somehow locked there and she was powerless to make her case. The more she tried the harder it was to transfer her thoughts into speech. She stuttered and stammered a few incoherent words then turned away from him and stormed off back to the bedroom, slamming the kitchen and bedroom doors as she went.

It was cold in the bedroom and she got back under the bedclothes fully clothed. She felt desperately miserable, irritated with herself and Ralph. "What a cheek he's got" she thought "putting all the blame on me". She brooded for some time bitterly despising him and wondering whether she'd made a mistake marrying him. She toyed with the idea of divorce, such was her pique. But as she calmed down and the anger subsided she started to feel lonely and wished Ralph would come to the bedroom to make up. She was unwilling to make the first move and go to Ralph, so she just lay immobile in the bed waiting for him to come to her. What seemed like hours but was only minutes passed by. She began to fear he was more upset than she had realised. Ralph never lost his temper; this was the angriest she had ever seen him. She debated what to do but remained immobile. Surely he would realise how nasty he had been and come to her? Suddenly she heard the front door slam shut. Ralph had gone out! She looked over to the drawer top where he kept his keys and saw they were still there. Now she had the upper hand! She imagined him pleading to get in when he returned later that day. Then she wondered what she would do if he didn't come back. A cold space opened up in the pit of her stomach as she imagined what it would be like if he left her! She put the thought out of her mind; she couldn't consider the possibility of them separating.

She slipped out of bed and listened at the bedroom door. She couldn't hear anything. She opened the door a fraction and looked out; nothing happening. She wandered down the hall to the closed kitchen door and stopped outside, again checking for signs of Ralph. She was creeping about like an imposter and told herself not to be so silly. She edged the door open and saw the kitchen was empty. The fire was still whirring and the warmth was like a blanket reaching out to her. She stepped in and closed the door to retain the heat. She made a pot of coffee and took a cup of it to the kitchen table. She sat sipping and contemplating how very different it had been sitting in this very same spot the night before. She realised that Ralph had made dinner to keep costs down and remembered how sweet and supportive he had been. Then another part of her resentfully wondered who had paid for the beers he and James had consumed whilst watching the rugby. Then she remembered the stack of beers left over from Christmas. She sighed. What a fool she had been to get so upset and where was Ralph now? She desperately wanted to see him and give him a hug.

Her thoughts were interrupted by a familiar, domestic sound; it was the toilet flushing! Soon she heard Ralph's footsteps in the hall and in no time his bulky figure was framed in the kitchen door. They stared at each other.

"Would you like a coffee?" she offered with a slight shiver as the cold hallway air rushed into the kitchen.

"Love one" he responded.

"Can we afford it?" she said with a playful edge.

"Only if I have it black!" he laughed.

She stood up and moved to fill a cup for him but he barred her way. She looked up at him and he took her into his arms, squeezing her so she could hardly breathe. She basked in the comfort of his strong embrace and when he let go they kissed as though they were long lost lovers that had been separated for years. They abandoned the coffee and made for the bedroom not emerging until well into the afternoon.

She never thought to wonder why the front door had been slammed shut.

***

"Brrrrrrrr, I think I'll shower at work tomorrow" said Mia that evening.

"Good idea" he answered then added as gently as he could "I don't want to resurrect the argument but if we ate home-cooked food more often we would save money, be healthier AND I like it."

"Yes OK, OK, I know, I get the message" she retorted then pro-nounced "a late New Year resolution! We'll cook at least four meals a week!"

"That would be a start" Ralph sighed "but maybe we should aim for five?"

"OK, five on the weeks I'm on early shift and four when I'm late" she proposed.

"It's a deal" he said.

***

It was Friday lunchtime and Pam Sayers sat at a window table waiting for her daughter to arrive. She looked forward to their meetings. They had busy lives but made a point of taking half a day's leave every other month to meet for lunch. It was a chance to catch up and spend time together.

Pam was a Senior Account Manager for a major bank. She was proud that she had attained this position in spite of having raised three children and not having any paper qualifications. With her clients she had a relaxed but professional attitude. She also had an eye for business and worked exceptionally hard. These attributes were ideal though she was well aware that for many years new recruits were expected to have a degree. She felt strongly that a degree was not a necessary or desirable requirement for her job. She was not perturbed by her lack of certification. She had unerring confidence in her abilities.

She considered it was important to be particular over her appearance. Every night she prepared the clothes she was going to wear the next day, pressing blouses and trousers, choosing jewellery, polishing shoes and laying everything out ready. At week-ends and holidays she was just as fussy. Even though she looked casual her clothes were designer brand, and her hair and make-up were impeccable.

Pam and Mia were of similar slim build. Both had deep brown eyes and though Pam now had her hair short and the colour restored, as a young woman it had been much like Mia's. The similarity was just physical. In personality Pam was more cynical, critical and less optimistic than her daughter. She was also bolder and more assertive. She worried about Mia because she thought people exploited her good nature.

She'd expressed her concerns several times to Mia's dad John. These conversations always resulted in John telling her Mia was fine and Pam blaming him for his daughter's easy-going personality!

John was a steady, honest person; the type others befriended because they could trust him. He was fair-skinned and although

Mia wasn't at all like him in appearance, they shared the same outlook. Before she left home for university Mia and John regularly sat and chatted together after their evening meal. There was a close father daughter relationship and although Mia met her mother for lunch she was always more pleased to see her father.

Pam sighed. Mia never arrived on time. There was always some needy person delaying her. Why couldn't she be bolder and tell them she had to leave? It was feeble not to be assertive to get what you wanted. Why were her daughter and husband always willing to sacrifice their own needs for the sake of others? Pam couldn't understand it. She conceded, however, that if she'd married someone of her own unforgiving disposition, it would have been a disaster, and Mia's reconciliatory nature had brought calm to the family especially when her older brothers started fighting.

She thought about Ralph. What did her daughter find attractive about him? He seemed to Pam to be an untidy hulk lumbering through life. She had hoped Mia would meet a go-getting doctor when she decided to study physiotherapy. Mia would have benefitted from somebody with drive to drag her out of her comfort zone. Instead she'd chosen Ralph. They'd peddle through life in the slow lane letting others pass them by, it was most frustrating.

She took another sip of the cool dry white wine she'd ordered while she waited and hoped that Mia would arrive soon. She made herself consider the positives in Ralph. He was after all a gentle man who wouldn't harm her daughter and he was able to earn a good living, if not stunning. He wasn't going to set the world on fire, but he certainly loved her daughter and Mia loved him.

With that thought she saw Mia coming through the restaurant door and felt a warm glow.

"Hello sweetie!" she said as she stood to give Mia a hug.

"Hi Mum" Mia replied returning the hug and taking a seat. "Sorry I'm late."

"That's OK" said Pam "I was just getting slowly drunk! You'd better have a glass of this before I finish the bottle! I haven't ordered yet but I know what I'm having."

Pam poured a glass of wine for Mia whilst she took off her coat and sat down. She picked up the menu and started to choose what to eat.

"How's work?" asked Pam.

"Good" answered Mia. "I've an interesting case, a sixteen-year-old with spinal injuries. The cord wasn't completely severed, just badly damaged, so there should be a fair chance of the nerve growing back. I have to stop her leg muscles wasting away. She's a great kid. She's so determined to do the exercises however hard they are. I wish all my patients were like her. How about you? What's new in the banking world?"

"Same old same old" answered Pam. "The waiter's coming over, have you decided what you're having?"

They ordered their food and raised their glasses to each other.

"Mum" faltered Mia awkwardly "I was going to call you and cancel today."

"What's the matter?" asked Pam concerned but thinking "what now?"

"The thing is Mum I'm a bit tight for money at the moment. We overspent at Christmas and there's nothing in our bank account until payday next week! Can you pay for lunch today?"

"I always do!" exclaimed Pam.

"I know but I don't like to assume anything" explained Mia apologetically.

"No problem" Pam said sharply. Mia assumed her mum was annoyed because she hadn't managed her finances properly; another black mark. In fact Pam was irritated by her daughter's apologetic manner, it got on her nerves. She looked at her daughter and thought she seemed a little dishevelled.

"Is everything alright?" she asked. "You look a bit hassled."

"I'm fine, it's probably because I showered at work and the hairdryers there are not as good as mine at home."

"Why didn't you shower at home?"

"Our heating's broken down so I'm using the shower at work until it's fixed."

"Well you must be careful about your appearance, Mia. You can't go to work looking like a scruff!"

"I don't look like a scruff!"

"If you don't look after yourself other people won't believe you're worth looking after. That's my motto."

"Yes, I know what you think Mum but I don't look *that* untidy, do I?"

Pam studied her daughter.

"No" she admitted "I'm just warning you to take care of your appearance, that's all."

Mia gave a little giggle and her mother conceded a short half laugh; she was nagging again.

They were quiet for a while then Mia asked after her father and brothers. She wanted an update on the latest addition to the family, her niece Carly, Neil's new baby daughter. Pam asked after Ralph and that reminded Mia she was going to tell her mother about Vicky's test.

"He's good" she said of Ralph then added excitedly "but I must tell you, a really strange thing has happened."

"Oh, what's that?" answered Pam.

"Well, you know Vicky manages the Genetic Diagnostic Department, sh.."

"Yes, didn't she do well?!" Pam interrupted. "Good for her! And she beat all those men as well. There's a girl after my own heart! She's got some drive and guts!"

"I know how much you like her Mum" Mia said with a tinge of bitterness "but let me finish. Vicky offered to give Ralph and me a free screening test to check our compatibility for having children."

"What on earth do you want to do that for!?" Pam exclaimed interrupting again. "Why can't you just go in for children like anyone else?" Then, as the full significance of the words sunk in, she added "You didn't tell me you were trying to have children!"

"We're not!" stated Mia getting exasperated. "It's just for when we do."

"But why do you need a test? There aren't any major problems I know of on our side of the family. Is there a problem on *his* side?"

There was a sneer in the way she said "his side" which Mia ignored.

"No, not that we know of, but that doesn't mean there aren't any."

Pam scoffed impatiently. "For goodness sake, Mia, why go looking for problems that aren't there!? If you don't look you won't find any! It seems to me you're looking for an excuse to prevaricate on making the decision to have children."

Mia sighed; this was so typical of her mother, judgmental and hijacking the conversation.

"I'm not looking for an excuse to put off the decision" she said wearily "we already know we want to have children; it's just a question of when."

"Exactly, you *are* putting off the decision!" Pam answered with self-satisfaction.

Mia felt so annoyed and frustrated with Pam she stopped speaking. She decided attempting to tell her mother about the test really wasn't worth the effort. Besides, the punch-line wouldn't be at all amusing now.

"I'm sorry love" Pam offered when she realised Mia was fed up. "Please go on; I promise not to butt in again."

Mia took a breath and reluctantly continued. "Let me explain" she said less eagerly "as Vicky has access to the equipment she offered to put our samples through. It seemed like a good opportunity. People pay hundreds of pounds to be screened and she offered it to us for free."

"You mean the National Health offered it for free! Won't she get into trouble for abusing her position? You shouldn't have allowed her to risk her job to do you a favour!"

Mia wanted to scream but the conversation was further interrupted by the waiter who had appeared with their lunches. Mia leaned back in her chair to allow him to reach over and put

Pam's plate down. Pam gave him a filthy look to convey outrage because, as she saw it, he used the opportunity to rub himself against her daughter; Mia didn't seem to have noticed.

After he'd gone Pam told Mia the waiter was a pervert; he should have walked round the back of Mia to serve, not throw his body all over her. In answer to this Mia pointed silently down to the space beside her. Pam half raised herself from her chair to see the top of the head of a Labrador and realised there was a blind person at the next table blocking the waiter's access. She still remained convinced the waiter could have served them without touching Mia and made her mind up that he wasn't going to get a tip.

"So" said Pam returning to their conversation "Has Vicky taken much of a risk on your behalf?"

"I didn't ask her to do it!" reiterated Mia. "She volunteered! She insisted there was no risk as nothing had to be recorded on the computer system. She did the testing in her own time so all it has cost the NHS is the price of two syringe needles."

There was a further silence between them as they started eating their lunches.

Mia contemplated their exchange. "She's completely ruined my story with all her annoying interruptions. Maybe I shouldn't have been so late. It's made her all tetchy from waiting and she's probably had too much to drink. Trust her to be all sanctimonious about the testing. I wish I hadn't mentioned it now."

Pam replayed the conversation in her head "Typical of Mia" she thought "has to analyse and dither about everything instead of just getting on with it like everyone else. I suppose Ralph just concurred for a quiet life. What a load of baloney." Then she was struck by the realisation that Mia hadn't told her the test results and was overwhelmed with a need to know.

She broke the silence between a mouthful of coleslaw and baked ham.

"So, what did this DNA test show?" she asked.

"Mum" answered Mia "that isn't the point and doesn't matter because something went wrong with the test. Really, I can't be bothered to talk about it anymore; let's just drop the subject."

"Aw, don't be like that! I want to know now; I won't interrupt, promise" Pam pleaded.

Mia hesitated but conceded to her mother's request. "Well you wouldn't believe what Vicky tried to tell us!" she said rekindling her quest to deliver the funny punch-line and pausing for effect.

"Go on!" Pam demanded.

"Well, she reckoned the test showed....." Mia paused again and got some satisfaction that her mum was getting agitated by the delay. She let her stew for a few more seconds before declaring "it showed we are half brother and sister! That we have the same father!"

Pam nearly choked on her wholegrain bap, some escaping as she tried to stop the coughing. It wasn't the reaction Mia had expected and she watched with concern as the blood drained from her mother's face.

"Are you alright?" she asked giving her Mum a pat on the back.

"Yes" Pam answered shakily "It's just that...."

"Don't you feel well? Shall I get you some water?"

"No, no I'll be fine in a minute."

They were quiet for a while and the colour started to return to Pam's cheeks. Mia returned to her lunch but Pam sat vacantly opposite.

"You look a bit better now, mum. You gave me quite a fright; you went as white as a sheet!"

"Sorry about that sweetie" Pam said composing herself. "It was just such a shock and I had to collect my thoughts."

It was only now that Mia sensed her mother may be about to drop a bombshell.

"I can't believe it" mumbled Pam mostly to herself, then straight to Mia "but you must be your father's girl, you're so much like him!"

"What are you saying mum?" Mia asked. A sick feeling of panic was welling up turning her tummy into a gurgling watery mass. She silently prayed this was a wind-up, but her mother looked more serious than she had ever seen her look before. "Are you saying there's a chance I'm not dad's daughter?!"

Pam took a deep breath. "I had a fling" she stated flatly. "I went to a party up in Liverpool. Your aunty Sheila invited me when she was at nursing college there. Dad and I were going through a rough patch. Don't look at me like that! You wait until you've got children you'll realise what a strain it is and how mundane it can be!" She shuffled in the seat, her half-finished lunch looking forlorn and unappetising in front of her. "Aunty Sheila knew I was low so she thought it would be good for me to have a break and go stay with her for the week-end. The party was great!" She smiled briefly at the thought of it. "There were loads of students there and as I'd not been to college I'd never experienced being with so many young people. Although I was a bit older, I was still only twenty-five."

"But you had two children!" said Mia; it was now her turn to be sanctimonious.

"It was only a week-end away! I'm sure young mums of today wouldn't think twice about leaving their husbands with the children for a week-end. In my office I hear it all the time, women demanding their husbands look after the children while they go off on a trip, sometimes for weeks!"

"I'm sure they don't all go shagging the first person they meet!" exclaimed Mia cruelly.

"He wasn't the first person I met!" Pam answered indignantly. "I met loads of people; I just ended up with him! It wasn't like I didn't know him, we chatted all night, off and on. He was a medical student" she stated as though that justified her behaviour. "Anyway, that's that and I can't say any more about it other than we were so careful, I can't believe I could have got pregnant."

They were both quiet for a moment then Mia relaxed.

"It's certainly a revelation mum and thanks for telling me about your fling!" she said impishly "But think about it. Was this man such an Adonis he made his way from Liverpool to Hillingdon to have a fling with Ralph's mum of all people?!"

Pam stared at Mia and relief crept onto her face. She had been leaning more and more forward but now she relaxed back.

"You're right!" she exclaimed "I've always been conscious of the fact I had a fling about the time I conceived you and I guess I got so wrapped up in the thought of it I lost all sense of well, common sense. Yes, that still wouldn't explain this result of Vicky's, thank goodness! You are your father's daughter!" She went quiet and mused "I can't imagine Ralph's mum having a fling with anyone, can you? Anyway, you couldn't possibly have been that man's daughter; he was a right pompous git!"

"Why did you go to bed with him if he was a pompous git?" asked Mia.

"You tell me" answered Pam. "Why do we do things like that? Drinking too much for one thing and I didn't realise how much he loved himself until the cold light of the next day. I was just thankful we'd used a condom."

"Let's move on from here" suggested Mia not wanting her Mother to go into any more detail "or do you want to finish your lunch?"

Pam looked at her plate. "No, let's go, my lunch doesn't look very appetising. We can get a cake or something later."

She waved to the waiter for the bill.

"You won't tell your Father, will you" she implored as she gave the waiter her credit card "there's no point in upsetting him over something that happened more than thirty years ago."

"Of course I won't say anything to Dad, sometimes I think you don't credit me with any sense at all" Mia answered scornfully.

They spent the rest of the day wandering around the shops in Oxford Street, enjoying each other's company and not talking any more about it.

Chapter 4
For Better or Worse

"A guilty conscience!" exclaimed Ralph. "She must have been plagued by that for all these years! Poor Pam has had to admit she isn't perfect after all! I bet she's kicking herself that she told you in the heat of the moment when she could have kept it secret!"

"Don't be mean" chided Mia. "I've never seen her look so unsure of herself. I'm so used to her being in control it was quite unnerving."

"Well I find her constant criticism of you annoying" persisted Ralph. "She never accepts you might be right or even just different. Look at how she tried to talk you out of living in Balham, you'd think we'd chosen to move into the Wild West the way she went on, advising us to put three locks on the door and not go out after eight at night! She'd have rather we spent all our time and money commuting back and forth to Dorking."

"She was only worried about us" defended Mia. "But could you imagine what it would have been like living near them? Dad would have been alright but Mum would have driven us crazy! Arm's length is where Mum needs to stay and lunch every other month is more than fulfilling my daughterly obligations. Now I feel guilty for saying that so we'd better drop the subject!"

Ralph had just come home from work. Mia had got home earlier following her lunch with Pam and had been reading in the living room sat up close to the gas fire. The heat was not reaching the rest of the room and she was wearing one of her thickest jumpers. Ralph went to get changed and Mia followed him into the cold bedroom.

"What shall we have for dinner tonight?" he asked as he quickly pulled on some warm clothes. "I don't suppose by any chance you've prepared anything?"

"No, I thought I'd wait for you" Mia answered. "Shall we go out?"

"Mia! How could you ask?! What did we row about on Sunday?! We can't eat out; we have NO money!"

"We have enough money for a simple meal out" Mia countered though she'd spoken without thinking. "We'd need to buy something to cook anyway. Come on Ralph, we haven't been out this week and it's not very friendly in here without the heating."

"We've been fine in the kitchen with the fan heater on" he answered determinedly.

"Alright, I'll go see what's in the freezer" she conceded dejectedly.

Ralph sighed as she left for the kitchen. He reflected ruefully again how they had got into the habit of living on convenience foods, takeaways and pub grub. He heard Mia rooting about in the freezer and then her light footsteps down the hall as she came back to report what was on offer.

"We've got some breaded fish and oven chips or we can have lasagne" she said.

"I don't think we've got any vegetables left" Ralph said.

"No, not fresh" answered Mia. "It's only six-thirty; shall we go and get some now?"

"No let's have the fish and chips for tonight" he answered "but I suggest we go to the supermarket tomorrow to pick up supplies and then we take it in turns to cook dinner."

Mia considered the idea. "Surely whoever gets home from work first should start the cooking" she suggested "the other one can do the clearing up."

Ralph nearly always got home before Mia. He couldn't argue with her logic but it looked like he'd be doing most of the cooking and, as he'd never leave her to do the clearing up alone, he'd be doing that too. It was the price he'd have to pay to get them into decent eating habits.

"OK" he agreed reluctantly and he made his way to the kitchen to put the oven on.

***

On the following Thursday it was Ralph's turn to be working alone in a deserted office block. The dark February night had closed in around the rest of the building and his lit office stood out like a beacon; it was nearly eight o'clock. Ostensibly he was sorting out an urgent problem but actually he was ensuring he got home later than Mia. He'd made dinner every night since their conversation and was determined to get a night off.

He was using the time to sort out a complicated problem and was totally absorbed in his monitor. He turned slightly then leapt back at the shock of seeing somebody in the doorway, it gave him such a start, he nearly fell off his chair.

"Vicky! You made me jump!"

"Sorry" she answered "I didn't mean to scare the wits out of you! I saw you were working late so came to say hello. Are you saving us from a system failure? I'm sure the hospital would close if the computers went down."

"No nothing that dramatic, just trying to stop one person from losing their lifeline tomorrow."

Ralph felt awkward. He was aware that Mia had been avoiding Vicky.

"I haven't seen you or Mia since I came over the other week. Is everything alright?"

"Fine, fine" Ralph answered quickly "we've just been very busy. You know how it is; what with working here all hours" he swept his arm vaguely around the office "and we're on a health kick. I've been going to the gym most nights and we're eating more healthily by cooking at home. The time just disappears."

"Oh, which gym do you go to?" asked Vicky.

"Tone Ups" he replied "as it's on my way home."

"I go there!" exclaimed Vicky. "That's funny; I've been most days this week, you'd think we would have bumped into each other!"

Ralph cursed; what bad luck she happened to go to the same

gym! He hadn't been since before Christmas.

"That *is* strange" he agreed. "What time do you go?"

"Varies" she said "sometimes I go before work and sometimes after."

"Well I'm sure we'll bump into each other sooner or later" he said evasively.

There was a short uncomfortable silence. Then Vicky looked at Ralph with an unusually bashful expression. "Actually" she said "I've been worried about you both. Since I came over with the test results Mia seems to have been avoiding me. You're not upset with me for telling you, are you?"

"No, no" Ralph answered reassuringly "not at all, we really have been very busy, honestly" then to add weight added "Mia's really getting into cooking, she seems to spend hours over preparing meals, it's become quite a hobby."

"That doesn't sound like Mia!" Vicky remarked. "I'd imagine she'd much rather go out or put her feet up whilst you did the dinner!"

Ralph started to rebuff her comment but Vicky had read his expression.

"That's why you're here!" she exclaimed, an understanding smile forming at the corners of her mouth. "You're hanging around so that she'll have to cook the dinner!"

Ralph was stunned at being rumbled. How transparent he must have been! His pink cheeks confirmed Vicky's accusation was on target. He'd managed to divert the conversation but had exposed himself as a liar and a schemer. He prided himself on his honesty and now he felt very uncomfortable. All he could do was to shrug his shoulders and come clean.

"You're right on both counts!" he admitted. "I am hoping to get back to a nice hot meal and no, cooking isn't Mia's forte!"

Vicky glowed with self-satisfaction. Ralph cringed at her relish in exposing his true reason for working late. He deeply regretted having been cornered by her. He was about to extricate himself but before he had the chance she came up with an idea.

"I know!" she said "Why don't you come over to mine this week-end? I'd enjoy cooking for you both, you can have a decent meal and it would be good to catch up."

Ralph couldn't accept the invitation without discussing it with Mia so was forced into telling more lies.

"That's very kind of you" he said "but we're pretty tied up this week-end. On Friday we're out with this lot" he waved at the empty desks again "we're seeing Mia's old college friends on Saturday and we're visiting my parents on Sunday. It would be good to meet up and take you up on the offer of a meal though. I'll get Mia to give you a bell to arrange a date."

"You ARE busy bees" said Vicky and in a sarcastic tone added "I'll wait for Mia to ring and find me a slot in your overloaded schedule."

"Thanks" Ralph said without knowing why, then aware that Vicky had probably also seen through these lies, tried to sound more convincing by adding "sorry we can't make it, you just happened to choose a particularly busy week-end. We don't usually live in such a whirl!"

"So long as you're both OK" replied Vicky half questioning.

"Yes, we're great" he answered.

Vicky hesitated then adopted a grave frown and her doctor's persona.

"You can't just ignore the test results" she stated. "You do know that, don't you?"

"Yes" he answered tersely. "You can leave that with us now, Vicky; we are grown-ups!"

"Just as I thought" she said. "You *are* angry with me."

"No, really we aren't" he asserted "we just want to deal with it in our own way and time. It is a private matter after all."

"Yes, you're right, of course it is" she conceded. "Sorry, I wasn't meaning to interfere. I was just concerned that you understood the seriousness of it."

Ralph didn't respond but allowed a pregnant pause to fall between them.

"We're still friends then?" she said breaking the impasse and moving towards him in an affable manner.

"Of course!" he replied instinctively adopting a board-like stance to stave off any possibility of physical contact.

"Oh well" she said understanding his body language and moving back towards the door "best be getting home else I won't have time to cook myself anything. Are you leaving now? We can walk to the station together."

"I'm not quite ready yet" he said. "I'll get Mia to ring you."

"OK" Vicky responded. "Have a nice night, what's left of it. Hope the meal Mia's cooked is worth being late for!"

She left the office and Ralph breathed a sigh of relief mixed with irritation. He was rattled by her haughtiness over the test result and the annoying way she'd unravelled his ploy not to cook dinner. They would have to make the effort to see her soon; she had been genuine in trying to help them and was one of Mia's closest friends. However, he was not prepared to hear any further reference to that bloody test and didn't want any mention of it when they were together.

***

It was just after nine o'clock when Ralph made his way through the main entrance to their block and was met by the familiar smell of cooked food that always lingered in the common hallway at night. Somebody was preparing grilled meat and it made his mouth water. The smell got stronger as he climbed the stairs and was reminiscent of a BBQ; his stomach rumbled. But by the time he reached their door his hunger was vanquished by fear; the smoke alarm was screaming and the smell was more bonfire than BBQ. He hurriedly turned his key, forced open the tight-fitting door and was engulfed in a tsunami of hazy, blue smoke swirling from the kitchen. He flew into find Mia standing in front of the sink with the grill pan in her hand. She looked hassled, hot and close to tears. He threw the kitchen window open allowing a cold breeze to invade the kitchen and chase the warm, smoky air away. He then went and stood behind her, putting his head over her shoulder so they were both staring into the ruined contents of the grill pan. He woefully observed two leather-like, dried-up pork chops, several blackened slices of onion, six mushrooms that could have passed as prunes and a number of charcoaled red pepper strips. The whole sorrowful platter was swimming in water. He was thankful the flat and Mia had survived, but grievous for the poor chops and trimmings that could have been so very, very tasty.

"Do you think we can salvage any of it?" she asked.

Ralph picked up a fork and tried to push it through one of the wet chops but it was as hard as a rock.

"No, afraid not" he concluded.

"I only left it for a minute whilst I went to watch the end of *Master Chef*" Mia whined ruefully. Ralph chuckled and she managed a smile as she saw the irony of what she had said.

She wiped her arm across her forehead. "I was so pleased with what I was cooking, now look at it!"

"Well at least the rest of the kitchen has survived!" Ralph consoled.

"What are we going to eat? It's so late" asked Mia dejectedly.

"We'll go vegetarian" stated Ralph "jacket potatoes with cheese and salad will be fine and won't take long."

"I'm sorry!" said Mia. She put the pan down and turned to face him, then put her arms around his waist and buried her head into his chest.

"Don't worry" he replied encircling her with his arms "just stay like this for a while and you'll more than make up for it!"

She pulled slightly away from him and looked into his eyes. He bent down and kissed her and they continued to kiss for a few minutes. Then Ralph, thinking he might die from hunger, suggested Mia proceed to put the potatoes in the microwave whilst he got changed.

They finally started eating at ten o'clock. By then the smoky air had been chased from the flat, the alarm had stopped crying and they had closed the windows. However, it still felt chilly in the kitchen so they took their meals into the lounge, where they could sit by the gas fire and eat from their laps in front of the TV.

"I saw Vicky tonight" Ralph said above the programme.

"Oh no!" answered Mia. "What did she say?"

"Just wondered how we were and whether we were OK after our meeting with her. She was a bit upset that we hadn't been in touch."

"I know I do feel guilty, I should ring or mail her but I'm scared she'll want to discuss that stupid test result. Did she mention it?"

"Yes, but I told her it was up to us."

"You didn't!"

"Well I didn't put it quite that directly. She asked whether we wanted to go to dinner at her house this week-end."

"Oh no!" Mia exclaimed "What did you say?"

"I fobbed her off. Said we were out with my office lot on Friday, your college friends on Saturday and my parents on Sunday."

"Ralph! That's a whopper! The only truth is the visit to your parents! Say she phones or passes by and sees we're here?!"

"That's not very likely! I think you're getting a bit paranoid now! Anyway, we can always tell her something was cancelled; did you want to see her this week-end?"

"No! Definitely not! I'm not ready for her yet."

Neither spoke for the next few minutes whilst they listened to a couple of politicians arguing over funding of the NHS.

"I'll mail Vicky next week" Mia continued. "I can't go on avoiding her. Once I repeat what you said she can't really ask again can she?"

"No, that should end any further conversation about it" Ralph stated.

***

Sunday morning was bright and sunny, feeling like spring. There had been no lingering in bed. Ralph had agreed they would be at his parents by ten thirty so they could visit his Grandmother before lunch. She was now ninety-four and had moved to a residential home for company more than any physical or mental incapacity; though she was getting a bit more forgetful these days. "I'm spending your inheritance!" she teased Ralph during one visit; the home was very expensive. She was happy there and well cared for. Ralph tried to visit when he could.

It was going to be a gruelling journey, a long tube ride between Balham and Hillingdon followed by a fifteen-minute walk to Ralph's parents' house. Sitting in the noisy, soot laden atmosphere of the underground for over an hour would be unpleasant, but more flexible and reliable than the alternative train and bus. At least it would be less crowded than on work days.

"I suggest we don't mention Vicky's test" said Ralph as they walked to the station.

"Definitely not" concurred Mia.

Mia didn't feel easy with her mother-in-law, finding her remote and difficult to read. Davina was a reserved person seemingly aloof and unfriendly. Mia had found her intimidating at first but familiarity had thawed the ice and there was now affability between them. Ralph's father David was much more welcoming than his wife, though also reserved. They were older than Mia's parents, both retired; they had obviously had Ralph late in life. Davina had been a Head Teacher at a private girls' school and David an Actuary, so they were relatively wealthy. Ralph, their only child, had been looked after by a Nanny and had a different relationship with his parents to the one Mia had with hers. She imagined it must have been very quiet growing up in the Davenport household in contrast to the Sayers', where there was a constant hubbub. What with her parents bickering and her brothers fighting, the TV in competition with guitar strumming, and music blaring out, it was a miracle she wasn't deaf. But that was what she was used to. It was alien to be in a tranquil home environment.

Ralph had told her of how he'd spent hours making model aeroplanes with his father, meticulously gluing the pieces together, whilst his Mum marked papers or read. As Ralph got older he and David went out cycling together and they also shared an interest in mathematics; deliberating for hours over complicated puzzles. He had a more remote relationship with his mother but it was clear Ralph was very much loved by both his parents and Mia was sure this had contributed to his quiet confidence and caring personality. Mia envied the individual attention and the broad education they'd given him; in music he seemed to know everything from jazz to the classics.

She didn't look forward to visiting David and Davina. They were kind but she felt she had to be on her best behaviour all the time. It was more of a strain than going to work. She didn't feel she'd had her week-end break when half of it had been spent visiting them.

"Do you think you could loosen up a bit today" Ralph said as if he had read her mind. "They won't bite your head off, they really are nice people."

"I know, I'll try to relax but when it's quiet I think I've done something wrong. When I was at home a quiet house was a warning to keep your head down. Tell me Ralph, how did your parents tell you off? What sort of punishment did they give you?"

"I don't remember getting told off" he answered.

"Well didn't they ever get cross, if not with you, with each other?" she said incredulously.

"If they argued it wasn't in front of me" he said "I think I was lucky."

They descended into the gloom of the underground and said little more until they emerged at the other end.

David opened the door with a welcoming grin. He shook Ralph's hand warmly and gave Mia a light kiss on the cheek as they passed into the hall where Davina was waiting her turn to peck them on the cheeks. They moved into the front lounge, which Mia found too tidy to be comfortable, sat in the leather suite and exchanged pleasantries. Davina then went to make tea and came back to the room holding a tray that contained an ornate china teapot, milk jug, sugar bowl and four delicate china cups and saucers. She went out again and returned with a fine china plate on which was a beautifully presented home-made cake with a layer of soft icing on top. She gave David instructions to fetch four tea plates, teaspoons and cake forks from the side-board.

Mia had seen the china before and had been told it was a family heirloom. It seemed to her that most of the Davenport's posses-sions were either inherited or purchased on holiday. Didn't they ever go shopping in the local high street? It was, in Mia's opin-ion, quite a to-do for a cup of tea and piece of cake; they even handed out napkins. It put Mia on edge as she worried about breaking the plate or spilling her tea. She had difficulty using the small fork; the cake broke up into crumbs and it was a job to keep them on the fork all the way to her mouth. She self-con-sciously picked up any pieces that fell on the settee or carpet. The cake was tasty but Mia wished she'd been able to eat it with her fingers. Her Mother never made cakes; Mr Kipling was the provider of such fare in the Sayers' household. Cakes were eaten straight from the box without the aid of implements or the use of serviettes.

"We wouldn't normally have cake in the morning" confessed Davina as though Mia might be critical "but as we'll be eating a late lunch I thought you might get hungry."

"Quite right Mum and this is lovely" answered Ralph. "We didn't have much breakfast either so it's much appreciated." Mia nod-ded in agreement as she shakily raised the delicate tea cup to her mouth.

They went on to catch up. Ralph and Mia talked about work, what exhibitions and films they'd seen and reported on how Mia's family were doing. David and Davina mainly talked about their latest holiday, they had just returned from Kenya, but also reported on various family friends, most of whom Mia had met at the wedding but couldn't remember.

As soon as they'd finished their tea they got ready to go to Rose Acres residential home to see Nanny Davenport. Davina stayed at home to prepare lunch whilst David drove Ralph and Mia the short journey there.

On Sundays there were always a number of visitors at Rose

Acres and all sorts of people were coming and going. Most of the residents were entertaining their guests in the large, communal lounge. Audrey Davenport was sitting with another couple of ladies in a corner of the room and Ralph thought she looked really well.

"Hello!" she said when she saw the three of them. "What a pleasant surprise! How nice it is to see my favourite grandson and his wife!"

"Hi Nan" Ralph replied as he bent down to the chair to give her a kiss. "How are you doing?"

"Can't grumble" she said but was just about to start when her neighbour butted in.

"I'm Vera" she stated. "I've moved into the room next to your Nan."

"How do you do Vera" smiled Ralph. "I'm Ralph, this is my wife Mia and my Father, Audrey's son, David."

"Have you come far?" Vera continued.

Ralph saw Audrey looking thunderous; she didn't want to share her visitors.

"I won the Bingo this week!" she said completely cutting across Vera.

Ralph was now in the difficult position of trying to talk to both ladies at once. He didn't know whether to be rude to Vera or upset Audrey. David came to the rescue by explaining to Vera that the "children" lived in South London but that he lived nearby, whilst Ralph asked Audrey what she had won. Now two conversations were going on at once and Mia felt at home. She was easily able to follow both exchanges as well as other peoples' chatter. A member of staff came around with the regular Sunday sherry and poured them a glass. Mia felt relaxed; she liked the general atmosphere in the home and the sherry was warming.

A few minutes later she heard Ralph agree to go to see his Nan's paintings in her room. She had never tried painting before but was thoroughly enjoying it now, taking part in a small class run at the home under the direction of a volunteer. As Mia was curious to see the paintings she chose to go with Ralph. David decided to leave them to it. He had already seen his mother's artwork so decided to stay with Vera. This may have been a mistake. As they left she was asking him for the third time where he lived.

Audrey's room was a good size though not huge. Knick-knacks and a few photographs, including one of Ralph and Mia at their wedding, adorned the top of a chest of drawers. In one corner there was a large TV with a recliner armchair in front of it. Audrey reached into a fitted wardrobe and pulled out a large folder in which there were a number of sheets of paper. She flicked through and chose one; a large, colourful painting of dancing couples. It was a good attempt for a ninety-four-year-old starter though it wasn't clear whether it was supposed to be impressionist or was how Audrey saw the world now her eyes were not so good.

They showered her with complements as they made their way through about a dozen paintings that all looked much the same as the first. They began to realise why David had chosen to stay with Vera; they were running out of flattering remarks to make.

"A new helper came yesterday" Audrey told them. "A very nice young lady; she thought I should try to sell my paintings!"

"Why not?" said Ralph thinking the helper had gone a step too far but happy to see Audrey looking so proud and pleased. "Maybe they would like to display one of them here?"

"I don't want *them* to have any of my paintings!" Audrey spat begrudgingly. "Why should I?"

"It was just a suggestion Nan" Ralph replied quickly, perplexed at her attitude.

At that point Audrey seemed to run out of steam and they agreed to go back downstairs. Audrey grabbed hold of Ralph's arm and held on to it as they walked slowly down the corridor from her room to the lift. Mia followed finding it difficult to walk at such a snail's pace, it made her muscles ache more than if she'd gone for a jog. They finally got to the lift.

"It's so lovely to see you Ralphie" Audrey said and Ralph felt guilty that he didn't come more often. "What would I do without you?" she added and then she started rambling on as she had a habit of doing. "As I told that young helper, you're my only grandchild so you're very precious. I didn't agree with it at the time but I'm so glad to have you. We couldn't have any more children, you see, not after Davie; he's the end of the line. It's not my fault. It's the Davenport men that let the side down."

Ralph had only been half listening but he caught the last thing she said. "What did you say about the Davenport men?" he asked and as he did he looked back at Mia who indicated she had heard it by giving a quizzical look.

"Eh, what? I wasn't saying anything love."

"Just then, Nan, something about dad and the male members of the family that let the side down."

"Not a big family are we son?"

"No, Nan. Why is that?"

"Just the way it is" she sounded tired of his questions and dismissive.

The three of them said nothing else as they waited for the lift and took it down the one floor of the two storied building. They continued the snail's pace along the corridor to the lounge where they saw David slouched in his chair trying to hold his eyelids open but not fully succeeding. Vera was still chatting away, seemingly oblivious to David's semi-comatose state.

"We're back!" bellowed Ralph and laughed as David nearly dropped his empty sherry glass.

"What's the time?" he said recovering his composure.

"Twelve-thirty, and some of the residents are already making their way into the dining room" answered Ralph.

"We have to wait for the Zimmer frames to go first" stated Vera begrudgingly. "It's not fair, us having to wait while they all go in front."

Audrey flopped heavily into a chair. "No" she agreed anger welling at the reminder of this injustice. "Yesterday I got a right telling off from "Miss Piggy" just because I pushed Mary; she'd purposely stood in the passage to stop me getting in! She's only just started using a Zimmer and was showing off!"

David had got up in readiness to leave and quickly glanced around to check whether Sue, the tubby care assistant, was within ear-shot; she would be offended by the "Miss Piggy" reference. He breathed a sigh of relief when he saw her some way away down the corridor, standing sentry at the dining room doorway.

"Don't be like that Mum" he said "Mary can't help not being as fit as you; you're the lucky one not needing a Zimmer frame. And don't be rude. If you go around upsetting the staff or other residents they may not let you stay."

"They won't throw me out! They like my money" Audrey answered defiantly.

"Just try to be nice" David pleaded "they only let the least able in first to allow them to get to their seats more easily. It's not as though you don't get anything to eat because you go in after them."

He raised his brows as he looked towards Mia and Ralph over Audrey's head. They exchanged a small grin with him.

"We'll be off now" David told his mother as he bent down to kiss her good-bye.

She looked as though she may protest at their departure but she became distracted by two elderly gentlemen who were making their way out of the lounge without Zimmer frames. It was evidently time for the "able" bodied residents to go for dinner.

"Thanks for coming" she said to Ralph and Mia as she determinedly lifted herself back out of the chair. "Try to come again soon."

"We will" promised Ralph as they kissed her goodbye.

"See you tomorrow" she said to David then she hurried off. They watched in amazement as she rushed towards the dining room, rudely barging past the two gentlemen. Mia was surprised; she'd thought their earlier snail's pace was all Audrey could manage.

They waited for her to disappear into the dining room and David shrugged his shoulders with a smile.

"The Manager called me in last week" he told them as they made their way back to the car. "It seems she and her friend Martha had been sitting in the lounge bitching about other residents loudly enough for everyone to hear, including the people they'd been talking about! I had to tell her not to be rude to the other residents! Nan thinks she's "saying it as it is." I told her "no Mum, it's just plain rude!"

"She didn't used to be like that" observed Ralph.

"I'm afraid it's a sign of dementia" answered David "it causes personality changes. Still she isn't bad for her age."

The smell of roast lamb floated into Ralph's nostrils as they came back into his parents' house; it reminded him of Sundays as a boy. His mouth watered and his stomach rumbled at the thought of roast dinner. They sat and had another sherry, Davina popping in and out between checking the vegetables. Mia made a polite offer to help but knew Davina would refuse. With the second sherry of the day she sat back in the sofa and unwound.

The dining table looked inviting with a lovely white lace table cloth (purchased on a holiday in Madeira), posy of small flowers in the centre (vase from Portugal) and knives and forks laid round exquisite place mats (purchased in Singapore). The polished wine glasses (Venice) sparkled in the low lighting needed as it was already getting dusky. Mia admitted it looked superb but couldn't help feeling they were what her Mum would call "standing on ceremony". She wished the Davenports could be less formal. Of course, they didn't realise they were "standing on ceremony". They were just trying to please.

"This all looks lovely Mum" complimented Ralph and Mia saw Davina's shoulders go back with pride. Mia inwardly conceded that there was no point in having lovely things if you didn't use them. A number of their wedding presents were still in boxes.

David went to help Davina serve the meal whilst Ralph poured the wine and soon they were all lifting glasses with Cheers! Good Health! Compliments to the cook! Good to see you! They helped themselves from terrines (inherited from Aunty Fanny) and tucked into their food.

Conversation continued much as before and they finished dinner and pudding. As they relaxed with a coffee the conversation turned to Audrey and the concerns David and Davina had for her mental state. They related how she was rambling more, forgetting things and getting a little aggressive.

"Yes, I know what you mean" said Ralph "she was perfectly fine most of the time we were there but when we went to look at her paintings she started going on about the Davenport men, and saying it was their fault she hadn't had many children. She said something about disapproving of you having me but pleased you did!"

Mia nodded in confirmation.

"Did she?!" David exclaimed. "That's weird."

"Yes, it is" agreed Davina. "Why would she mention that after all these years?"

"You know what she was going on about then?" said Ralph.

Davina sighed, she wasn't prepared for this.

"Yes" she answered "I do."

There was a really silent pause; more silent than the usual Davenport silences. If it were possible to grade silence this would be at the extreme. Mia couldn't bear it and having had a couple of glasses of wine spoke up.

"Why did she disapprove of you having Ralph?" she asked.

Davina looked at David. He took a huge intake of air. A knot started to form in Mia's stomach.

"The truth is that over the generations the male side of my family haven't been very productive as far as children are concerned" David told them "and it has become progressively more problematical for each new generation."

"Oh, so you only managed one, and I'm not likely to manage any" Ralph interrupted with an edge to his tone close to anger.

"Oh no, no" interceded Davina reassuringly "YOU should be fine!"

She looked at David again but this time she decided to take over. "Darling" she addressed Ralph and placed her hand over his on the table "we always meant to tell you but somehow it never seemed important. The truth is we discovered that Dad couldn't have children because of this genetic problem. We wanted children so we agreed to try artificial insemination. You were what we called a test tube baby! That means you won't have inherited the Davenport reproduction disorder."

She said it as though he should be pleased, David nodded in agreement. They watched their son as he digested the information.

"What you're telling me" Ralph said slowly and tight-lipped as though the words were freezing in his mouth "is that Dad, well he isn't my Dad?!"

He looked from one parent to the other as he spoke. His head was spinning, his heart was thumping. He reached out to take Mia's hand.

"Of course he's your Dad!" Davina said offended. "Who else raised you all those years. There can't be many fathers as dedicated to their sons as yours has been Ralph."

Ralph looked at Mia and saw his fear and shock reflected in her face. First, he had to absorb the fact that he was not genetically related to his father, which was a bolt from the blue, but at the same time he needed to take in the implications of such a discovery as related to that dreaded test. He realised his parents were not privy to the test results and would think he and Mia were overreacting. He was amazed at his parent's casual attitude although when he looked more closely there were lines of anxiety across his father's face.

Ralph couldn't bring himself to start talking about the test and its implications and was sure Mia didn't want to either. It was all too complicated and he just needed time with Mia alone to consider what this all meant. He looked towards his parents.

"No, no of course you're right" he stuttered "there would never be anyone else I could think of as my Dad, it's just a shock to suddenly find out I'm the genetic son of somebody else. I wish you'd told me before."

"What would have been the point, Ralph?" said Davina in her typical practical and insensitive manner. "The donor had the right to complete anonymity, which was fair in my opinion. If not, who would have been prepared to donate sperm?" She was repeating an old, well aired argument and momentarily forgot Ralph was not an acquaintance but her son who had only just been told the truth about his father. She was alarmed to see he looked tearful and very pale; she hadn't seen him so upset since his grandfather died.

She continued in a more sympathetic tone. "All I'm saying Ralph is that as you were never going to be able to trace the donor we didn't think it was worth chancing any psychological problems or insecurities by telling you when you were young. Once you'd grown up it didn't seem relevant."

"It was all new when we went in for it" David came in, also seeing his son's distress. "In fact we had to go up to Manchester as no other hospitals were able to carry out the procedure. The consultants were well ahead in the field; the first test tube baby was born there. You were one of the first to be ..." he searched for the words "well, grown from a donor. I'm sorry Ralph, I guess we didn't spend much time thinking about when and what we were going to tell you, we were just so pleased to have you!"

There was a pause. Ralph tried to keep calm but what he had just heard seemed unreal. He wanted to leave straight away, be on his own with Mia, but knew it would upset his parents and that would be unfair.

Mia sat in silence throughout the exchange watching Ralph's distress and feeling panicked. Her mother's words "pompous git" were reverberating through her head; "pompous git! pompous git! pompous git!" Could this really be true? She, like Ralph, was desperate to leave but also didn't want to upset his parents. She started an exit strategy.

"Loads of people have artificial insemination now" she said moving the conversation on from the personal to the general "some women pay to have babies when they don't even have a partner."

"I know" agreed Davina pleased to progress to generalities "and there are gay couples that have children that way too."

This allowed the four to spend a few minutes discussing the morals of these cases and then move on to more general subjects like how things had changed over the years. When Ralph judged there had been enough conversation to dispel the thought there was a problem between him and his parents he looked at his watch and indicated it was time they should leave.

"Work for us tomorrow!" he said "and a long ride on the tube so we'd best be on our way."

"Let us help you with the washing up before we go" offered Mia knowing very well they wouldn't accept.

"No don't worry about that!" answered Davina "most of it will go in the dishwasher and we don't have to get up for work to-morrow!"

They thanked his parents for the lovely meal and finally got out of the house, waving goodbye until they had turned the corner.

"I was surprised how badly Ralph took that" Davina said as she closed the door "and did you see Mia? She went white."

"It wasn't the best way to tell him" answered David feeling sick with guilt. "It must have been a shock. Fancy Audrey mention-ing it! I hope it doesn't make any difference to our relationship. He will understand why we didn't tell him, don't you think?" He wasn't sure and wrung his hands nervously.

"Yes, don't worry about it" Davina answered consolingly "I doubt they'll think any more of it." She put her arm around his shoulder but he didn't respond so she left him with his thoughts and headed back to the kitchen to start clearing up.

Part 2

Breaking the Vows

Chapter 5

In the Delight and Tenderness of Sexual Union

The promise of spring had given way to the raw cold of winter by the time they made their way back to Hillingdon station. Mia lifted her coat collar against the chill wind and Ralph put his broad arm around her shoulders. They walked the whole distance without speaking.

On the train they sat together silently gripping hands, a pair of frightened souls reflecting on how the last few hours had catapulted their lives into an unknown space. Back home there was the relief and pleasure of being safely in their own little castle where they could relax and speak freely but it was tainted with an underlying fear that the ramparts had been breached and a strange enemy was within.

Neither wanted to start the inevitable conversation so they busied themselves with small tasks like putting their coats away and filling the kettle. In the end it was Mia that spoke.

"So" she said leaning back against the kitchen cupboard "it looks like you've got a pompous git for a father as well!"

"Looks like it, though you take after him more than I do" answered Ralph following Mia's attempt to lighten the mood.

"So, after all our piss taking" reflected Mia "Vicky was right!"

"I still can't believe it!" sighed Ralph bewildered. "What must the chances of this happening be? It must be more remote than winning the lottery!"

"I know" Mia concurred. "But when you think of it maybe we were attracted to each other because we were .... it's hard to say … related."

"Maybe it isn't right, maybe this is all a mistake" said Ralph in denial. "You don't *know* your mother got pregnant from that fling; it's supposition."

"I wish so much I could believe that!" Mia cried. "But you can't get away from the facts, Ralph. My Mum shagged a student doctor in Liverpool; your Mum had you through a donor in Manchester. Medical students often act as donors for money or the good of the human race and Manchester and Liverpool are neighbours. And, of course, we can't forget the final piece of evidence, that damned DNA test!"

Ralph remained quiet. He'd reached the same conclusion but didn't want to believe it.

"What are we going to do!?" wailed Mia, tears forming in her eyes.

"We don't have to do anything" Ralph answered moving forwards and folding his arms around her. "We'll carry on just as before. Vicky's the only one that knows and she's not going to say anything. We can just ignore it."

"But what about having children?" Mia asked.

"We can do as my parents did or adopt" answered Ralph "I'm sure we can find a way."

They remained cuddled together. Mia felt safe and consoled; Ralph enjoyed the comfort of her body held close to him.

"What shall we say to Vicky?" asked Mia eventually pulling away.

"Same as before" he replied. "What we do is private; that's that! Now, let's make ourselves a sandwich and have a strong cup of tea."

***

The next day they set off for work as usual, elbowing their way onto the tube, Ralph clearing a space for Mia. Everything was normal and the couple smiled at each other and kissed goodbye as they went their separate ways at the hospital. But there was something; something not quite right; not quite as it had been before. Something so subtle it wasn't noticeable to the outside and was barely evident to the couple themselves. But the slim, thin end of a wedge had been driven between them and now it had a foothold it was only a matter of time before it split them apart completely.

***

A couple of days later Mia and Vicky were back in the Black Cat cafe, Mia not being able to stave off the meeting any longer. After some general conversation Vicky suddenly waded into the subject Mia was dreading.

"Are you going to do anything about the results of that test?" she asked blatantly. "I went to a lot of trouble and took some risk doing it for you. It wouldn't be a good idea to ignore it."

"We're not ignoring it!" answered Mia unnerved by Vicky's boldness. "We are looking into it but it's a private matter and I don't want to discuss it." She tried to recite the agreed line but sounded feeble.

"What's there to look into?" persisted Vicky ignoring the private bit. "You think I got it wrong, don't you? You think I don't know what I'm doing!"

"No, no I'm not saying that" Mia answered.

"Well, you can't just ignore it, Mia. Having children with a sibling can cause all sorts of problems, as you well know."

"We can adopt children" Mia blurted out.

"OK, so that's the plan is it? Hmm, should be alright so long as they don't delve too closely into why you are adopting. I suppose you can tell them you're unable to have children; but do they ask for clinical confirmation?"

"I don't know" stuttered Mia, starting to feel irritated with Vicky's apparent search for hurdles. "It wouldn't matter anyway. Ralph and I will stay together whether we have any children or not."

"Of course you will! I'd never imagine you two to part!" Vicky said reassuringly.

They were quiet for a moment then Vicky continued earnestly.

"Look Mia, I'm your closest friend and I'm so sorry to have been the person to have brought the bad news. I'm just as shocked and upset as you by the result! I'd always imagined you and Ralph happily raising your own children. I'm devastated that you can't."

The words cut through Mia like a razor. That was the stark truth. They would never have a family of their own. Was she deluding herself that everything could carry on as before? Did she really want to adopt someone else's children when she'd always envisaged small versions of Ralph to look after? Would she be allowed to adopt? Vicky had a point about the depth of investigations carried out. What's more she knew she'd been avoiding any sexual contact with Ralph since Sunday. She couldn't imagine living with her brothers, the thought of sex with either of them was abhorrent; unthinkable. Now she found she was picturing her brother Tony whenever Ralph made any kind of sexual advance. That repulsed her. Would she be able to continue her marriage with Ralph now she knew he was her brother? But how could she consider life without being married to Ralph? A little tear welled in the corner of her eye and she quickly wiped it with a tissue.

"Sorry" said Vicky sympathetically "I'm sure it will all work out for you."

They were quiet for a while then Vicky started again.

"It must seem strange though, doesn't it? I mean now you know Ralph's your brother, being married to him."

"It doesn't make any difference to how I feel" Mia lied defiantly.

"That's good" Vicky said placing a consolatory hand on Mia's shoulder. "I must admit if I were you I'd find it hard to have sex now I knew he was my brother, but we're all different aren't we. Anyway, don't worry, your secret's safe with me" she smiled "I won't tell anyone about it."

"I didn't think you would" answered Mia absently, dwelling on her friend's comment about the sex.

"Cheer up Mia!" said Vicky removing her hand and sitting back, "I'll come and visit you in prison!"

"What's that supposed to mean?" said Mia flaring at Vicky's flippancy. It was hardly the time for jokes. Did Vicky imagine she could instantly drop Ralph and move on? Vicky could never have been in love else she'd have more compassion.

"Sorry, I was just trying to cheer you up" continued Vicky. "I was just kidding because marrying your brother is illegal but I'm sure they wouldn't put you in prison, you didn't know when you got married."

"Thanks a bunch!" Mia said now completely pissed off with Vicky.

"I'm sorry Mia, really" Vicky frowned. "I just don't know what to say to try to cheer you up. Part of me wishes I'd never volunteered to test you and Ralph, I feel like it's my fault that you're related. But I still think it's a good job I did test you rather than you find out later when you have children. You *do* agree" she implored "it *is* better to know don't you think?"

"Yes" Mia conceded dejectedly "I suppose it is."

Vicky looked at her watch.

"I've got to get back" she said, then looking deep into Mia's eyes added "you know I'm always here for you. If you need to talk about it or I can be of any help please just ask me. That's what friends are for isn't it?"

"Thanks" answered Mia. "Sorry to give you a hard time because I've had bad news. I do appreciate having you as my friend."

They said no more about it as they headed back to work.

**

On Saturday Ralph and Mia had arranged to meet up with Ralph's old university friend John and his wife Sarah. Mia didn't want to see them or anybody else. She was in a complete state of flux, unable to concentrate on anything for any length of time. For some unexplained reason she was able to absorb herself at work but she couldn't face ordinary social interaction.

"Why don't you want to see them?" asked Ralph. "It'll do us both good to get out and talk to people that don't know we're not normal."

"You don't think we're normal?"

"You know what I mean, they don't know anything about our discovery." He chose the word carefully.

"I don't know how you can just carry on as though nothing has happened!" Mia said. "I'm finding it very hard. I don't know what to think."

"Look, if Vicky hadn't done the test we wouldn't have known!" Ralph pointed out.

"But she DID do the test and we DO know!" exclaimed Mia. "I can't just ignore it."

"What do you want to do?" asked Ralph.

"I don't know!" wailed Mia. "I just need time."

"Well while you think about it do you think we can have some sort of life?" Ralph asked.

"OK, we'll go to the pub and see John and Sarah" conceded Mia "but we're going to be living a lie, Ralph, sharing a secret that we can't impart to anyone else."

***

John and Sarah soon realised all was not well with their friends, Mia was quiet and pre-occupied whilst Ralph was overbearingly jolly.

At the bar John asked Ralph what was wrong but Ralph insisted everything was fine. John placed his hand on his friend's shoulder and offered to meet him for a chat. Ralph would have dearly liked to off-load his problems but he knew that would be impossible. How would it look? The whole idea of telling his mate he'd accidently married his sister was preposterous!

However, towards the end of the evening, after several glasses of wine, Mia relaxed and some sense of normality resumed, laughing at shared anecdotes and discussing shows watched on TV. By the time they said goodbye to John and Sarah they were feeling good and made their way back home in high spirits.

As soon as they got into the flat Ralph took Mia in his arms and kissed her passionately. She responded positively and their lips locked together for several lingering, sensual seconds. He unbuttoned her coat and slid his hands around her waist, then gently reached inside the back of her thin jumper to unfasten her bra. He continued to kiss her as his right hand felt for and found her left breast. He cupped the soft flesh and was roused by the touch of her hard nipple. His whole body tensed with excited anticipation, he needed to get inside Mia now. He freed his hands and pushed her coat off her shoulders so it fell to the hall floor. She willingly allowed him to gently lay her down on the coat. He unzipped her jeans and ran his hands around the waistband. She raised herself from the floor to enable him to pull them down. He eagerly wriggled out of his trousers and laid half way over her. She could feel his erect penis against her leg and his hot breath as he kissed her again. He manoeuvred himself over her leg. She looked into his face but bang! She was hit by the image of her brother. The spell was broken, she started pushing Ralph away.

"I can't Ralph" she whimpered then more assertively added "Stop!"

"I can't stop now!" he said desperately.

"I'm so sorry, Ralph, but you must. I can't do this."

"What do you mean you can't?" He was sounding angry now.

"I'm sorry" she repeated "but it doesn't feel right."

"For God's sake, Mia, you can't leave me high and dry like this!"

"I'll help you" she said as she gently pushed him back and rolled towards him, reversing their positions. She kissed and caressed him until he ejaculated.

She lay back beside him and held his hand in silence for a while. Then she lifted herself off the floor, pulled her trousers up and made her way to the bathroom to get Ralph a towel.

He remained silent and motionless. In the moment of passion, he'd forgotten how cold it was in their unheated hall. Now he lay half naked feeling foolish and pathetic, his deflated penis sapped of virility. He was humiliated and frustrated by Mia's rejection and gripped by a sickening fear. She had been repulsed at the thought of sex with him! He gritted his teeth. His throat felt tight. He mourned the lost opportunity of getting their relationship back on track. He told himself to be patient with Mia, it had only been a week. But her behaviour made him pessimistic for their future.

The wedge was being driven further between them. Ralph was distraught at the prospect of his marriage failing but was beginning to accept the possibility.

***

Mia was pleased to be at work the following week; it occupied her enough to chase away the discord in her head. On Monday she found a small potted plant on her desk with a thank-you note from Analyn.

"That was nice of you" Mia said "but you really shouldn't have."

"It's just a small gift" answered Analyn "for being so kind to me. I don't know how I would have coped without your help."

"I'm sure you would have!" Mia told her kindly.

They agreed to find time to share a lunch break soon and Mia felt momentarily boosted by the new friendship; she really had been hard on Analyn who had now settled in very well, just as Bina had predicted.

Later in the week Mia had a last session with her young, feisty accident victim who was fit enough to be discharged. Her parents thanked Mia profusely. Mia had become attached to them and their daughter. Although it was brilliant news for the family, a tribute to her own efforts and those of the girl, instead of being pleased Mia felt a curious sense of loss and abandonment. She made the right noises, bidding them farewell and good luck, but as they left a cold and hollow loneliness crept through her.

After lunch Bina asked Mia into her office. Bina was a short stocky lady of mixed race, possibly some African blood mixed with Caucasian, maybe a bit of Arab thrown in. She had a light olive skin and fairly large nose. Endless grips and combs couldn't control her mop of dark brown frizzy hair. She ceaselessly attempted to contain it by pushing the escaping strands back under the grips, but they always managed to escape again. She was in her forties and had two children from two failed relationships, the stress of which showed on her prematurely lined face. She was not embittered by her experiences but they had left her wiser than most. She was a kind and empathetic person.

"Mia is there anything the matter with you?" Bina asked. "You don't seem to be yourself lately. You're usually such a cheerful soul; you light up the place. But recently you've been distracted and, well, something seems to be upsetting you."

Mia was disturbed by Bina's observation. Was her tension that apparent? She knew it was pointless to claim there was nothing wrong so chose to tell part of the story.

"I've had a shock" she confided. "I've found out that my father isn't actually my father."

"Heavens!" Bina exclaimed. "Yes, that must be a shock! But what difference does it make? I mean the man that brought you up, cared and provided for you and all that; he's really your father. Don't you think?"

"I know but I've always been so close to my dad I just can't believe I'm not his actual daughter and I know next to nothing about my blood father" explained Mia.

"How much would you want to know?" posed Bina. "I don't want to pry or anything, but it would appear he hasn't been bothered to stay in touch so why would you bother to want to know him?"

"He doesn't know I exist! My mother had an affair and it was over before she realised she was pregnant. She didn't tell him or my dad. She's lived with the lie for years!"

"Why has she decided to tell you now?" Bina asked.

"She let it slip out by accident" Mia replied "but I think it must have been at the back of her mind for ages."

"Does your father know now?"

"No."

"And is it your intention to find your real father?" asked Bina.
Mia hadn't given any thought to her real father but she was suddenly overcome by a huge wave of anger. Now she found a focus for her problems; someone to take the blame for this terrible situation. "What sort of man donates his sperm without worrying about the consequences?" she thought angrily. "What sort of Narcissist is he? Pompous Git!"
She realised Bina was waiting for an answer.
"Yes" she said "I do plan to find him and give him a piece of my mind!"
Bina was miffed. What was the poor man supposed to have done!? He had an affair; hardly a capital offence. She suspected there was more in this than Mia was admitting. Maybe her mother had been raped or jilted. She knew Mia could get wound up; she'd witnessed all that upset over her friend's gossiping colleagues. She was however very fond of Mia. She thought her a good person and liked her sunny disposition. She didn't like to see her so down.
"What does Ralph think?" she asked.
Mia hadn't contemplated the question.
"He doesn't think anything" she answered, pinking slightly.
Bina knew that Ralph would never disregard anything that affected Mia; she'd never seen such a pair of love-buds. Now she was convinced something strange was going on but Mia's reticence stopped her probing further even though she was bursting with curiosity.
"Well, my view is this" she ventured as she returned a wayward lock to its grip, "there must be hundreds of people walking around thinking their fathers are their fathers when they aren't. It's a known fact that some women have long term relationships with lovers they don't marry because they wouldn't be good providers. Their husbands do all the hard work raising the children, unaware! Think of your father. How will he feel if he finds out? What good would it do to find this stranger?"
Mia thought for a while.
"I agree I wouldn't want to upset my dad" she conceded "but he

doesn't need to find out. My mother won't even know what I'm doing as I don't intend to tell her."

Bina saw several flaws in Mia's proposal. She didn't appear to have considered how her "new" father might react to her exist-ence and, in Bina's experience, facts you wanted to keep buried had an uncanny way of coming out into the open. She didn't voice these reservations but kept to practicalities.

"How can you find your Mum's old lover without admitting you're going to look for him?" she pointed out.

"Well, I know he was a medical student" Mia answered, thinking on the hoof. "I can go to see my Aunt on my day off next Friday; I think she may know his name. Then I can look him up. If he's a practising doctor he should be on the internet."

"Why don't you just ask your mum for his name?" asked Bina exasperated.

"I can't" Mia answered simply and Bina was sure her theory of rape or rejection was right.

"Well, if I can be of any help let me know" Bina offered genu-inely. "But think carefully about contacting your true father. In my experience it isn't worth scratching at old sores."

"Thanks" answered Mia grateful for Bina's concern. "I will think about it."

She left Bina's office and headed back to continue her ward rounds.

***

She spent the following week-end turning over Bina's words and considering whether it was wise to pursue her genetic father. In the end she felt overwhelmingly curious to find out what he was like and was willing to risk the consequences. Ralph had a right to know what she was up to, it was his father too, but she de-layed discussing it with him. It was likely he wouldn't approve and she decided to see what she could find out before telling him.

Meanwhile Ralph noted with concern how quiet and preoccupied she was; it was becoming her normal persona. He tried to bring her round by suggesting things they could do and by cooking all the meals but she was oblivious to his endeavours. She wasn't unfriendly, just distracted. Without the passion he felt flat and lonely. There was no connection between them. Mia was somewhere out of reach.

***

On Wednesday Mia's shift allowed her to be home for the boiler engineer's morning appointment. Thank God pay day had arrived. She was fed up with showering at work and being cold at home.

She used the quiet moment to ring Aunty Sheila and was lucky to get a reply. She told Sheila she was coming to Lewisham hospital for a morning course on Friday week and suggested they meet for lunch. Sheila worked at the hospital but was on nights so suggested Mia came to lunch at her house, a short walk from the hospital.

As Mia finished talking to Sheila there was a long continuous buzz on the intercom. Before she had a chance to answer it another, longer buzz sounded. "Alright, give us a chance!" she thought as she pressed the intercom.

"In The Heat; come to repair the boiler" a deep voice stated.

"Come in" Mia answered as she pressed the release to the main entrance door.

She went and opened her front door and saw a very chubby man making his way slowly up the stairs. He was gripping the balustrade with all his might and puffing and wheezing with each step.

"Arthritic knees" Mia surmised as she watched his painful progression "carrying all that weight doesn't help."

He finally got to her landing.

"You, *puff*, could, *wheeze*, do, *wince*, wif a lift 'ere!" he spluttered.

"Yes" agreed Mia in sympathy. "Good job I'm only on the first floor!"

They made their way through the flat and he dropped his heavy holdall of tools on the kitchen floor with a thump. His face was bright red, beads of sweat were running down his forehead and he was breathless. Mia thought he might collapse so offered him a drink and pointed to a kitchen chair.

"I 'aven't 'ad a break all day" he told her as he plonked himself down. "I could just do wif a cuppa cha."

She wondered whether she'd made a mistake with the tea as he looked as though he could get settled in her kitchen for the day. Meanwhile the offending boiler sat uselessly in its recess waiting for his attention.

She gave him the tea and sat opposite with hers.

"How long do you think it will take?" she asked "only I'm due to be at work by two."

"I'll be finished by then" he assured her not moving.

"I'll need to leave here by one to get there for two" she pointed out.

"That'll be fine" he reassured her, remaining in the seat. He sipped his tea quietly then reached into his work bag and pulled out a pasty. He bit into it with gusto as though he hadn't eaten for weeks. Her heart sank. She wanted him to get on with fixing the boiler.

"Where do you work?" he asked conversationally, crumbs spraying onto his belly as though looking for a short cut.

"I'm at Brentfield" she said trying to keep it short.

"What do you do?" he asked.

Mia inwardly groaned; she didn't want a conversation.

"I'm in the Physiotherapy Department" she said. "That's why I have to get back. I have to cover a shift."

"I expect that's interesting" he said apparently oblivious to her concern for the time. "My son wanted to go in for that but he didn't get the grades."

"Oh dear" she answered.

"He's a personal trainer now, at the gym."

"Oh, that's good" she said then to herself "he should give you some time!"

"Well, this won't do!" he commented as he finished his tea. He wiped his mouth on the tissue supplied with the pasty and lifted himself from the chair. "Let's 'ave a look at this 'ere boiler then shall we?"

"That's what you're here for!" Mia thought "It's over there" she said pointing.

He sauntered over to look at the boiler and immediately sucked air back through his teeth, making a whistling sound, and shook his head from side to side.

"This is an old 'un!" he exclaimed. "I 'aven't seen one like this fer years! Do you know 'ow old it is?"

"No, it was here when we came" she answered sullenly.

"Tut tut tut" he clucked "it's gonna be 'ard to get parts fer this. Still let's see what we can do."

"Do me a favour!" Mia thought irritably as she watched him take the front cover off.

He drew in another large intake of air through his teeth; more head shaking.

"Blimey! Titch! Titch! When was this last serviced?"

"I don't know" Mia answered "we've only been here a couple of years."

"See these burners?" he said beckoning her towards the boiler. "See all that black stuff on 'em? That shouldn't be there. They're all gummed up and filfy."

"Oh dear" she answered standing well back and making no attempt to look. "Is that the problem? It just needs cleaning?"

"I wish it were, luv!" he answered "but it looks like you've got more of a problem than that. See that old staining down there?" he pointed to the base of the casing "'ave you ever seen wa'er dripping awt?"

She was really losing patience with the inquisition. She just wanted him to tell her what was wrong.

"Yes, I may have" she answered.

"Well, yer main gasket's gone" he told her.

"Can you fix it?" she asked.

"Not today, and if I can't get the part; not at all."

"Are you likely to be able to get the part?"

Another suck of breath.

"I'll do me best luv but I can't promise anyfink."

"So what do we do if you can't get the part?"

"You'll 'ave to 'ave a new boiler" he told her.

"How much would that be roughly?"

Another suck of breath. "Depends" he paused "fifteen to eighteen 'undred."

Mia's mouth dropped; they couldn't find that sort of money!

The boiler had become symbolic of their problems. She had, with no logic whatsoever, thought fixing the heating might help sort out their troubles. The idea that it couldn't be fixed flooded her with melancholy and she burst into tears.

The fitter was shocked. He didn't know how to react. In all his years of work he'd only had one other client cry like this. That was the lady that answered the door looking like a gigantic caterpillar, dressed in a bright green sleeping bag with her feet sticking out the bottom.

"Don't worry" he said kindly "I'll 'ave a good go at gitting the gasket. There's more chance these days wif evryfink on line. Any'ow, you can get the boiler done on tic, the Company do low interest rates 'n all that. You mustn't get yerself upset over it!"

He looked at the young lady in front of him and noted how thin she was. No wonder she felt the cold! She could do with feeding up. A layer of fat would do her good!

She soon pulled herself together, drying her eyes on a tissue.

"I'm sorry" she said "I'm not feeling very well today."

"Look luv" he ventured "evryfink works out fer the best in the end. In fact, you'd be be'er off wif a new boiler! It'd be cheaper to run so you'd get yer money back long term and it'd work better. I'm sure "In the Heat" can come to a deal about the dough. It's not wurf you ge'in in a state o'er it!"

"No, I know" she said "Thank you."

He looked at her to check she was alright and she managed a thin smile.

"I'll letch yer know if I get the part" he said. "I've got this mobile

number fer yer. Is it correct?"
She saw it was Ralph's.
"Yes, that's my husband's number, it's best to talk to him."
He put the boiler back together whistling an extra cheery tune. Then he packed his tools into his bag and she showed him to the front door. He wanted to tell her she wouldn't feel so miserable and cold if she had some decent food inside her, but he just politely bade her farewell and plodded heavily back down the stairs.

**

On Saturday night Ralph and Mia set out to visit Vicky. She lived in a flat above a shop in Clapham South which was a fairly long walk for Mia and Ralph or one stop on the tube; they took the second option. They arrived early evening, as agreed, to allow time to watch a film after dinner. Vicky had obtained "The King's Speech" as Mia had told her it was a film they'd missed.
They greeted each other warmly at the front door then made their way up the narrow staircase to the flat. They were met with the mouth-watering smell of something delicious cooking and were informed it was "*only* beouf-en-croute with roasted vegetables and crispy fried cabbage." Clearly Vicky had made a lot of effort.
Ralph had never been to Vicky's flat so now he surveyed the lounge and was impressed. There were flowers in a vase on the hearthside and one or two pieces of modern china on an oak cabinet. The room was slightly under-furnished but comfortable with a settee and armchair arranged around a large, low, teak coffee table. Everything was neat and tidy, not like their flat which looked like a war zone most of the time. It reminded him of a smaller, more modern version of his parents' house.
He also noticed how great Vicky looked. She was wearing a pair of snug-fitting jeans framing her firm, rounded buttocks and a tight, fluffy, pink, V-necked pullover that exhibited her ample cleavage. He hadn't had sex for over three weeks and was

pleased to rest his eyes upon Vicky's chest.

Mia saw Ralph survey the room and look at her friend's cleavage. A pang of jealousy ripped through her whilst at the same time she felt plain and dowdy. Her shoulders drooped and she curled into herself. Her hair was lank and dull compared to Vicky's glistening and vibrant short bob. She wished she'd taken more care and not donned an old, comfy jumper. It hung loosely over her shoulders, effectively concealing any hint of her body shape, unlike Vicky's skimpy top. Not only that but Vicky was in super-drive; making jokes, telling stories and giggling at everything Ralph said. She was openly flirting, thrusting her chest forward as she offered Ralph snacks.

"She's making a play for MY husband!" Mia thought, infuriated.

Things got more maddening when dinner was served. She thought Ralph was going to have an orgasm over that bloody beef pie. The way he kept going on you'd think he hadn't had anything home-cooked for years! And fancy her doing rice pudding because she'd noticed Ralph always chose it when available in the canteen! And saying how her mum always said the way to a man's heart is through his stomach! She knows I can't cook! Bitch! The marriage hasn't even gone cold and she's jumping in!

They cleared away and started to get ready for the film. Mia made a quick move for the sofa; she didn't trust Vicky to sit with Ralph and wanted to relax and give her attention to the film. However, during the movie she kept ruminating on Vicky's behaviour and became so distracted and agitated she hardly watched it. Afterwards Vicky and Ralph waxed on about this and that part, mutually agreeing with each other's opinion and sounding like a pair of art critics. Mia felt totally left out.

The test didn't get mentioned until the end of the evening. Vicky was curious to know how they had happened to have the same father. Ralph enlightened her by saying in a child-like robotic voice "she from fling, me from test tube." Mia was miffed at his stupid behaviour and shocked at his flippancy. Vicky laughed at him in a flirty way and that was the end of the subject.

"Bitch!" Mia thought. "Maybe Alan was right!"

However, in her heart she knew there was nothing constructive Vicky could have said and she couldn't even blame her for coming on to Ralph, after all he was special.

On the way home Ralph bombarded Mia with complimentary remarks about Vicky, yelling to be heard above the tube noise. He finally ran out of steam when they got home but then went quiet, his mood a stark contrast to that of earlier. He turned on Mia with a dark expression she'd never seen before.

"Are we going to get back to where we were?" he said aggressively.

"I told you Ralph, I need time" Mia answered, caught off balance by his tone and threatened by the latent spite in his voice. "I want to pretend nothing has happened, really I do" she continued "but when we start to have sex a horrible image comes to me; I see one of my brothers, Neil or Tony, and it puts me off. I'm so sorry, really I am."

"If we're going to behave like brother and sister we may as well *be* brother and sister" he said resentfully.

"Please Ralph, just give me some time."

"How long do you think I can wait!" his voice was raised. He'd never verbally attacked her like this before.

"Is it any coincidence that you're getting all angry after seeing Vicky?" she retaliated, unusually finding the words. "You've been all over her this evening! Yes Vicky, lovely meal Vicky, anything you say Vicky" she mimicked viciously. "Maybe you'd rather I just got out of the way and let you two get on with it!"

"Well that's what you seem to want!" he hit back. "I'd be better off if you were my sister; at least I'd have some sort of relationship with you!"

They stood looking at each other, chins out, shoulders back. There was a stand-off; then Ralph relented.

"Listen" he said "there'll NEVER be ANYONE I'll love as much as you Mia. This whole situation is tearing me apart. I admit I enjoyed Vicky's attention today, God knows I haven't had much from you recently, but truthfully she nor anyone else could ever be as precious to me as you are."

It was too much for Mia. She threw herself towards him and he took her in his arms. He felt her body shudder and she sobbed as though she would never stop, shoulders heaving. He held on to her, large teardrops falling silently down his cheeks. Finally, he composed himself and held Mia at arms' length to look into her face. They could see the pain in each other's eyes; they knew they were in an impossible situation.

"What are we going to do?!" wept Mia not expecting an answer.

"I don't know" said Ralph "but we can't go on like this."

In the end they agreed to give it another month, to the end of March, and if by then Mia was still unable to reconcile the situation they would discuss how they were going to part.

The words of their agreement hung in Mia's head like the date of a death sentence. She wasn't confident she would feel any different in a year's time never mind a month. It was likely the marriage would finish in just a few weeks and that made her stomach turn. She could tell Ralph was just as miserable at the prospect of separating, but she knew he couldn't understand why she wasn't able to carry on as though nothing had happened. Over the last few weeks he had tried seduction, emotional blackmail and even begged her to return to their former relationship; but she just couldn't. Recently she'd noticed he'd become cooler and there was an air of resignation about him. No wonder he had enjoyed Vicky's attention. What did she expect of him?

They had staved off further penetration of the wedge, staunching its progress for now; but they were beginning to picture a life outside of their marriage and becoming physically distant, their body language reflecting their state of mind.

Chapter 6

In Faithfulness and Trust

The daffodils were in bud, the winter had gone and another spring was here. Ralph was working from home. The engineer had managed to obtain the relevant part and was coming to repair the boiler, hurray! Mia could have covered the appointment but she hadn't admitted it was her day off. For the first time since they'd been married she was deceiving him. She had told him she was attending a course and visiting her Aunt afterwards. As she left she felt guilty for her dishonesty.

Now she wandered aimlessly around the shops killing time and thinking. Since their agreement Ralph had been even cooler towards her. She believed this was due to the absence of sex. She found it inconceivable that at a time like this all he could think about was getting his leg over! She was wrong and underestimated her husband. Ralph's behaviour stemmed from a deep belief she no longer loved him. If she loved him there would be no obstacle too large but she wasn't willing to compromise at all.

Mia felt lifted at the prospect of seeing her Aunt who was kind, crazy and always had an amusing repertoire of stories to tell. She'd been a nurse for nearly thirty years and if there were no new yarns the old ones were always worth another hearing, especially as they became more embellished and bizarre with each retelling.

Mia knew she must be careful not to let anything slip out. If any revelations were to be made her parents must be the first to hear. She couldn't risk her father finding out through an intermediary. If she "went public" it would start a deluge of questions and opinions which she couldn't cope with, especially as she felt embarrassed to be married to her half-brother even though by accident. She doubted she would ever be able to admit the truth, whatever happened between her and Ralph.

Extracting information without directly asking her aunt or causing her aunt to be suspicious was going to be tricky. She'd a few ideas up her sleeve and was relying on her aunt's passion for story-telling to help.

Aunty Sheila was a different shape to her sister Pam, being shorter and rounder, but she had the same dark colouring. She was cuddlier and more maternal than Pam, and much less interested in her appearance; she didn't care if her clothes were out of fashion, mismatched or crumpled. Sheila usually wore the first thing she could lay her hands on, the only considerations being practical ones like the weather. Her friends weren't bothered about her appearance. They were more interested in her personality and sincerity. She was easy to talk to and less judgemental than Mia's mother.

Aunty Sheila's husband had died of a heart attack when he was only forty-five, leaving her with their two children, Lucy and Simon, aged thirteen and eleven. Sheila worked nights so that she could be with the children during the afternoon and early evening. They were on their own at night but their paternal grandparents lived nearby to cover emergencies. Mia remembered her mother pontificating about how irresponsible Sheila was and suggesting all sorts of horrors that may befall the children. Nothing ever did happen; "by the grace of God" her mother had said. However, her cousins had grown up quickly and showed incredible independence, rallying around their mother to complete chores in the house. This attracted further criticism from Pam. "What sort of life is she giving those children?" she'd say to Mia's Dad.

Mia found her mother's condemnation of Sheila annoying. What right did she have to pass opinions when she had no idea what it would be like not to have a husband around? Mia admired Sheila and the way she had battled on alone to raise the children without asking for help from anybody. There must have been times when she was exhausted, working nights and dealing with everything else in the day.

Now as Mia approached her Auntie's unassuming house, in the middle of a Victorian terrace, she tried to appear cheerful. This morning she had been shocked at her reflection, her cheeks were hollow and she had black circles under her dark brown eyes. To accentuate this, her skin had taken on an unhealthy white and sallow appearance; she looked like an emaciated panda! She'd spent a considerable amount of time using make-up to lighten the blackness and add colour to the rest of her face without turning herself into a clown. She was satisfied she'd achieved the cover-up. Anyone looking below the surface would detect the distress and lack of sleep but only Ralph looked at her that closely. She was confident she would be able to look happy for Auntie Sheila who made her laugh anyway. Coming here was already a tonic and distraction from her woes.

Sheila opened the door and Mia wondered if the green jumper with a frog motive on the front was the same as the one she remembered her Aunt wearing at least fifteen years ago. They kissed each other affectionately and went through to a small, cosy sitting room warmed by a gas fire. Lucy was married and Simon was working in Korea so Sheila was living in the house by herself. She had abandoned her front living room to chilly redundancy, choosing to live in the confines of the small rear lounge. This was barely large enough to accommodate her settee, armchair, TV, wall cabinet, coffee table and dining table with two chairs tucked under it. It was also full of clutter. A pile of magazines and books were stacked up on one end of the dining table, more magazines littered the coffee table, there was wool and knitting needles spread over the settee, the mantelpiece and surfaces of the cabinet were chock-a-block with pictures and knick-knacks, a mixture of shoes were piled up near the entrance door to the hall and a washing basket full of ironing sat awaiting attention by the kitchen door.

Sheila shoved the wool and needles to one end of the settee so that Mia could sit down and went to make tea in the adjoining kitchen. They carried out their conversation between the two rooms.

"How's work at Brentfield?" Sheila called out above the noise of the kettle.

"Good" answered Mia "though the proposals for restructuring are causing a few headaches. How are they coping with that at Lewisham?"

"I've seen so many reorganisations and restructures over the years I can hardly be bothered to think about it" admitted Sheila. "I know I should be more interested but it's sooo boooring! I just want to get on with the job. Have you noticed how every time there's a change they get rid of more jobs at the bottom and hardly any at the top?"

"Yes" concurred Mia "there seems to be a moratorium on reduction of management posts; as they're the ones making the decisions that's no surprise!"

They carried on putting the NHS to rights for a bit longer then they asked after each other's families. Mia went through these niceties looking for a chance to somehow turn the conversation to her mother and Sheila's youth. It wasn't proving easy. Then Sheila went into a story about how she had gone to buy a dress for last New Year's Eve. She explained she'd tried on a black, cocktail dress that looked good on the hanger but when she put it on the front drooped down below her bust.

"I thought that's a strange design" she told Mia "then the shop assistant called through the curtain to see how I was doing, you know what they're like, so I told her I thought the dress was odd and opened the curtain to let her see." Sheila paused and started to laugh, it was enough to spread a smile over Mia's face. "You've got it on back-to-front she told me!"

They both laughed. "How could you?" asked Mia through her giggles. "Wasn't it obvious?"

"Yes, once she'd told me!" answered Sheila. "I felt a proper twit!"

"You didn't buy it then?"

"No, it didn't suit me even the right way around!"

They exchanged a few dressing room stories and Mia tried her first attempt at steering the conversation in her desired direction.

"I expect you and mum used to go shopping together when you were young" she offered.

"We did have a couple of outings" answered Sheila. "I remember going to buy "hot pants" together. You know "hot pants"? They're like a fancy pair of shorts. Looking back on it I don't know how we had the nerve to wear them! Some of us, including me, shouldn't have worn them! It was great for your mum though. She was tall with long legs and strutted about the changing rooms looking great; I looked more like a garden gnome!"

"I'm sure you didn't!" objected Mia. "From what mum tells me you were the one that was the party goer with all the friends."

"You don't have to be glamorous for that!" said Sheila "and, as you know, your mum was young when she had Neil, only twenty, so she didn't have much time for partying."

Mia's heart started thumping. An opportunity! She couldn't afford to miss it.

"I'm sure that's something mum regrets" she told Sheila. "She's often lectured me about not getting tied down in a relationship too early. She told me about one of your parties when you were at college." Mia tried to sound casual and unscripted. "Told me how good it was to be with a load of young people even though she was a few years older."

"Yes, I remember that" said Sheila reddening a little at the memory. "She came for the week-end."

"Was it hard having your big sister stay? Did you feel you had to be on best behaviour?!" Mia goaded.

"*Me* on best behaviour!?" exclaimed Sheila indignantly, taking the bait. "Your mum wasn't exactly an angel!"

"Ooh, that sounds interesting! What do you mean by that!?"

"Nothing I'd tell you!"

"Mum did mention meeting someone that was her age, a mature student, studying to be a doctor?"

"Yes, I remember."

Sheila was tight lipped. Mia knew she had to crack it now. She mentally apologised to her mother.

"I think it would have suited Mum to leave Dad for a doctor" she said. "I reckon she probably considered it!"

"Mia! How could you say such a thing! Anyway, that doctor was already married with children. It was just a one-night thing, that's all. It wasn't a *Brief Encounter* moment if that's what you're thinking."

There was a pause. Mia racked her brains to think of something to prolong the conversation and tease out more detail. She was so desperate she feared Sheila would see her heart pounding. As usual in her panic her mind went blank. Think of something! Think of something!

Then, suddenly, out of the blue, bingo!

"Your mum would never have left your dad for him" Sheila mused with a mischievous grin upon her face. "Who could possibly want to live with someone called Sandy Balls!"

Mia took in a huge intake of breath.

"Sandy Balls!" she repeated. "But that wasn't his real name was it?"

"Well that's what he called himself. I bet your mum never admitted to that!" Sheila started to laugh again. Mia joined her though didn't think it particularly funny. Hopefully it would be enough to use as a trace; it was all she was going to get.

They had lunch perched either side of the dining table and Mia relaxed. By the end of the afternoon she had almost forgotten her problems and she thanked Sheila more than usual for her hospitality. There were promises to not leave it so long before their next get-together and requests to pass on best wishes to cousins and parents. Mia left temporarily lifted by the visit.

***

It was Saturday and Mia was on her way home from her shift. Although the days were lengthening and warmer, the nights were still chilly and she looked forward to the warmth of the flat now that the heating had been fixed. Three weeks to the end of March and the thought weighed heavily. Her plan to find Sandy Balls was a welcome distraction but didn't take away her feelings of impending doom. For tonight she had decided to park the problem and spend some time enjoying Ralph's company.

As she turned the key she heard conversation. She walked into the kitchen and found Vicky and Ralph crouched over a game of chess.

"Hi" said Ralph not looking up "how was work?"

"Quiet" she answered to the side of his head.

He was totally absorbed in the game. By the number of pieces taken he was trailing by a rook. Mia waited for Vicky to make her move before asking if either wanted a tea. They shook their heads. Then Vicky explained she'd made a Tagine she'd brought over for them to try. Mia saw a pot on the stove and couscous in a bowl. She went to lift the lid but Vicky jumped at her warning it could get ruined. Mia sat with her tea watching the game in silence.

Ralph moved his bishop and Vicky immediately lifted her queen across the board. "Check mate!" she announced triumphantly.

"How did I miss that?" Ralph exclaimed. "You're a good player. Where did you learn?"

"At university but I haven't played for years" she told him.

"Let's have another game" he proposed.

"I think we should eat" Mia cut in.

"Yes, we should" agreed Ralph. "We can resume play after."

"I'll do the couscous then" said Vicky and she proceeded to dominate the kitchen leaving Mia sat at the table whilst Ralph put the board aside and found a bottle of wine.

Predictably, Ralph praised Vicky's cooking excessively. Mia didn't get angry or jealous. She was overcome by an unexpected weariness; any fight had left her.

After watching a couple more games she went to bed saying she had a headache. She tried to read but couldn't concentrate. She was sure they would stop playing chess and progress to a more intimate activity. She felt miserable and abandoned. Ralph had ignored and marginalised her. He knew she was hardly ever ill yet hadn't bothered to come and see how she was. She contemplated going to get a drink of water so that she could spy but feared what she may find. She stayed in bed, brooding.

Ralph thought Mia was being childish making a protest about him playing chess with Vicky. He knew she didn't have a headache when she sulked off to bed. What did she imagine he should have done when Vicky turned up? Tell her to bugger off? Now he was enjoying the distraction of playing chess with Vicky knowing the alternative would be an emotionally draining evening of deep soul searching with Mia who was becoming more and more morose. He again questioned whether she truly loved him. Time was slipping by quickly since their agreement and he didn't feel optimistic. Whatever he did seemed to be wrong. He decided to park the problem, ignore Mia's tantrum and carry on playing chess.

In due course Vicky exclaimed it was late and she really should go. She gave Ralph a pat on the shoulder and assured him everything would be alright. It was a hollow comfort but he knew she was trying to be kind. Her absence left a lonely silence in the flat and Ralph sighed as he headed to the bathroom to get ready for bed.

Mia heard Vicky leave and Ralph go into the bathroom. She pretended to be asleep when he came into the bedroom and listened to him fumble about in the dark trying not to disturb her. As he climbed into bed all she could smell was Vicky's perfume. He rolled into a ball away from her and was fast asleep in minutes. She stayed awake for most of the night.

***

Sundays had lost their appeal. The couple play-acted; going through the motions of deciding what to do. They wandered around The Tate Gallery with no enthusiasm for the art works. On the way home Mia received a text from Vicky. She'd left her reading glasses at their flat and wanted to pop round to collect them. Mia had endured more than enough of Vicky for one week-end so Ralph agreed to take the glasses back whilst Mia prepared dinner.

As soon as he'd gone Mia doubted the wisdom of the arrangement. After an hour he hadn't come back. Where was he? She pictured him flirting with Vicky and it made her seethe. She tried calling his mobile but couldn't get through. He must have turned it off! She angrily sat to eat alone, though had no appetite so left most of it. She left Ralph's dinner drying out in the warm oven.

He got home about half an hour later and was narked to find Mia had already eaten. He tried to explain there had been a delay on the tube but she refused to listen and sulked off to the lounge. He sat down alone to eat the breaded fish that was like a crisp, mashed potato that had a crust on top and withered broccoli. Vicky had offered him a meal but he'd refused knowing Mia was cooking. Now he wished he'd taken Vicky up on her offer.

***

On Monday morning Mia opened her computer to see Bina had entered an appointment for a one-to-one interview. She sighed, were things going to start going wrong at work as well? Pete arrived and immediately started grumbling about his estranged wife. Their divorce was in process and he regularly related the details of their conflicts.

"She's a selfish bitch!" he said venomously after telling Mia about how awkward she'd been when he'd collected the children yesterday.

Mia hardly responded but kept her eyes fixed on her computer screen. To get her attention he carried on, adding more lurid details in an ever more indignant tone. At last he succeeded.

"I've got too much to do to listen to your woes!" she snapped.

Pete was completely taken aback. He was used to Mia being kind when he offloaded; her shortness was like a slap in the face. He wasn't interested in and didn't question the fact that Mia did something out of character. He took it personally and, like a wounded animal, went to get himself a coffee and find someone else to listen to his troubles. Mia felt guilty for barking at him but she was not in the mood today to cope with his grievances.

In the late afternoon she found herself once again sitting opposite her manager watching the struggle between hair and grips. Bina informed Mia a complaint had been made by one of her patients. He had alleged Mia made personal comments about his family. Mia was totally affronted. She had no idea what she could have said to offend anyone and was upset by the accusation.

"Who has complained?" she asked.

"First let me tell you not to get worried about this" answered Bina. "I've worked with you for long enough to know that you don't make a habit of upsetting people but I'm obliged to investigate and resolve the matter. The complaint was made by Mr Robson in G ward."

"Eric!" exclaimed Mia. "But he's a lovely old boy! What on earth am I supposed to have said to him?"

"He says you made remarks about his granddaughter and he didn't like it."

"What?!" said Mia screwing her nose up. "He showed me a picture of his grandchildren and I told him his granddaughter was a pretty girl. What's wrong with that?"

"He says you insinuated she was "flirty" and that she should be married off!"

"Er? What *is* he talking about?" said Mia perplexed as she tried to recall the conversation. "Yes, I remember, I said she was pretty and would be breaking a few boys' hearts. I really wasn't suggesting she was going to act like a Lolita or that she should be married off! Truthfully, that's all I said."

There were a few minutes silence whilst Bina considered what Mia had told her.

"Look" she said "I'll talk to Eric again and explain there's been a misunderstanding. I'll probably be able to smooth it over and I don't expect it to go any further. I would add a word of advice though. It's best not to make *any* comments to patients about *anything* other than their physiotherapy. I've experienced this sort of thing myself. Someone can appear to be friendly and nice but after you've left they brood over what you've said and misconstrue it. The public are a very strange bunch. Most are reasonable but the odd few can make life difficult. It's best to maintain a professional distance."

"I am professional" Mia protested.

"I know" countered Bina "and it is a shame that the awkward minority mean you have to remain detached from everyone, but I strongly advise you not to let yourself be drawn into any personal conversations, however minor you think they are."

"Will this go on my record?" Mia asked, concerned.

"It shouldn't" Bina replied "so long as he doesn't want to take it further. I can't see there's much for you to worry about even if he did."

Mia didn't find that very reassuring and felt completely fed up with everything.

"Can Pete take on Eric?" she asked. "I don't think I want to see him again."

"Yes" answered Bina "I'd already thought of that and asked Pete, he's fine about it."

They were quiet again and Mia felt like crying but managed to hold back.

"I'm glad for the chance to have this one-to-one" said Bina. "I've noticed you've been very quiet and snappy lately. I know we spoke the other day about your father, is there anything else up-setting you?"

Mia didn't answer so Bina continued.

"I manage a team" she said "and it's important you all get on as a team. Only this morning I heard you bite Pete's head off and other people in the office have noticed you ignoring requests for help."

"I think that's unfair" Mia retorted indignantly. "I am the most willing member of the team! I do the majority of the unsocial and emergency shifts!"

Vicky's words echoed in Mia's head "So you cover for other peoples' child care issues and incompetence!" Resentment welled up inside her.

"I do appreciate your willingness to cover more than your share of the rota" Bina responded "and your colleagues only commented out of concern for you; you're usually so cheerful and helpful."

Mia remained silent.

"So" Bina continued "there's nothing else worrying you other than what we discussed the other day?"

Mia felt like telling her to mind her own flippin' business. "No" she mumbled then added to herself "Isn't that enough?"

Bina caught the whisper. "How did you get on with finding out about your genetic father?" she asked. "Any luck?"

Mia sighed. "Well I've got a name but nothing else. Google didn't get me anywhere and I don't know how else to try to trace him"

"You said he was a doctor, didn't you? Have you thought of searching the NHS staff database?" Bina asked.

"I'm not authorised" Mia answered.

"I am!" said Bina. "Give it to me and I'll look it up."

Mia was reluctant to share the information but couldn't waste the opportunity.

"Sandy Balls" she announced.

"Sandy Balls" Bina repeated. "Is that his real name?"

"I don't know, it's all I have."

"I'd guess the Sandy part is a nick-name which would explain why you couldn't find him on the public lists. We may not be able to find him on the staff list but let's start with Balls and see what we get."

Mia felt a sudden wave of warmth towards her manager and waited hopefully as Bina opened the programme and started searching for the surname.

"There are no Balls listed" Bina reported "but there are three doctors with the name Ball."

"Maybe it's spelt differently" Mia suggested. "How about b-a-w-l-s"

"No, nothing for that either" Bina said as she typed. "Nor under Bulls."

They paused to think of any other variations but they were short of ideas. Bina went into the details for the first Ball on the list. Mia moved to look at the screen.

"This one's only forty-five" Bina said as she pointed to the first doctor's details. She turned and smiled at Mia "I don't think he could be your father!"

"This one's possible" she commented as she scrutinised the second doctor's details "about the right age."

"No good" Mia jumped in "those are Australian qualifications."

Bina sighed "Oh well, third time lucky" she said as the third set of details appeared on screen.

"Hmm, this one looks promising. He's in his late 50s, so about the right age, he trained in Liverpool. His first name is Edward and he's currently working at the Royal Liverpool University Hospital."

She carried on scrolling through his details then pointed to the screen and looked back at Mia.

"Look!" she said excitedly "the earlier records refer to him as Edward Balls! It looks like over his career he's dropped the s."

"It could be him" Mia agreed more doubtful than Bina "but we can't be sure we've got the right name and we don't even know if our Mr Balls works for the NHS, for all we know he's working abroad!"

"That's true, but it is quite common for doctors to stay in the place where they were trained" Bina advised with more optimism. "I agree we can't be absolutely sure."

Further delving revealed Edward was an orthopaedic surgeon of some status.

"If you got the opportunity to meet Sandy you wouldn't confront him, would you?" Bina asked.

"No" answered Mia "I just want to see what he's like."

"That's OK then" Bina said. "You don't know how he'd react to such an accusation. I wouldn't want to be party to this if I thought there'd be any trouble."

They discussed how they might establish whether Edward was also known as Sandy. That was the first dilemma. The second was to work out how Mia might be able to meet him without showing her hand.

"I've an idea!" said Bina. "I'll contact the orthopaedic department in Liverpool. I'll say you're doing a study for the Department and request a short interview with Mr Ball to get his expert opinion on whatever it is we think up. Consultants always like to be asked for their expert opinion. In my experience most of them can't resist the chance to show off. But we don't want you to go if he isn't Sandy. I'll see if I can wheedle anything out of his secretary before making the request."

She paused and looked at Mia. "This could all come to nothing, you know that don't you?"

"Yes, of course" Mia answered.

Mia was grateful. She appreciated Bina's attention and willingness to bend the rules. There was an element of risk in what she was doing. It was good to feel there was somebody on her side. She'd been feeling very isolated lately.

"Thank you so much" she said.

"No prob" answered Bina. "Now will you go home, relax with a glass of wine or something and get a good night's sleep. I'd like to see you at work tomorrow as your old self."

"Will do" smiled Mia realising Bina imagined this would fix everything. As she got to the door she added "I'm still miffed about Eric, he seemed so friendly and nice to my face. Why didn't he tell me if he thought I'd said something offensive instead of going behind my back and making it so formal?"

"As my old manager used to say" answered Bina "there's nought so queer as folk!"

With that Mia smiled weakly and left for home.

***

She was more relaxed that night and sat with Ralph sipping wine; it almost felt like old times. She told him about the complaint but didn't mention the search for their father. For the first time in their relationship she was wary of Ralph's reaction. He was supportively outraged by the complaint but didn't think there was a case to answer. He had news himself. His manager was leaving, having found a promotional job, so there would be a vacancy. Ralph would have to decide whether to apply. He wasn't sure how much he'd enjoy managing people but didn't want to pass up the opportunity. Mia thought he'd be an excellent boss and boosted his confidence making him feel good for the first time in weeks.

In bed they embraced each other fondly but when he started to touch her more ardently she pulled away. The old wall came up between them. The wedge persisted, slowly pressing onwards, tenaciously pushing its way between them.

***

At work the next day Mia was immediately called into Bina's office. Bina's excitement was reflected in her hair; clumps were escaping their grips with abandon. She'd come to work early to contact the administration section for Liverpool's orthopaedic department. She couldn't restrain the broad grin from spreading over her face as she proudly recounted how she had feigned possibly having met the consultant years ago and had asked if he was also known as Sandy. The admin manager had laughed and admitted they do call him Sandy because he used to have light ginger hair. They still used the nick-name even though he was almost bald. Bina had got on so well with the lady she had fitted Mia in for an appointment next Thursday!

Mia was shaken. A wave of nerves washed over her. Doubt rushed in. Had she really thought this through? Bina had gone full pelt ahead and Mia wasn't ready. The shock of it showed on her face.

"You can't get cold feet now!" exclaimed Bina. "It's all arranged."

"No, sorry" answered Mia. "But it's a bit scary, the thought of actually meeting him. What am I going to say my project is about?

I'll have to do some background research. I can't just turn up clueless!"

"Don't panic!" commanded Bina. "I've looked up a paper he wrote some years ago on bunion operations."

"Bunion operations!" repeated Mia.

"I know, not the sexiest subject but you can tell him your project is about how useful physiotherapy may be for post bunion op patients."

"I can't! I've never seen a patient recovering from a bunion op! Do they even need physio!?"

"It is rare but I have seen a couple over the years. Maybe we should see more. So many people have that op there must be plenty that would benefit from physio. You could say you're comparing different recovery rates for those that receive physio and those that don't. Use your imagination! Remember, he'll be more interested in lecturing than hearing anything you've got to say! At least he's working in a field we can hook on to, you're lucky he isn't a brain surgeon!"

That made Mia smile. She graciously thanked Bina for her help. However back on her rounds she dwelt on the consequences of the plan. She was distracted and her mind was only half on her job. How was she going to face this consultant knowing he was her father? Would she be able to discuss a bogus project with him? She felt sick with anxiety. She also considered Ralph. She wished she'd told him what she'd been up to. How devious she'd appear having got so far without mentioning it. She feared his reaction. Almost certainly he would be irked. She couldn't see a way of approaching him without there being friction. She considered not telling him but that would mean more deceit. She was sliding down a slippery slope. Ideally, she would have loved him to go with her but her plan already excluded him. Then there was her father to think about. What if he found out? How would he feel? What *was* she doing?

In spite of all these doubts she was gripped by her desire to meet her genetic father. She determined to put the anxieties aside and proceed with her "project".

Chapter 7

To Be United in Heart, Body and Mind

Mia was up at five on Thursday morning in order to catch the train to Liverpool and be on time for her eleven thirty appointment. As predicted, Ralph had been outraged by her clandestine behaviour and wasn't at all interested in joining her. He told her he didn't feel any desire to meet his genetic father. His real father was the person that had raised him and he would rather spend time with him. He made Mia feel guilty but at the same time she was perplexed that he didn't share her curiosity.

Her stomach was tied in a knot by the time she arrived at the reception area for Mr Ball where his friendly admin manager told her to take a seat. She sat mulling over the encyclopaedia of facts she had looked up about bunions! She'd never realised how complicated bunion operations were. There were about a hundred and thirty different operations for correcting the condition! She'd read the paper Edward had written. He'd called his operating procedure a Ballsectomy which amused her more than she thought it should. Now she hoped not to be questioned too closely about her bogus project; she dreaded being exposed as an idiot or a fraud.

Alongside these fears she was bursting with anticipation. What would Sandy Balls be like? She knew he was bald and had been ginger, but that was the extent of her knowledge. Both she and Ralph had dark brown eyes; what colour eyes would he have? Unlike any of their parents they both had small hands; had they inherited them from Sandy? Her mother had said he was pompous; would Mia find him like that now?

These thoughts and more tumbled round her head. She contemplated what might happen if she gave away her real reason for coming. She feared her tendency to speak on impulse. But where would that lead? What could she expect from him and what did she want? He was a stranger even though they were blood relatives. Her non-genetic father was in ignorance; she couldn't bear the thought of causing him any pain. Mr Ball had a wife and children, what effect would such a revelation have on them? No, for everybody's sake, she must stick purely to observation and make no slip-ups.

She felt shaky when told she could go in and she opened the door tentatively. Her nerves were raw, her mouth was dry. She looked into the room and saw it was dominated by a huge old-fashioned desk behind which there was an equally large chair occupied by a giant of a man. He stood up as she came in and held out a hefty hand for her to shake. She had a rush of adrenalin and her mind, going into super-drive, took in every detail at once. He was well over six foot, broad and portly. As she shook his large, freckled hand she noticed his nails were clipped short and he wore a ring on his little finger. He had rusty brown eyes under thick ginger eyebrows but no hair on his head. His lips were thin but broad and when he smiled she noticed there was a prominent gap between his front two teeth. He had a wide-bridged nose on which sat a pair of frameless spectacles. His cheeks were ruddy against his pale skin and there was a large mole below his left ear. He looked civil but business-like; she was after all here for work not pleasure.

Her first impression? He was a *complete* and *utter* stranger. She had imagined experiencing a sense of affinity but, in reality, she felt devoid of any emotion.

She sat as directed in the chair on the other side of the desk and explained to him the basis of her project. She felt herself go pink. Now she was face-to-face with him the project sounded even less plausible. However, Bina was right in her assessment of consultants and Mr Ball was no exception. After allowing Mia just a few minutes to explain what she wanted he waded into a long monologue about bunion operations. His voice was deep and soft with a slight Scottish intonation. Mia strained to hear but couldn't catch all the words. She didn't feel bold enough to ask him to speak up but worried she'd miss something and not be able to respond intelligently.

After some time she realised he wasn't going to ask her anything or expect her to comment; he was just going to lecture her in the advantages of the Ballsectomy. She fixed her eyes in his general direction and let her mind drift. She watched his lips move but only heard the occasional word.

He wasn't handsome and seemed a bit straight-laced, what would it have been like to have been raised by him? *"Big toe lateral deviation"* He seemed serious but maybe he was more fun-loving at home. *"Bony lump Hallux Valgus"* Did she share any features with his children? *"Joint stress"* She tried to imagine him as a younger man and wondered what her mother had seen in him. *"Plaster cast"* She pictured Auntie Sheila laughing over his name. What would she think if she knew her mum had got pregnant that week-end? *"X-ray"* Most of all she searched for some sign he was her father but couldn't find any; even his hands were huge! *"arthritic condition"*

The warm, stuffy room, his soporific voice, the early start, her poor night's sleep and the nervous energy she'd expended brought on a huge weariness. She shuffled in the seat and tried stretching her eyes apart but the lids kept drooping. He didn't seem to notice or if he did he ignored it, continuing his dialogue in the same soft, monotonous tone. His voice droned on and on and her eye lids got heavier and heavier. She was trapped, imprisoned in the chair obliged to listen to him for goodness knows how long. She should have excused herself and gone for some fresh air but she thought it would be rude to interrupt him. She knew she MUST keep her eyes open but they felt like lead. His voice continued to drone on and on and on. Suddenly, she was overcome with a peculiar sensation. The room and Sandy faded away from her, as though she'd gone to a distant place. She didn't remember anything else.

Edward got a shock when the young physiotherapist fell from

her chair. He'd been explaining one of the most interesting details of his Ballsectomy when suddenly she crashed to the floor. He rushed round the desk and finding her pulse concluded she had fainted. He put her in a recovery position and called through to his admin manager, Penny, to get help. He left a junior doctor to check her over as she regained consciousness and went out. He told Penny he would be back to finish his talk with the "young lass". He wanted to outline some case histories he was sure would be of value to her project.

"No bones broken!" the young doctor declared after checking over Mia.

"What happened?" she asked.

"You fainted" he answered. "You'll probably have a bruise on your left shoulder but you don't need any medical attention so I'll be on my way. It's best if you just rest up here a bit. I'll ask Penny to get you a drink."

Mia had been lifted onto a couch in the consultant's office. Penny came in and offered to get her a cup of tea. Mia accepted gratefully.

"What happened to Mr Ball?" Mia asked.

"He's just popped out" Penny answered "but don't you worry, he told me to tell you he would be back by one thirty. He wants to make sure you get all the facts you need for your project"

Mia groaned and worried that she might not be able to stay awake for another session; she would be even more tired. She couldn't faint again!

"That's very kind of him" she told Penny. "I hope I didn't give him too much of a fright. Maybe I shouldn't take any more of his time."

"That's not a problem" Penny said. "Mr Ball enjoys sharing knowledge with young professionals."

Mia detected an edge of derision in Penny's tone and it was easy to imagine her sharing a joke with Bina. Now she kindly offered to get Mia a sandwich suggesting it would be a good idea for her to eat something. Mia accepted the offer gratefully.

She sighed as Penny left. She had never fainted before; it must have been the stress of the situation. She wanted more time with Edward but not for listening to him prattling on about bunions. At the moment it looked as though that was about the best she was going to achieve.

She gingerly rose from the sofa; she felt very light-headed. She wandered towards the book shelves and ran her eye over the titles. There were various volumes on the subject of orthopaedics, one of which she noticed Sandy had co-authored. It was a thick tome and, although still feeling weak, Mia took it down from the shelf. Inside the back cover was a photo of a younger Edward with a head of hair. He looked more handsome but not, in Mia's view, very sexy. He wore an arrogant expression. What had attracted her mother to him? There must have been something. After all this was her genetic father! Until now it had pleased her to think she'd inherited more of her father's genes than her mother's; there were a lot of her mother's characteristics she didn't like. Now she found herself wanting to believe she'd inherited most of her genes from her mother. She couldn't imagine she'd been built with fifty percent of this man's genes. The thought of it made her feel queasy again and she put the book back.

She moved to Edward's side of the desk where she saw two framed photographs of his daughters. Both girls were in their respective graduation garb. Mia looked closely at the photos but saw no resemblance to either of her half-sisters. One of the girls had inherited many of Edward's features which Mia thought was very unlucky. Her eyes looked small behind the thick rimmed glasses and she had a huge number of freckles over a very broad nose. She looked affable though with a broad grin across her face and Mia sensed she would be easy to befriend. Having been raised with two older, ultra-self-confident brothers she felt a desire to make herself known to this estranged half-sister. The other girl was more attractive but looked aloof. Both girls had elements of their father's ginger colouring, albeit more auburn than orange, presumably their mother was of a darker complexion. Mia compared herself with these half-siblings. Why didn't she have any hint of ginger in her colouring? Ralph had no trace of ginger either. She and Ralph were of remarkably similar colouring. Davina did not look at all like Mia's mum Pam so it would stand to reason any likeness between them came from Edward. Mia pondered that genetics was an interesting science and maybe she should study it; Vicky certainly found it totally absorbing. She surmised there were evidently genes carried in Edward that had been passed on to Ralph and her but not the two daughters in the photographs.

She was so engrossed in her thoughts she didn't hear Penny come back into the office with a large mug of tea and a BLT sandwich and she gave a startled jump.

"Sorry," said Penny "did I give you a fright?"

"Yes" answered Mia "I was miles away then. I was just looking at these photos; are they Mr Ball's daughters?"

"Yes, they were taken a few years ago now" replied Penny. "He's very proud that they both followed him into the medical profession, though with him as a father I don't suppose they had much choice."

Mia noticed a hint of disdain in the tone. She mused briefly whether she too might have qualified to be a doctor had she been raised by Edward. She looked at Penny. "Thanks for getting me the sandwich, what do I owe you?"

"Don't worry" answered Penny "it's on the house. You deserve it after listening to Sandy for the best part of an hour. I'm not surprised you passed out!"

"You don't like him much do you?"

"Oh, he's not a bad sort really. I just find him more than a bit superior. He sometimes talks to me as though I'm a child! Just because I don't have a string of qualifications doesn't mean I'm stupid or my opinion should be ignored!"

Mia was surprised by Penny's openness and disturbed Edward was someone people didn't like. Such a contrast to her father John whom she loved dearly; he was such a wonderful person.

"You sound like my mum" she told Penny "she's always on her high horse about people thinking they know everything because they have a degree."

Penny was about to say something else when Edward came in, earlier than expected. Mia hoped he hadn't heard too much of their conversation. Penny hastily retreated out of the office.

"How's the patient?" he asked.

"Much better, thank you" answered Mia. "I'm so sorry to have been such a lot of trouble."

"Don't worry about it" consoled Edward, then seeing she hadn't eaten her sandwich told her she should eat up whilst he did a few things at his desk. They could return to her project when she was ready. He was kind and considerate. Maybe he wasn't so bad after all.

A quiet period followed then Edward broke the silence.

"My wife fainted two or three times when she was younger" he told Mia "when she was pregnant, it was very worrying."

"That must have been difficult" Mia answered sympathetically, then added "how many children do you have?"

"Just two daughters" he replied and went back to the papers on his desk.

There was a silence again.

"Just two daughters, that's what you think!" Mia reflected as her resolve to remain distant evaporated.

"My Auntie was a trainee nurse up here" she stated to the crown of his head. "I mentioned your name and she thought she remembered you being at one of her parties. It sounds like you all had a riotous time in your college days."

"I don't know why she would have given you that impression" he said looking up from his paperwork "I certainly didn't have a riotous time; it was all study and long hours on the wards. But as she was a trainee nurse she wouldn't have been under the same pressure as us doctors."

Penny's words echoed in Mia's head.

"Well she thought she remembered you" Mia repeated.

"What's her name?" he asked.

"Sheila" Mia said "Sheila Cummings."

"Hmm, no" he said slowly "don't recall her. She trained up here you said?" Mia nodded.

"No, don't remember her, sorry."

He went back to his paperwork.

"I suppose I didn't enjoy my student days as much as many of my contemporaries" he said as a contemplative rejoinder towards Mia but keeping his eyes down on his papers. "I was a mature student and already had two children by the time I got my place at the university."

"Hmmm, that would cramp your style!" Mia agreed light-heartedly as she swallowed a mouthful of sandwich.

There was another brief silence between them. Edward sneaked a peek over his papers at the young lady sat on his office sofa. He remembered all too well that party at her aunt's lodgings. He'd been going through a bad patch with his wife at the time; the tie of young children, long working hours, study and lack of money had not been conducive to a happy marriage. He'd gone to the party to get a break and met the host's sister who was visiting from London. She was an attractive lady, equally fed up with marriage and children. They were both at a low ebb. They'd talked throughout the night and ended up in bed together. It was a one-night stand; neither had any intension of leaving their partner. Now he realised that Mia must be the daughter of that lady. What was her name? He wracked his brain. Pamela; that was it! Yes, Pamela. Now he looked at Mia he could see she was like her mother; carrying many of her fine features. Was it just chance that her project had brought her to him? Could she have a hidden agenda in arranging to see him? Alarm bells sounded.

"It was hard work raising my daughters when I was studying" he volunteered casually. "In fact immediately after my second child I decided to have a vasectomy."

"Goodness" Mia said taken aback by the admission.

"Well we didn't want any more children" he stated.

Mia didn't comment. She sat quietly finishing her lunch thinking. Had he had the vasectomy before sex with her mother? If so, why would he have used a condom? Could it have been to protect against infection? She could imagine him thinking in those terms. She felt offended at the idea of him treating her mother like some common trollop. But more important was the vasectomy; it might mean he couldn't be her father. She felt a wave of hope. Maybe Vicky had been wrong and the nightmare was over. She finished her tea and sandwich and Edward suggested they resume. To her relief he could only spare another half an hour. She casually went to the waste bin by his desk to dispose of the sandwich wrapper then asked him whether the photos on his desk were of his daughters. She sensed him tense up and thought he was irritated by her being more interested in tittle-tattle than his pioneering bunion operation. This was partly true; he did think some women tended to lose focus and shouldn't be in the medical profession. But mostly he was more convinced than ever she had a hidden agenda. He hoped she'd believed him about the vasectomy and was doing the maths.

"Yes" he said looking up at her through his spectacles "they are both qualified doctors."

She sensed he was getting impatient with her questions but she continued.

"How old are they?" she ventured.

He relaxed a little as he answered "thirty-five and thirty-three" then returning to his formal stance added "now, shall we continue?"

***

On the train home Mia was ecstatic. She tried to suppress the huge grin that wanted to plant itself over her face. The pompous git wasn't her dad after all! There was no reason to assume he was Ralph's dad! Edward had a vasectomy "immediately after his second child was born". She was thirty-three, two years older than Mia, so born well before his chance sexual escapade with Pam. He must have worn the condom for fear of getting a disease from her mum! She felt offended by the inference but mostly she felt relief and excitement. Now she would be able to resume her relationship with Ralph. She loved him so much.

She wanted to call him on her mobile straight away but knew it would be impossible to explain what had happened in public on the train. No, she would just have to wait until she got home. She would buy a bottle of bubbly to celebrate! Damn the expense! She couldn't wait to see Ralph & tell him the good news.

***

It was nearly seven o'clock by the time she turned into her road, swinging the champagne in its carrier bag. On nearing their block, she looked up to the lounge and it was in darkness, Ralph must be in the kitchen at the back of the flat. She quickened her step. Then she noticed a familiar figure standing in the shadows outside. Her heart sank. It was Vicky. Vicky waved and waited.

"What are you doing here?" Mia said as soon as she was in earshot.

"Thanks for the welcome!" Vicky answered sarcastically. "Ralph and I have been trying to reach you all day. Has your phone been switched off?"

Mia had turned her mobile off when she went into Sandy's office and now she realised she hadn't switched it back on. Her mood changed.

"What's happened?" she asked.

"It's Ralph's dad" answered Vicky "he's had a heart attack. He's in intensive care in Hillingdon Hospital. Ralph's gone to see him and be with his mum."

"I'd better get over there" Mia stated turning to go back up the road.

"Wooo, no rush" answered Vicky placing a retraining hand on Mia's arm "I think they're happy to be on their own."

Mia looked back at her, puzzled.

"Ralph told me about your trip today, he was quite upset about it" Vicky explained. "In the circumstances it'd be less stressful for him and his mum to be given a bit of space; some peace and quiet."

"What?" Mia demanded. "Does he think I'm completely insensitive?"

"Don't get all uptight Mia. It's perfectly natural for people not to want to cope with outsiders when there's a family crisis going on."

"But I *am* family!" Mia exclaimed.

"Yes, I know, and it may seem hard but you're not exactly close to your mum-in-law, are you? Maybe at a time like this she doesn't want to have the strain of having to think about visitors."

"Visitors?" repeated Mia insulted.

Vicky looked awkward.

"Well maybe you should have thought more about Ralph when you went gallivanting off on your mad goose chase today" she offered.

"It was anything but a mad goose chase" retorted Mia. "I found out today that Ralph and I aren't half siblings after all!"

As soon as the words left her mouth she wished she could grab them back. Vicky would want an explanation and she really didn't have the energy for any more discussion about genetics or anything else for that matter. She suddenly realised how extremely tired she felt. It had been a long day in more ways than one.

"How so?" asked Vicky.

"Look Vicky I'm sorry but I'm really tired and don't want to talk about it. I just want to go in, ring Ralph and get some sleep."

"Ok" Vicky conceded "but those test results were pretty conclusive."

The words agitated Mia.

"I think a vasectomy before sex with my mum is pretty conclusive!" she countered triumphantly.

"How did *you* find out *that*!?" challenged Vicky wide-eyed.

"We had a friendly chat" answered Mia swelling with pride at the sight of her friend's bewilderment "and he mentioned he'd had a vasectomy immediately after his second daughter was born."

Vicky remained astounded. "Mia" she exclaimed "people don't

just tell strangers about having vasectomies! It's hardly every-day conversation! How on earth did you get him to tell you?"

"I made a casual remark about young doctors having a great time at college and asked whether he remembered going to my Aunt's party and ..."

She was cut short by a hoot of derisive laughter.

"Mia, you are so naive!" Vicky spluttered. "You don't think he suspected anything!?"

"It was all very natural!" Mia cried indignantly.

"Yeah sure it was" Vicky sneered.

There was an impasse between them for a few seconds.

"I'd better get going" Vicky said, then added casually "by the way I've been in the flat and got some clothes for Ralph" she pointed to a sports bag by her feet. "I left you a note on the kit-chen table in case I missed you."

"You went in?" Mia repeated shocked. "Did Ralph give you our key?"

"No of course not" Vicky assured her. "I've just used his key to get him a change of clothes. I'm giving the keys back; he'd hardly give me the keys to your place."

"But" Mia faltered trying to understand the situation "that means you'll be visiting Ralph; he doesn't think of you as a vis-itor or outsider!"

Vicky sighed. "Don't be like that Mia" she stated. "It's an *emer-gency.* I told him I was in Hillingdon tomorrow night so could drop his stuff over. I won't be staying. Don't get yourself all wound up! I'm trying to be helpful."

"I see" whispered Mia, but her heart ached at the sight of Ralph's gym bag between Vicky's feet.

"Are you OK?" Vicky asked. "You've gone very pale."

"Just tired" answered Mia. "Think I'll go in, call Ralph and get an early night."

"He'll be at the hospital until at least 8.30" Vicky told her "so probably best to ring after nine to give him a chance to have something to eat."

Mia prickled but nodded acceptance.

"See you next week" she said as she turned away from Vicky who picked up the bag and strode off with it slung over her shoulder.

***

Inside the flat Mia found Vicky's note and tore it up into tiny pieces. She looked at the kitchen table and recalled the image of Ralph head to head with Vicky over the chess board. What an idiot she'd been! She'd thought they might be starting something; she was well behind. She saw now that they'd spent the day together whilst she was at work. How could she have believed Vicky brought that Tagine from home? It was obvious she'd made it here. What had they got up to whilst it bubbled and simmered on the cooker? Ralph had turned to Vicky in his time of need. That hurt. And what was he doing giving Vicky the key of their flat? He had no right to hand their key to anybody else, even in an emergency. She thought of Vicky going through Ralph's clothes and packing a bag for him; it was such an intimate task. It was evident they had become close; closer than she had thought possible in such a short time. No wonder he'd been cool towards her. She felt dizzy and disorientated.

But what weighed just as heavily on her mind was Vicky's derision over Sandy's vasectomy revelation. She now recalled with incredible clarity and excruciating embarrassment Edward's denial of knowing Sheila and his quiet contemplation afterwards. Why *should* he volunteer all that information? Vicky was right; she had been naive and stupid to imagine he'd casually mention something so personal. She'd been fooling herself.

She sat on the sofa and wept. The flat was silent, empty and hollow. It felt sullied by Vicky's presence. She wanted to ring Ralph now. She was desperate to hear his voice. But Vicky had warned her to wait and ringing at an inconvenient time would only exacerbate the probability of an argument. She yearned to be with Ralph and comfort him but he blatantly didn't want to see her. She wished to know how David was, maybe visit him in hospital, but she'd been excommunicated from the Davenport family and didn't have the confidence to force her presence upon them.

If only she'd been at work today and not chasing after Sandy. It had been a whim, a distraction. No good had come from the visit. She recalled Ralph telling her he was only willing to spend time on one father and that was David. She had thought him strange but now she wondered whether she was the weird one pursuing an oblivious genetic father. She should tell Ralph she had changed her mind. He was right. They should carry on as before but adopt children. She thought about Ralph; his big broad shoulders and friendly grin. She wanted to run her fingers through his hair and feel him hug her tight. Yet in her heart she knew she may have pushed him too far away to get him back.

She flopped across the sofa and fell asleep. Her phone remained in her handbag switched off.

***

Ralph wondered what had happened to Mia. He'd been trying to contact her all day. It had been difficult at the A & E Department; they didn't allow mobile phones to be switched on so he'd repeatedly popped outside to try. Now it was nearly nine o'clock and he'd been home with his mother for hours. He tried Mia's mobile yet again but it was still switched off!

He felt a mixture of worry and anger. Part of him feared that something awful had happened. He imagined her being attacked or falling ill and the thought made him feel anxious and restless. He wouldn't be able to cope with something dreadful happening to her as well as his father. The other part of him wondered whether she just didn't care about him enough to bother ringing. Maybe she hadn't received his messages asking her to call. But surely by now she'd be wondering why he hadn't come home? Wasn't she concerned about him? He knew they were struggling at the moment but he thought she might have shown some interest in his welfare. Anger welled in him.

He thought back over the day. It was unfortunate that Mia had been absent and he hadn't been able to see her at work or speak to her. Don, his manager, had been very sympathetic and understanding, telling him to take whatever time was necessary and sort out leave later. Vicky had happened to come by his office and he'd told her he hadn't been able to contact Mia. She had agreed to keep trying and if she got through to tell Mia to ring him. She'd looked questioning when he said Mia was in Liverpool for the day so in a low whisper he'd told her Mia was pursuing their genetic father.

Everyone had been so supportive but what he wanted more than anything was to have Mia here with him. He had never felt so insecure and he ached for her to be in his arms. He yearned to rid himself of the strange, vacuous feeling that had taken hold of him. He was sure Mia was the only person that could chase it away. Where was she? It was then that his mobile rang and he rushed to answer; all would be forgiven and she'd be on her way to him.

As he picked up the phone his heart sank; number not recognised. The sound of Vicky's voice rekindled his fears for Mia's safety but Vicky soon dispelled those. She told him she'd been to the flat and seen Mia hours ago. She was just as surprised as him that Mia hadn't phoned but she assured him Mia was fine, just very tired after her long day. That angered Ralph. Too tired to ring him? His father had suffered a heart attack! Vicky went on to tell him she was in his neck of the woods tomorrow evening so had agreed with Mia to drop a bag of clothes over to him.

Ralph was *very* upset. Mia had packed clothes for him! Couldn't wait to get him out of the flat! And she couldn't even be bothered to bring the bag of clothes herself. She obviously didn't care for him at all.

He thanked Vicky for ringing and just as he was about to hang up she broke in:

"Ralph, are you still there? Oh good. I nearly forgot. You left your keys at work today, they'll be in the side zipped pocket of your bag."

"Oh! I must have left them on my desk in all the panic. Thanks Vicky."

"That's OK, just thought you should know in case you started looking for them."

"Yes of course, thanks again. See you tomorrow night."

***

Mia woke with a stiff neck. The harsh sofa fabric had left an imprint the length of her cheek and she was cold. She looked at the time; five past eleven! Was it too late to call Ralph? She decided better to ring late than wait 'til tomorrow.

Meanwhile Ralph had given up on Mia and taken consolation in several glasses of whisky. Davina and he had virtually finished a bottle between them. When the phone rang Ralph jumped out of his semi-comatose state and in spite of the time was pleased to see it was Mia calling.

"Hi Angel Cake" he said. "You eventually got around to calling me then."

"Hi love" answered Mia pleased he'd used her pet name but at the same time registering the use of the word eventually. "Yes, sorry it's so late, I fell asleep when I got back and I've only just woken up. How are you doing? How is Dad?"

"I'm physically and mentally exhausted" he admitted. "Dad's what they call comfortable and looks like he'll pull through, though we're not over the worst yet. Mum's bearing up but I'm pleased I'm here for her."

There was an awkward pause. A myriad of incoherent thoughts rushed into Mia's head. She knew she should ask more about David but she was too preoccupied with her own hurt and rage. Was Ralph ready to throw her over for Vicky?

"Hello Mia, are you there?" Ralph questioned the silent phone.

"Yes, I'm here" came back Mia then added hesitantly "I hope I can come and see Dad soon."

This inflamed Ralph. "Hope I can come and see Dad soon?!" he thought. "You should be here now! My father nearly died today and all you can say is you might try to visit soon!"

Stress and whisky colluded to cloud Ralph's mind. Instead of questioning Mia's uncharacteristic behaviour he became aggressive.

"I don't want to put you to any trouble" he told her harshly. "Just make sure you leave your mobile switched off then you won't have to get involved! I'll know not to expect moral support from you!"

She was incensed by his tirade. He spoke as though she'd intentionally been out of contact, insinuating she was disinterested. She hadn't known when she left that morning her father-in-law was going to have a flipping heart attack! Was she supposed to repent for ever for not having her mobile switched on?!

"You've got plenty of moral support from Vicky" she answered in bitter retaliation. "She'll bring your clothes over, that should make you feel better!"

"For God's sake Mia, this is hardly the time for petty jealousies!" he retorted.

She was struck dumb. Petty jealousies! Vicky had packed his clothes! How would he like it if James packed a bag for her?! She was seething.

Ralph was equally confounded. Had Mia got Vicky to deliver the bag as some kind of test? Was he supposed to have told Vicky not to come? He could do without Mia playing silly childish games. She was attention seeking and selfish. His attitude hardened.

A long pregnant pause fell across the airwaves, both parties too blinded with anger to speak. Eventually Ralph broke the stand-off.

"Look, we're both tired" he said. "Let's call it a day and catch up again tomorrow."

"OK" she answered quietly.

She could have told him she wanted to be with him, she loved him so very deeply. He could have told her how much he had yearned to hold her in his arms. But neither was prepared or able to continue the conversation. Ralph angrily disconnected. Mia waited for the line to die then switched off.

Chapter 8
To be Life-Giving and Life-Long

Mia had a painfully long, dismal week following their argument. She expected Ralph to call but as the days went by she realised he wasn't going to. She didn't feel able to take the initiative and contact him. Vicky mailed her mid-week and Mia agreed to meet for lunch. It was a mistake. Vicky apparently imagined Mia would welcome updates about her husband and in-laws from a third party! She spoke excitedly about Ralph as though Mia hardly knew him. She was like a teenager with a new boyfriend.

She told Mia before the test she'd never considered Ralph as anything other than a friend; he was after all her best friend's husband. However, when she saw those test results she knew Mia "would never be able to remain married to her brother". She spoke the words with disgust, reinforcing feelings previously seeded.

Mia pointed out that as her "best friend" Vicky should have given her time to sort things out instead of charging in on Ralph like a "bitch on heat". Vicky ignored the insult and pointed out it was best she was with Ralph; at least Mia would be able to stay in touch with him. Mia was mystified with Vicky's attitude.

Although angry, Mia continued to overlook Vicky's treacherous behaviour mainly because she didn't have any other close friends. Since the wedding she had lost contact with her three best girlfriends. One had moved away and she had become lazy about meeting up with the other two. Her singles lifestyle had been exchanged for her marriage to Ralph and friendship with Vicky. Now she'd lost Ralph and Vicky had become her only friend.

However, the lunch date had made her feel worse than ever. She knew she shouldn't begrudge Vicky the chance to be happy with Ralph but she raged with jealousy at the thought of them together. She was appalled with herself for being so spiteful and resentful towards Vicky. She felt ugly and unwanted. Without Ralph her life was bleak, empty and pointless.

The week dragged on with no word from Ralph. She cried herself to sleep and struggled to find the motivation to get up in the morning. She felt physically sick at the thought of never being with Ralph again, everything had become mundane and difficult. Her light and zestful step had turned into a lumbering plod. One morning the short lady with the thick-rimmed glasses and Cossack hat was on the tube again, fighting her way through the train, knocking into other passengers, just as she had before. What had Mia found so funny? All she saw now was a pathetic, little old lady with no manners.

At work Mia didn't want to socialize and she particularly avoided Bina. Bina would want to hear all about the meeting with Sandy Balls and Mia couldn't face talking about it. With the aid of increasingly more make-up, and by restricting herself to pleasantries, she hid her state of mind from her colleagues. The work itself was her only respite. It was a life-raft she must cling to or she would surely sink into oblivion.

She finally heard from Ralph on Saturday morning but was not comforted by the contact. He texted to say he wanted to pick up some more clothes. She had volunteered to work that day so he came whilst she was out; he evidently wanted to avoid her.

Now she trudged back from the Saturday shift and climbed the stairs with no enthusiasm to be home. She carried a bag of food she'd bought at the local store; snacks purchased with no interest. She was intensely lonely. She pictured people out socialising or at home with friends or partners, grateful for the weekend, and felt totally cut off. She momentarily considered going to a local pub or restaurant, but being surrounded by people laughing and chatting would only make her feel conspicuous and exacerbate her sense of isolation.

She entered the dark, silent flat and made for the bedroom where she opened Ralph's wardrobe. His remaining clothes hung forlorn on the virtually empty rail. She shut the door but the image of the bare cupboard remained. She quickly moved to the lounge and put the television on, finding a chat show spewing out friendly but banal conversation. It was a poor substitute for the company of real people but better than silence.

She dumped the shopping on the floor, threw her coat over the back of the chair and slumped onto the sofa. Momentarily the host show held her attention and she was able to forget her solitude, but the minute she let her attention turn away from the programme she became painfully aware of Ralph's absence and the hollowness of the flat. The light and sound from the television was like the glow of a fire, reaching to the centre of the room but leaving the perimeter and the rest of the flat cold, dark and silent. The ghostly spaces sent a shiver down her back. She considered ringing Ralph. But he would be with Vicky and his unwelcoming mother. She felt utterly forlorn.

She stared at the faces on the telly without taking anything in. She sat frozen to the sofa, unwilling to move even to get a drink. She felt repulsive and useless. Ralph was better off without her. She'd been a dreadful wife. She'd repeatedly rejected him even though he'd tried so hard to win her round. She had got what she deserved; to be discarded for somebody better. Who would want to be with her? She was thoughtless and selfish. She wasn't even pleased for his happiness. Ralph had made her feel special and loved. Without that she was nothing.

She sat in this introspective state for some time but was roused out of it by the buzz of the intercom. She ignored it. It buzzed again. She ignored it. It buzzed persistently for the third time. She forced herself out of the sofa and sauntered to the speaker.

"Who is it?" she barked.

"My-mi?" a male responded.

"Tony!" she exclaimed. "What are you doing here?"

"I've come to see you!" he answered. "Are you going to let me in?"

"Sorry!" she exclaimed as she pressed the door release. She went to the front door and watched him sprint up the stairs two at a time. When he reached her they gave each other a big hug.

She was so very, very pleased to see him; tears welled in her eyes. The security and assurance of a pair of familiar strong arms was so comforting she was reluctant to let go.

"What are you doing in this neck of the woods?" she asked as they moved into the flat and he off-loaded his small back-pack and a carrier bag. "I am so pleased to see you! I really, really needed a friendly face; you have been heaven sent!"

"Not exactly heaven sent" answered Tony. "Mother sent!"

He explained Pam had been worried about Mia for the last few weeks saying things like "she isn't herself" and "something's up, I know it!" Then a couple of days ago Auntie Sheila phoned and mentioned Mia's visit. She told Pam she thought Mia hadn't looked well and seemed distracted. Pam had already been sceptical of Mia's explanation for Ralph staying at his parent's house, dismissing Mia's assertion he needed to be there for his mother. She'd gone into action mode. She knew her daughter wouldn't open up to her and decided the best person to find out what was going on would be her closest brother.

"So here I am!" stated Tony with a broad grin. "Of course I'm not supposed to have told you all that but I couldn't go along with the "working in the area" excuse Mum suggested."

"But I was so cool at Auntie Sheila's" stated Mia. "How could she have known there was something wrong?"

"Ah, you failed to notice something!" he told her, then mimicking Sheila added "and 'er being such a sensitive girl too, it wasn't like 'er not to notice."

"What didn't I notice?" asked Mia perplexed.

"Think" coaxed Tony. "What was missing?"

Mia still looked blank.

Tony poked out his tongue, lifted his curled hands to his chest and panted.

"Rex!" exclaimed Mia. "Where was Rex the dog!? I didn't notice he wasn't there even though he usually jumps all over me. I must have been so preoccupied."

"Exactly! They were right! You would normally have asked where he was. That was the give-away!"

"Well, where was he?" she asked concerned.

"Old age got him" Tony told her. "He was sixteen and that's like you or me being eighty in terrier years."

"Poor Auntie Sheila; she would have been so upset and I didn't even miss him! I feel really bad now. I'll have to ring her to apologise. I can't seem to do a thing right at the moment. To think she didn't even take offence but was only worried about me."

A wave of gratitude overcame her. She often complained about her family but here they were worrying and wanting to help in her time of need. She tried not to cry but couldn't control the tears and in no time was sobbing on her brother's shoulder. He just held her and when he thought she was gathering herself together held her out at arm's length. "I think it's a good job I came" he said.

Mia went to get beers and Tony wandered into the lounge. He cringed at the mindless chat show Mia had been watching and noted her coat slung over the sofa. He was nosey enough to peer into the bag and examine the strange assortment of chocolate bars and crisps. He was shocked at Mia's appearance; he'd never seen her so gaunt. For once his mother had not been over-dramatic when she'd talked him into coming.

They chatted generally, Mia having turned off the telly and put away the bag of goodies and her coat. She apologised that she only had snacks to eat and was surprised when he declared he had brought something. He fetched his carrier bag to reveal a couple of steaks, jacket potatoes, some ready prepared salad and a bottle of wine. They moved to the kitchen where Mia watched him stab the potatoes and stick them in the microwave, then turn on the grill ready for the steaks. She had some old mushrooms that were a bit past their best but Tony chopped them with some onion and fried them with a dash of the wine and a little mustard; it was an excellent topping for the beef.

For the first time she saw Tony as a man. He was about five foot nine with broad shoulders and slim hips. He'd inherited his father's colouring and wore his light brown hair swept back off his forehead emphasising his round hazel-green eyes. He and Mia shared the same shaped nose, long and slightly turned up at the end. They also shared the same high cheek bones. These were attractive features in Mia and, although not as appealing in Tony, he was still a handsome man. Watching him now, confidently working around the kitchen, Mia could see he would be quite a catch for somebody and wondered why he wasn't already hooked, though she knew he had suffered a couple of disastrous relationships. She suddenly pulled herself together. What was she thinking? It must be the discovery about Ralph that made her think of Tony in this way.

They sat down to eat and for the first time in weeks Mia enjoyed a proper meal. They stayed seated at the table and chatted well into the night. Mia told him everything. About the test and how they'd ridiculed Vicky and then the steady revelations that followed.

"Mum, having an affair!" exclaimed Tony. "Wicked woman! And knowing how sanctimonious she can be!"

"Sworn to secrecy" Mia reminded him "remember dad doesn't know."

"Naturally" he confirmed but there was a large twinkle in his eye.

His visit was proving to be more profound than he'd anticipated. He'd expected to listen to a load of boring piffle about some silly argument with Ralph, comfort his little sister with a few encouraging words, then get away as soon as he could. Instead Mia was truly in need of help, the problem was weirder than he could ever have supposed and, to top it all, there were some family skeletons coming out of the cupboard.

He was incredulous about nanny Davenport. The co-incidence of Ralph being given the unsolicited information about his father at that particular point in time was extraordinary, too uncanny to believe. Mia pointed out that he had often suspected conspiracies that didn't exist and after some discussion they agreed co-incidence was the only reasonable explanation, what else could it be?

Tony laughed at Mia's account of her visit to Sandy Balls and he again referred to their mum's infidelity. Mia felt uncomfortable and disloyal but she was relieved to off-load. Pam would be able to look after herself should Tony decide to throw it in her face during some future altercation. Those two were like peas in a pod as far as verbal acrobatics were concerned. Mia was well out of their league.

She told him about Sandy's revelation and Vicky's derision. Tony agreed with Vicky on that point. "Sandy may be a pompous git" he said "but he wouldn't be a consultant if he was stupid enough not to smell a rat when it was standing in front of him, sorry about the analogy."

He was surprised about Vicky having the key to the flat. He'd always thought Ralph a good sort, nice and steady, ideal for his sister. He was shocked by Ralph's speedy leap into a new relationship and felt angrily defensive on his sister's behalf. But then she admitted she'd refused sexual contact with Ralph for weeks and Tony became more sympathetic towards his fellow male.

"What would your best outcome be now?" he asked her. "Go back with Ralph and pretend as he has suggested?"

"I think it's too late for that" she answered regretfully. "He'd prefer to be with Vicky, she makes him feel good and I don't."

"But if he *did* want you back, is that what *you* want?" Tony persisted.

"I'm not sure now" she admitted "but I do know I miss him so much. I don't think I can carry on without him" a tear formed in her eye.

"Don't talk like that!" he demanded. "You mustn't be so defeatist My-mi."

They were children again.

"I'm sorry" she responded. "It's just how I feel. I feel like shit."

"Look" she added as she slowly rolled her sleeve over her wrist. Tony's heart raced.

"I've come out in this horrible itchy rash" she said.

He exhaled with relief and studied the fierce looking red welts on her inner arm.

"They're on my legs as well" she told him "and I even have one up my nose! They're really itchy."

"You'll have to go to the doctor" he declared, then added "I must admit you do look like shit!"

"Thanks!" she said.

"We need to sort you out, sis. First, you've got to start eating properly. Tomorrow we'll go to the supermarket and get in a few supplies."

"I'm useless at cooking" she whined.

"Don't be silly" he told her "nobody's useless at cooking! You just need to learn a few tricks."

"That's one of the things Ralph likes about Vicky" Mia said "she cooks good meals for him."

"As can you!"

"I nearly set fire to the kitchen recently" she said. "Poor Ralph, all he came home to was a burnt chop soaked in tap water."

Tony chuckled and in spite of her mood she managed a weak smile.

"I'd be pleased for the tips" she conceded more positively.

"And we're going to visit David" he stated.

"I can't!" she answered. "I'm not welcome!"

"Who says? Just because you're arguing with Ralph doesn't mean you don't want to see his dad. You DO want to see him, don't you?"

"Yes, I really do" she said.

"That's tomorrow's plan then" he concluded. "And on Monday you're going to make an appointment to see the doctor. I'll soon have you sorted out, My-mi, and I'm not leaving until I know you're OK. I've got a few days off work so I should be able to concentrate on getting you straight."

It sounded like an army exercise but Mia was grateful for his company and to be taken under his wing.

***

The next day, Sunday, Tony wanted to go back to his flat in Twickenham to pick up some more clothes; this was going to be a longer visit than he had envisaged. They'd decided to go to Twickenham by train, collect his clothes and then drive to the hospital. Tony was keen to show Mia his new car, his pride and joy. He hadn't brought it to Balham because of all the parking restrictions and although he didn't admit it to Mia (for fear of sounding like their mother) he worried it might get vandalised. There was also the risk of it being damaged because of the double parking in Balham's narrow back streets.

Mia made all the right noises when she saw the black, low slung, long bonneted sports car. It had a customised number plate, TKS 007, and flashy silver and red stripes along the sides. Tony gleamed with excitement as he showed her the leather upholstery. She feigned enthusiasm.

She lowered herself into the passenger seat; it was like sitting on the ground. The throaty engine jumped into life, sending shudders through the car and Mia's body. Once on the main road Tony hit the accelerator and the car roared off, leaving a cloud of exhaust fume and most of Mia's breath in its wake. She was pinned to the back of the bucket seat, her legs flaying and her hands reaching out for anything to steady herself. Tony laughed at Mia's shocked face; his sister had never been a dare-devil. He swung the car around corners making the tyres screech. His foot hopped between the accelerator and brake, he was testing the seat belts to their limit.

Mia could hardly see out of the window, she was practically horizontal! The jerks and skids made her feel sick. She was sure they were going to crash. Her life was in peril! She was relieved when Tony found a parking place and she could get out of the car.

It started to rain as they neared the hospital and they ran the last few metres to the entrance. They didn't see a pair of cold, steel blue eyes intently watching them from the shadows of the hospital building.

Mia was nervous when they got to the ward anticipating Ralph might be in there, though she half-hoped he would be. She also wondered how badly affected her father-in-law had been and what reception he might give her. She spotted David and saw he was alone; she drew a breath and bravely walked over to his bed, Tony a step behind. Her apprehension was dispelled by David's obvious pleasure at seeing her. He looked weak but he hadn't lost any of his faculties and they immediately got into easy conversation about his treatment and present prognosis. That developed into a general discussion about the National Health Service; a subject always close to Mia's heart and now of infinitely more interest to David. Before long David tired and they decided to go, wishing him a speedy recovery and promising to come again soon.

As they reached the hospital exit it was raining harder. Mia reached into her cavernous handbag and pulled out a small umbrella. They tussled to get the lion's share as they huddled under it and headed for the car; giggling over their childish behaviour. At the car Tony held the umbrella whilst Mia got in. He then ran around and climbed into the driver's side, closing the umbrella behind him.

Ralph looked on from the end of the road. He'd seen them leave the hospital and followed unseen until they turned down the side street, where he waited at the corner. He hadn't recognised Tony whose face was obscured by the umbrella. All he saw was a young man with an expensive leather jacket having an intimate joke with his wife and gallantly opening the door for her so she could ride in his sleek, posh, penis extension of a car. A cocktail of jealousy and anger welled in the pit of his stomach.

"So" he thought bitterly "Vicky was right. Mia was visiting dad with a new man. It didn't take her long to start dating someone else! She must have been seeing him before all this blew up. What a nerve she's got bringing him here!"

The wedge had almost completely forced itself between them. It was now pressing against the very root of their relationship; their love for each other. But there were still feelings staving off their absolute separation. Until they were mutually indifferent, the wedge would not succeed.

***

David was asleep when Ralph got to the ward so he sat next to the bed and brooded over Mia. He'd so misjudged her and was heartbroken. Eventually his father woke up and gave Ralph a broad smile.

"Did you see Mia?" he asked straight away. "She just left."

"No" Ralph lied "but I've been here watching you sleep for some time."

"I must have been asleep longer than I realised" David stated. "It's your wife, she tired me out!" He was trying to sound upbeat but as Ralph remained stony-faced he added ruefully "I know it's none of my business but I'd be really pleased if you could patch up your argument with Mia. I feel responsible for you falling out. I'm sure things went wrong after that Sunday. I wish I'd told you before but I really didn't think it would be that important. That was stupid of me and I'm so sorry. It's been worrying me since you left that day but I don't know how to make it up to you."

"Please don't think you caused our problems dad" Ralph answered hastily. "We were having difficulties before that day. You mustn't think it was your fault. You're the best father I could wish for and it makes NO difference to me that we aren't genetically linked."

"Thank you" whispered David as he nodded off to sleep again.

***

Ralph got back from the hospital just after Davina had returned from visiting Audrey. They shared a simple meal and exchanged news about their visits. Davina noticed Ralph was distracted and asked if there was anything wrong. He admitted he was feeling down because he'd found out Mia had visited David today with a new boyfriend. Davina suggested this man could just be a friend but Ralph told her he'd bumped into Vicky, the friend of Mia's that dropped his stuff round. She'd told him she had just seen Mia going into the hospital with her new man. She'd suggested they go for a coffee to avoid any hurt or embarrassment. However, after leaving Vicky he'd seen Mia arm in arm with this man and watched her get into his posh car. He admitted to his mother he was devastated.

Davina felt Ralph's pain as though it were her own. She ached for him. What with her husband seriously ill and her son having problems, she was finding it difficult to stay strong. She wasn't privy to what had happened but found it hard to believe Mia would go with somebody else so soon after splitting up with Ralph. She wished with all her heart Ralph and Mia would get back together and be happy again.

She thought she might distract him with some newspaper cuttings she had rooted out. She handed them to him excitedly. He wasn't in the mood but felt obliged to show an interest. There were three articles all relating to the first ladies in Britain to have received artificial insemination from donated sperm. Two outlined the moral dilemma and possible problems that could arise. Ralph was sympathetic with their views! In the third was a large photo of four women. Each held a baby wrapped in a shawl. A doctor stood at the end of the group. Written above in bold, large type was the caption "**Monty's Mums Make History**". The articles were fascinating but at this moment Ralph didn't want to discuss artificial insemination, genetics or any other birth related matter. He was sick and tired of the whole subject. He knew his mother was eager to see his reaction so he mustered up the energy to study them for long enough not to offend her then handed them back.

"Cool!" he said.

Davina looked cress-fallen as she took them from him so he added "I'd like to get them copied some time if you don't mind."

That seemed to cheer her and she agreed she would get them copied for him; she didn't trust him with the originals.

Ralph was returning to work the next day. He asked Davina if he could stay for a while longer until he got his personal life sorted out. She was concerned about the long commute to South London but was more worried about her son's health; he looked pale and was obviously low. If he stayed she would be able to keep an eye on him. She would also appreciate having his company and help whilst David was in hospital. She readily agreed.

***

Wednesday evening and Mia sat in the doctors' waiting room. On the phone the receptionist had suggested Mia should seek advice from a chemist but Mia had insisted on seeing a doctor. Now she sat opposite the snooty receptionist and tried to avoid making eye contact.

The wait in the crowded, germ-laden room gave her time to reflect. Ralph was back at work. He had told her by e-mail he was not moving back to the flat; he didn't bother to come to see her. She didn't attempt to see him.

Tony had been brilliant. She'd come home on Monday to find a "Forman Grill" and "Slow Cooker" in the kitchen. He insisted on paying for them saying they were "his treat" and proceeded to show her how easy it was to cook salmon fillets in the grill, "even she couldn't set fire to them!" After eating the salmon, which was delicious, they piled chicken and various other ingredients into the slow cooker and put it in the fridge. All she had to do on Tuesday morning was place it on its stand and switch on. It gently cooked throughout the day and was also delicious.

Tony had extended his leave to cover the whole week. He was adamant he was going to stay until she was fighting fit. She knew it would be unreasonable to expect him to stay longer; he would have to go home soon. She needed to show him she was strong enough to cope on her own even though she wasn't.

Eventually her name was called. She'd not seen Dr Patel before as she hardly came to the surgery, but was pleased to find a female with a kind welcoming manner. In contrast to the receptionist, Dr Patel was not dismissive of Mia's rash and after a short examination pronounced it to be Psoriasis. She informed Mia this was a genetic condition brought on by, amongst other things, stress. She asked Mia whether she had been suffering from any stressful situations recently. Mia admitted she had and fought to hold back the tears. Dr Patel asked if Mia would like to see a counsellor; Mia refused.

The doctor then started to type out a prescription for cream, explaining there was no cure for the condition but the cream should help.

"Are you pregnant?" she asked routinely.

"Not as far as I know" answered Mia then gave a little breath as though she had something to add that didn't reach her lips.

"Are you sure?" pursued Dr Patel. "You shouldn't use this cream if you are."

Mia hesitated. When was her last period? She couldn't remember. Suddenly reality hit her like a wrecking ball and the blood drained from her face. She felt herself slipping away and for the second time in her life she fainted in front of a doctor.

Chapter 9
To Defend in Adversity

She caused quite a stir at the surgery, more than enough to justify her visit and put the snotty receptionist in her place. She had been gone for over an hour and Tony was starting to worry. Then he heard her come in and followed her as she tumbled through the hall to the lounge where she dropped onto the couch without saying a word.

"Well?" he asked.

"Psoriasis" she answered without looking at him "hereditary and not curable."

"There must be something they could give you" he said to the top of her head.

"Cream, with no guarantee of success" she stated then, looking up, added "have you ever suffered anything like this?"

"No" he stated.

"I don't know anyone in the family that's had it" she said resentfully "bloody Sandy Balls!"

"Come on My-mi, it's only a rash! It won't kill you and isn't the end of the world!"

"That's not all" she told him hanging her head down again.

"What?" he asked getting impatient.

She lifted her head and looked straight at him.

"I'm pregnant!" she told him and she started to sob.

For once Tony was lost for words. All the implications ran through his head just as he knew they would have gone through Mia's. He sat next to her and put his arm around her shuddering shoulders. Eventually she calmed down and turned her red, raw eyes towards him.

"What am I going to do?" she pleaded.

"Well" he hesitated as he considered what to say, then choosing a pragmatic approach answered. "As far as I can see you have three options. One; you can have the baby and raise it by yourself."

She didn't look too enamoured at that idea so he continued.

"Two; you can talk to Ralph and see whether he wants to get back together and have the child like a normal couple."

She shook her head despondently.

"Or three" he hesitated "well, I suppose you could have the pregnancy terminated."

She shuddered.

"I've dreamt of having a baby with Ralph" she told him "but not like this. I can't tell him, Tony, because I'd be obliging him to come back to me when I know he's happy with Vicky" her voice was breaking up "and I'm not sure I'd be able to carry on a normal marital relationship anyway."

"How can you be sure he's happy with Vicky?" Tony asked her.

Mia looked at him and wondered how he could ask such a stupid question. She didn't say anything.

Tony resigned himself to spending another week sleeping on the couch and commuting between Slough and Balham. He wondered how long it would be before he would be able to go home.

***

Mia swore Tony to secrecy about her pregnancy; she didn't want her mother to know until she'd decided what to do. She felt composed when she went to work the next day but also strange to think she had a baby growing inside her. She couldn't really believe it.

Bina made a point of catching her that evening; they were the last two in the office.

"Mia" she said "we haven't spoken for a while. How is your father-in-law? I'm so sorry to hear he's been unwell."

"He's recovering but it looks like it'll take some time" answered Mia. "Fortunately he doesn't seem to have lost his mental faculties which is a blessing."

"That's good" Bina commented, then added "we haven't had a chance to catch up since you went to see that doctor, Sandy Ball. I'm dead curious to know, how did you get on?"

That episode seemed a lifetime ago. Naturally Bina would be interested having made the arrangements.

"To be honest Bina" she said "I couldn't relate to him at all. I don't know what I expected but I couldn't find anything in common with him; neither in personality nor in looks. He had photographs of his two daughters on his desk and considering they are my half-sisters I expected to see some likeness to me. But no, there was nothing. It was weird."

"Are you sure he IS your father?" asked Bina.

"Well on the day I was convinced he wasn't, but now I'm sure he is."

"Why?" Bina asked curious about the whole business.

"I can't go into it" Mia stated "but I did feel a fool because I passed out!"

"Passed out?! What in front of him?"

Mia nodded.

"That MUST have been embarrassing. Have you ever passed out before?"

"No" she answered "but I managed to do so again last night at my doctors' surgery!"

"Did they check you over?" asked Bina concerned.

"Sort of" answered Mia then for some reason she didn't know added "I'm pregnant."

Bina was momentarily taken aback but soon found her voice.

"Congratulations!" she exclaimed. "That's great news! What does Ralph think?"

"That's the problem; he and I have split up. He hasn't been home since his father had the heart attack."

"Oh" answered Bina "I am sorry to hear that, you seemed so happy together. Surely it can't be anything so serious that you can't make up. Is there anyone else involved?"

Mia hesitated. "Well, Vicky is with Ralph; but we had already split up before they got together."

"Vicky!?" exclaimed Bina in feigned shock; she'd heard rumours. "She's supposed to be your best friend!"

"It's not like that" Mia said defending Vicky. "I can't go into it but there is a reason Ralph and I can't stay together. If he's with Vicky I know he's with somebody close, so I won't lose contact with him altogether."

She was unconsciously trotting out Vicky's words.

Bina was appalled. It was clear Mia wanted to be with Ralph and was putting a brave face on it.

"I must say you're being more than a bit generous to Vicky" she said. "If I were you I'd be fuming! Especially now you're pregnant! It is Ralph's isn't it?"

"Of course!" answered Mia indignantly "but please don't tell anyone I'm pregnant. I'm not sure what I'm going to do about it yet."

"Do about it?" repeated Bina. "You're not thinking of a termination, are you?"

"I'm not sure" answered Mia. "I would like the baby but ....." Mia couldn't tell Bina the whole truth so continued "I can't imagine having Ralph's child without him being with me. I don't want to face raising a child on my own without a father; it's not fair on the child."

At this point Mia pinked; Bina was a single parent.

"Not from birth anyway" she added.

"What does Ralph think?" Bina asked ignoring the unintended slight.

Mia didn't answer.

"You HAVE told him, haven't you?"

"No" Mia admitted "I haven't. What would be the point? It would only make life difficult for him. He's happy with Vicky. Why should I spoil it all for him?"

Bina could hardly believe what she was hearing. Mia was so resigned to the situation; it was extraordinary. And how could she be so forgiving of Vicky?

"What makes you think he's so happy with Vicky?" she asked.

"It's obvious from what Vicky tells me. And I've seen the way Ralph tucks into her beef pie!"

"Come on!" laughed Bina in spite of Mia's seriousness. "You can't tell me it's all down to a pie! You've GOT to tell him Mia" she implored "it's his right to know, it's his child. Maybe if he knows you're pregnant he'll come back. All relationships go through rough patches; you can't just give up!"

"That's ripe coming from you!" Mia retaliated. "You gave up on two!"

Bina held her hands up. "Fair dos" she said. "I just think, well, I thought you were different. I suppose I'm just disappointed for you."

They reflected over their conversation for a while, both saying nothing. Then Mia decided she should be going.

"I must make my way" she told Bina. "My brother's staying and I'm doing dinner."

"OK" answered Bina. "Let me know if you need any help. I'll always lend a friendly ear. After all, as you just pointed out, I've been there twice myself."

Mia apologised for the reference to Bina's failed relationships and thanked her for her support. She made her way out into the light but cold April evening.

***

The friends were back in the Black Cat Cafe on Friday for lunch. Mia had wanted to meet Vicky to discuss her pregnancy. Bina made her doubt her decision not to tell Ralph. Tony was reticent on this particular subject, for once admitting he was out of his depth. So here she was now, stirring her Cappuccino listening to Vicky waxing on about Ralph.

She got some pleasure at momentarily silencing Vicky with her news. But Vicky soon found her voice.

"What are you going to do?" it was a challenge more than a

question.

"I'm not sure" dithered Mia. "I feel really pleased but obviously there are complications."

"I'll say!" concurred Vicky. "I don't need to remind you of all the problems I see in the lab because of incestuous relationships." She said incestuous with a sneer that made Mia feel unclean and look around self-consciously to see if anyone had heard.

"You don't want the baby, do you?" Vicky asked repugnantly.

"Well" stuttered Mia. Vicky made the baby sound like a monster. But her talk with Bina yesterday had brought home the reality of a termination, and what it meant. It WAS hers and Ralph's baby. How would she feel after having their baby aborted?

"I think I should discuss it with Ralph" she said.

"Yes, I suppose you should" answered Vicky. She was silent for a few seconds then added pensively "though he does have a lot on his plate at the moment. What with his father's illness and that long daily commute. Still I expect you're right, it's not just *your* problem."

She insinuated Mia was being selfish.

"Well David's over the worst" Mia explained defensively "and Ralph's welcome to come back to our flat; it's his choice to commute."

"I suppose you could think of it like that" said Vicky "but he tells me the commute is less stressful than living with you! I was thinking of asking if he wants to move in with me. The poor man will wear himself to a frazzle if he's not careful. I want to look after him, Mia. I'm worried about his health. It's been very hard for him to cope over the last few weeks; what with his father's illness on top of finding out about being your brother. Also, his manager is leaving; Ralph's having to make sure his work is up to scratch or he'll have no chance of promotion. It's not all about *you* Mia and *you* having to cope; you could think of Ralph and shoulder the responsibility."

Mia was shocked. She'd never thought of herself as being selfish. But now she could see how caring and concerned Vicky was for

Ralph. Her mind raced back over the last few months. Vicky was right; she did only think of herself. She'd spent money they didn't have, arranged to see Sandy Balls behind his back *and* she'd shunned him in bed; even Tony had winced at that. She realised again what a poor wife she'd been.

"Go on then, you tell Ralph if that's what you need to do" Vicky continued.

"No, no ... you're right" Mia conceded. "I should take responsibility; Ralph does have a lot on his plate. It's just that..... I do miss him Vicky! I want to talk to him again." She sounded pained.

Vicky softened. "I know" she said reaching over the table to put her hand over Mia's. "It's tough for you both; I can't imagine how devastating it must be for you. Eventually though you will move on. Both of you will start afresh. It may not seem possible at the moment but you will be able to find somebody else."

"I can't imagine being with anyone else" said Mia.

"I know" Vicky said "but it's not good for you to dwell on what's happened. It's just one of those strange coincidences and you have to accept it. You're thinking of keeping this baby? First, it's likely to be disabled in some way so imagine bringing it up by yourself. You'll never find another partner once you're saddled with a child, especially a disabled one. Ralph will be forced to visit and become resentful paying for a child he didn't want. I'm not telling you what to do, it's your business, but you should think carefully about this, Mia."

Mia considered her friend's counsel and decided she was right. She had, after all, agreed this in principle with Ralph ages ago.

"I can't bear the thought of an abortion" she admitted in a whisper.

"I do know how you feel" said Vicky. She bent towards Mia who did likewise; their heads almost touching across the table. "Listen" she whispered furtively "I've never told you this before because I'm not proud of it but I had an abortion when I was at university."

Mia was astonished. "Really?" she said "what happened?"

"It was an accident" answered Vicky. "I was on the pill but somehow still got pregnant. I didn't tell the man concerned. It would have meant giving up my medical course; I just couldn't do that."

"Oh Vicky!" exclaimed Mia. "That must have been awful!"

"I don't think about it much. I went before I was nine weeks; it's much easier then. They give you a pill to make everything happen and it's a bit like having a heavy period. If you leave it until after nine weeks they have to carry out a "procedure" and it's much more dramatic. How many weeks are you?"

"Eight!" answered Mia and the number hung in the air between them.

"You'd better get moving" Vicky advised. "Go privately. You don't want NHS questions and delays."

"I don't know where to start!" Mia answered feeling panicked.

"Well, although it's something I'd rather not be able to advise you on, having been through the same thing I can make enquiries for you if you like."

"That's kind of you but I'd better do it myself. As you said earlier, I've got to take responsibility. You did it by yourself when you were only in your twenties, so I should be able to take care of it in my thirties! Are you sure about the nine week deadline?"

"Afraid so."

They sat back in their seats. The fact there was little time focused Mia and strangely she felt better. She now had a plan and there was no more indecision. She was pleased she'd spoken to Vicky; everything seemed clearer now. Vicky had been through the same experience and that gave Mia confidence. Vicky was right, all the reasons she gave for terminating the pregnancy were true; it would be easier to move on without the encumbrance of a child, especially a disabled one. Ralph need never know so would not have to worry about it. Yes, she knew now what she had to do. It was only like a heavy period after all.

"Thanks for being such a good friend" she said to Vicky.

"No trouble" answered Vicky. "I tell you what, I'll come with you to the clinic if you like."

"Would you? Thanks! It would be really good to have you there for moral support."

"Pleased to be of help" Vicky stated and gave her friend a pat on the shoulder. "We'll soon get you back to normal. Let me know when you get your first appointment so I can arrange time off and come with you."

Mia felt much more positive as they made their way back to work.

***

On Saturday Mia telephoned a private abortion clinic. She made an appointment for Wednesday morning to see the clinic's counsellor and undergo a brief medical. The receptionist was very reassuring and told Mia her details would be kept confidential and not passed to her GP. However, the procedure cost between £450 and £700 so Mia may wish to visit her doctor and arrange to have the abortion on the NHS.

Mia knew a large bill would weigh heavily on her stretched credit card account but now her mind was made up she just wanted to get on with it.

The receptionist also explained that unless Mia gave her specific agreement no member of her family, including her husband, could be informed of the abortion. She told Mia that if possible they would carry out a medical abortion whereby they would give her pills; she confirmed this was only suitable for pregnancies of less than nine weeks.

Mia had researched the types of abortion available and knew it was more common for women to be given surgical ones that consisted of a quick, simple procedure taking about five minutes and requiring a few hours stay at the clinic. She thought this might be preferable to taking pills and being at home. She relaxed about the nine-week time limit and was consoled to have the appointment with the counsellor.

***

On Monday Mia went to lunch with Bina. She wanted to keep her manager up to date and ensure she didn't tell anyone else, especially Ralph, about the pregnancy. She was beginning to regard Bina as a friend.

They were making their way along the canteen service counter, looking at the hot and cold options, when Mia became aware that Alan Harper was standing behind her. She tried to ignore him but he spoke loudly to her back.

"I'm not one to enjoy saying I told you so, but I did warn you about your so-called friend Vicky!" he sneered.

Mia didn't respond.

"Off with your old man now; with friends like her who needs enemies!?" he continued.

"You don't know anything!" Mia retaliated rising to the bait. "You're an old gossip with nothing better to do than poke your nose into other peoples' business!"

He ignored her comment and sniggered. "They're exercising at Tone Ups gym tomorrow night; you think they'll enjoy their work-out together!? I'm sure he'll be pumping more than his muscles!"

"For God's sake, Alan, put a sock in it!" Bina intervened "or I'll be reporting you for harassment!"

This stopped Alan but he continued to shake his head from side to side and tut mockingly.

Mia was grateful to get away from him as she followed Bina to a table at the far end of the canteen. Bina didn't think Alan would pursue them but if he did she was ready to give him a severe verbal lashing. But Alan had finished his gloating and went to join his cronies elsewhere. Mia saw him say something and they turned to look at her. Her face burned red.

"Arsehole!" Bina exclaimed angrily. "What an *arsehole*!"

"He must have overheard Vicky arrange something with Ralph" Mia said in a defeated tone.

"Or made it up" answered Bina now knowing the root of the rumours about Vicky and Ralph.

"They probably are going to the gym together" said Mia.

"It's still none of his business" insisted Bina calming down. "If I were you I wouldn't believe anything he says."

"Bina, I know Vicky and Ralph are together; I don't need to disbelieve Alan. It's just embarrassing knowing everyone's talking about me and I can't tell them what's really happened."

There was an awkward pause while Bina waited for Mia to expand on "what really happened" but Mia just looked down at her sandwich and shifted in her seat. Bina didn't take offence at being excluded from the intimate details. It was Mia's choice. She did however have a feeling that Mia was not necessarily right about Ralph and Vicky.

"I've been looking into terminating the pregnancy" Mia told Bina. "This incident with Alan has just about made my mind up. Can you imagine the gossip if I was walking around with a lump? I don't think I could bear it. I've got an appointment to see a counsellor on Wednesday but I've pretty much decided."

Bina went cold at the thought of an abortion and was shocked by how casual Mia was about it.

"You shouldn't base your decision on the fact that you don't want people to gossip" she said. "I know you may disagree with what I did but I've raised two children that on your basis I shouldn't have had. I'm very pleased I did and frankly can't imagine life without them."

Mia realised she'd been insensitive.

"Sorry Bina" she said. "I wasn't getting at you in any way. In different circumstances I'm sure I'd make the same choice as you. I admire the way you've looked after George and Lizzie. I hope I'll be as good a Mum as you someday."

Bina held back from telling Mia she had that opportunity now.

"Let me know what you decide" she said. "I'll arrange cover so you can have the time off."

"Thanks, Bina."

They finished their lunches and started to make their way back to the office. As they reached the canteen door they came face to face with Ralph. He and Mia both made a little jump as though a small electric shock had passed between them.

"Hello Mia" Ralph said softly. "How are you?"

"I'm fine" she answered automatically even though she wasn't. "How about you?"

"Surviving" he answered.

She had an enormous urge to fling her arms around him and he moved fractionally forward as though he was going to embrace her. Bina silently willed them, "go on for goodness sake, hug each other!" But the moment was interrupted by a shout from the other side of the canteen. All eyes were drawn to a young waiter who was teetering with a tray of dirty crockery he held above his shoulder. A man had propelled himself on his chair into the path of the waiter who'd made a desperate cry to "look out!" He was doing a kind of weird dance in an effort to maintain his balance and keep the tray flat. A lady nearby attempted to get hold of the tray. She held her hands either side, shadowing its movement and looking like a vaudeville dancer, whilst the young man's body curled back and forth from the waist. The man that had caused the incident sat immobile. The crockery shifted precariously inches above his head and he raised his arms to protect himself. There was a hushed silence as the diners watched the salsa and wondered where the tray would finish up. After what seemed ages, but was only seconds, the waiter found his balance and took control of the tray, keeping the dirty crockery on board. There was a spontaneous round of applause. The waiter smiled and gave a short bow then carried on towards the kitchen.

Ralph and Mia looked at each other and smiled. The expression of the waiter as he grappled with the tray, the lady with her hands in the air, the way they moved around each other, the man taking cover, it looked so very, very, funny!

Bina saw them smiling and again she secretly willed them to get hold of each other. But the invisible wedge of misunderstanding and misinformation was planted firmly between them. Their interchange resumed with a stilted conversation about David's health, followed by Ralph politely giving his excuses and continuing to the service counter.

Bina was almost as disappointed as Mia. On the way back to the office they didn't speak. Bina reflected on a meeting she had attended recently, called to inform managers about the proposed reorganisation. It was a large gathering and all present wore worried faces except Vicky. She was positively glowing. "She looks pleased with herself" Bina had thought "I expect she's already wormed herself a good job out of all this."

Now she realised Vicky's glow may have been because her plans to steal her friend's husband were going well! She thought about Ralph's expression just now. A light had gone out. He looked lost and sad. Bina was convinced he still loved Mia. She was sure he wasn't in an intimate relationship with Vicky. She was itching with curiosity and resolved to see for herself if these two people were lovers. During the afternoon she found time to get hold of her friend Joanna who worked in x-ray. Joanna was a member of Tone Ups gym and was happy to arrange for Bina to have a visitor pass for tomorrow evening.

***

Tony took a call from Pam before Mia got home from work that night. He found it very difficult not to tell her the root of Mia and Ralph's problems. He also would have liked her advice on the pregnancy.

He did mention his hunch that Vicky was fabricating her relationship with Ralph. Pam thought it was unlikely a "go-getter like Vicky" would be interested in somebody with no ambition, such as Ralph. Tony reiterated it was Vicky herself that professed to be in the relationship. She again expressed surprise that Ralph would interest Vicky and continued to go on about what good fun Vicky had been at the hen party; it was clear Vicky could do no wrong as far as Pam was concerned.

Tony was exasperated with his mother and sister; they appeared to be besotted by Vicky. It was as though she had got into their very souls.

***

"You? Going to a Gym!?" It was sixteen-year-old George's response when his mother told him why she was going to be late home from work tomorrow. He was sat at the kitchen table doing his homework whilst Bina prepared dinner.

"Why not?!" said Bina indignantly.

"You never exercise" he stated. "You're like the fat dietician; a physiotherapist telling people they should exercise."

"I'm glad you clarified that bit about being fat" she told him playfully smacking him on the head with a carrot "you nearly forfeited your dinner! You're right though, I haven't done anything like this for years. What am I going to wear?"

She continued to peel the carrots in silence not wanting to disturb this rare occasion of him doing his homework without prompting; one of his teachers must be truly inspirational! She mulled over her wardrobe; she had tea-shirts but what could she wear on her bottom half? She put the carrots on the hob and went in search of Lizzie.

Lizzie was a mature twelve-year-old and spoke to Bina like a sister. She thought it was a great idea for her Mum to try the gym; she didn't ridicule the proposal at all. Her brow knitted whilst she thought about suitable gym wear and what might be in either of their wardrobes.

"What about those black leggings you had a few years ago? Won't they do?" Lizzie asked.

"I threw them away" answered Bina. "They showed parts I didn't want seen. I need to be covered up!"

"I could go and see Shelly" Lizzie suggested. "Her sister's bigger than you and may have something suitably baggy."

Shelly was Lizzie's friend. She and her obese sister lived nearby. With no other option it was agreed Lizzie would go after dinner to see what was on offer. Bina was worried about borrowing clothes; she gave Lizzie strict instructions to check it was OK with their mother. Crafty Lizzie negotiated being excused from the washing up in return for the favour of going on the search for a gym kit.

Later Lizzie came back with three pairs of joggers in a carrier bag. She explained that Shelly's sister had grown out of them almost as soon as they were bought (maybe at an optimistic size) and her mum was going to put them in the charity box so was happy for Bina to have them. She hesitantly passed them to Bina stating she wasn't sure how suitable they were. Bina proceeded to open the bag. George turned from the TV to watch the "fashion show".

Shelly's sister hadn't chosen the joggers with a gym in mind. The first ones Bina pulled out of the bag were bright pink with the words "hot stuff" embroidered boldly down one leg; Bina put them to one side. The second had glittery star shapes all over them; they joined the pink pair. The last ones were not loose joggers but were tight fitting leggings patterned like a zebra's coat; Bina threw them with the others.

"I can't wear any of them!" she exclaimed with a desperate edge.

"Why don't you just go and buy a pair in one of the cheap shops?" suggested Lizzie as she exchanged a glance with George. "They don't cost much."

"I'm going tomorrow night!" retorted Bina as though it was Lizzie's fault. "When do you think I'll be able to get to the shops?"

"Well why don't you try the pink ones on?" Lizzie suggested remaining calm in the face of her mother's paddy. "They might look better than you think."

Bina took the pants and went to the bedroom where she sorted through her tea-shirts. None went with the lurid pink but she selected the purple as the best of the bunch and put it on with the joggers. She looked in the mirror and decided she didn't look too bad; after all she was only going once. "What the heck!" she thought. "It'll do."

She rummaged through the bottom of her wardrobe and found a pair of trainers that had hardly been worn. She put these on and returned to the lounge where her children were waiting. She jogged round the room in a jokey silly run.

"Well? What do you think?" she asked them.

"Fine, good" they said in unison; they couldn't really say anything else.

***

Bina left work dead on time the next day as she wanted to get to Tone Ups before Ralph and Vicky. She changed into her garish kit as quickly as she could, shoved her untameable hair into a headband Lizzie had provided and rushed into the gym.

She looked near the entrance for a suitable place to skulk but had no luck. She went further into the gym and found a recess that contained a single piece of equipment. She had no idea how to use the apparatus but the recess was ideal as it allowed her to see a large part of the gym without being seen herself.

She sat immobile on the hard, leather seat. When anybody walked by she pretended to be adjusting the machine, pulling at a lethal looking handle with feigned confidence. She prayed Ralph and Vicky would arrive soon before someone ousted her from the hidey-hole.

"Please come soon, please" she whispered to herself.

Minutes seemed like hours. She went through the adjustment routine four or five times, twice to the same person! Then, with some relief she saw Vicky coming in.

Vicky went to a cycle near the entrance and started a slow exercise, not putting in much effort. It soon became obvious to Bina they were both waiting for Ralph, neither doing any exercise! About five minutes later Ralph arrived. He acknowledged Vicky but didn't stop to talk. He passed by the recess; she got her head down and fiddled with the big black lever yet again. She saw him walk to the treadmills at the far end. Vicky waited a while then casually moved to a "leg press" near Ralph's treadmill. Bina crept out of her hide-away and slipped round the other side of the gym. Luckily, something called a "lateral pull down" was free. It was positioned behind a pillar where she was able to get close up to the pair without being seen. She sat with bated breath; a long pole suspended above her head that she assumed, by the name, she was supposed to be pulling down. She anticipated Vicky would catch Ralph when he finished running and was poised ready to listen in on their conversation.

Stomp, stomp, stomp Ralph pounded on the treadmill. Eek, eek squeaked the leg press as Vicky pushed it back and forth with more conviction than she'd cycled. No sound came from the lateral pull down! As hard as she tried Bina couldn't move the damned thing and the very man that had twice looked in on her in the recess was giving her a very strange look now. She kept her head down to avoid eye contact but she could feel him hovering. Eventually he moved off to another part of the gym and she heaved a sigh of relief.

She was nearly nodding off when the stomping finally slowed down to a halt. She heard Ralph step off of the treadmill and manoeuvred herself into a position where she could just see his reflection in the mirror opposite. At the same time, predictably, the eek, eek of the leg press stopped and Vicky came into view.

"Ralph" she said "How are things going?"

"What do you think?" he answered a bit sharply.

"Sorry, yes, it was a stupid question" she apologised.

"No, I'm sorry to bite your head off; it's not your fault my life has fallen apart!"

She shuffled on the spot for a few seconds.

"I suppose the commute from Hillingdon isn't helping" she said.

"No, you're right there; it's adding an hour each way to my day" he admitted.

"You poor thing" she sympathised. "You must be exhausted!"

"You poor thing, you must be exhausted" Bina mimicked under her breath "isn't she the angel!"

"It must be very annoying having to commute when you're paying for a flat so near the hospital" Vicky continued in the same sympathetic tone "have you spoken to Mia about it?"

"Crafty, stirring, two faced cow!" thought Bina.

"It's hard to talk to Mia at all at the moment" he admitted and again Bina caught sight of his lonely, sad face "but I suppose we'll have to speak about it soon."

"I've got an idea!" Vicky said as though the thought had just occurred to her.

"I bet you have!" thought Bina.

"I've got a spare room and I could do with more cash coming in. Why don't you come and lodge at my place? You can always go back to Hillingdon at the week-ends, if you want to."

"Oh" he said taken aback "that's very kind of you but I don't want to burden you with my troubles and I'm not sure what Mia would think."

"I'm surprised you're worried about what Mia thinks; she doesn't seem bothered about you! Anyway, it wouldn't be a burden for me. In fact, it would be nice to have your company. Maybe I could throw in a few meals as part of the rent! It's boring cooking for one!"

Bina turned puce with rage. What a scumbag Vicky was! That was a bare-faced lie that Mia didn't care! Vicky was trying to lure Ralph into living with her by offering cheap rent and home cooking! She's supposed to be Mia's friend. Alan was right after all. Poor Mia! Poor Ralph! She had to grit her teeth and hold tight to the seat to stop herself from leaping round the pillar and giving Vicky a piece of her mind. Surely Ralph could see through such a blatant come-on!? But Bina knew how easily men fell for the charms of women like Vicky; she'd lost her first husband like that.

Ralph chewed over the offer for a few moments.

"Thanks again Vicky" he said. "I'll give it some consideration, if you're absolutely sure."

"I'm absolutely sure" she repeated giving a broad smile and clapping him on the shoulder. "Everything will work out, you'll see."

"It'll all work out for you!" thought Bina then she nearly fell off the seat as a man tapped her on the shoulder.

"Hello Hot Stuff!" he said reading the large lettering on her joggers. "You seem to have taken root on this equipment, do you have squatters' rights?!"

Bina turned to see a rather handsome looking barrel-chested man. He was wearing a sports shirt bearing the Tone Ups logo, so was evidently a member of staff. Bina couldn't answer as she feared Ralph and Vicky would recognise her voice; they were only feet away. She ducked further behind the pillar to make sure they didn't see her. She looked at the instructor and didn't know what to do so she feigned a high-pitched foreign accent.

"Me no understand how work the machine" she almost whispered.

"Have you had an induction?" he asked.

Bina had told the reception she attended another gym so didn't need an induction; she was just using the guest pass to decide whether she was going to change gyms. They hadn't argued but now she was face to face with an instructor who could see she didn't have a clue.

"Shit!" she thought.

"Me not come here before" she told him "but go other gym. Me go now."

"You haven't done anything in the twenty odd minutes I've been watching you!" he told her.

"Shit again" she thought. Out of the corner of her eye she could see Vicky and Ralph parting company and Vicky heading for the exit. She had lost track of their conversation because of this damned jobs-worth! Still, she'd witnessed enough to know there was no romantic connection between them but that Vicky was doing her level best to create one. All she wanted to do now was make her way home but she had this hulk breathing down her neck!

"I'll show you how to use the equipment" he told her. "First you have to set the lifting weight here" he pointed to a marker at the bottom and she saw it was set at sixty kilos, no wonder she couldn't shift it! He made her sit properly in the seat and set the weight to five kilos, then showed her the correct way of pulling the bar down, explaining how she should breath as she did so. She became self-conscious of her ridiculous outfit and her flabby body in contrast to his top of the range sports gear and toned muscles. She realised he was actually being friendly and not a jobs-worth. She regretted the foreign accent rouse as she was stuck with it. She said as little as possible and smiled sweetly as he took her from one piece of equipment to the next. For the following hour he had Bina running, rowing, lifting, balancing, bending and stretching. She was hot and sweaty but had enjoyed it, not the exercise, that would always be a chore, but this was the most attention a man had shown her for years!

"Now you've earned the label "hot stuff"!" he told her with a smile. "I hope you'll be back soon for another work-out."

"I don't think so" thought Bina but said "OK, very good, muchus thankis."

Pride kept her upright as she walked back to the changing room but the minute she got behind the closed door she collapsed on a bench. She eventually recovered enough to head for the showers. As she stood she was hit by a bank of wall mirrors and endless images of her red, sweat strewn face topped by a headband with "I'm all yours" printed across the front! Why hadn't she looked at Lizzie's headband before she put it on?! To add to her humiliation, she saw her hair had gone completely wild and was a frizzing mass cascading over the headband. Her purple top had ridden up exposing the baggy joggers stretched over her flabby belly. She'd just spent an hour with the most handsome man she'd met in years looking like a cross between a seventies afro band member and an Umpa Lumpa!

***

"What happened to you?!" exclaimed Pete when he saw Bina limping into the office on Wednesday. "You look like one of the patients!"

"Very funny!" Bina replied. "I just overdid it a bit at the gym last night."

"The gym!? What's come over you? You can't start getting fit; who will I find to share a comfort binge if you start going all healthy on me?!"

"Don't worry Pete; there's absolutely no chance I'll be getting the fitness bug. Last night just about finished me off! Has Mia been in yet?"

"She just phoned to ask if she could take the morning off. She was already off this afternoon and there was cover for her morning schedule so I thought it would be OK. I told her you would contact her if it wasn't."

"No problem" answered Bina disappointed she couldn't tell Mia what she had found out last night. She knew Mia was going to the clinic and wondered whether she should speak to her now. But it wasn't something easily discussed over the phone so she decided to wait until tomorrow.

Chapter 10

To Lead in Truth

Mia was pleased to have Vicky's support for her clinic visit though their rules dictated she must see the counsellor alone. After lunch they made their way by tube and were well on time when they emerged from the station. Vicky consulted her phone to get directions and they were soon turning into the clinic road. They immediately noticed a group of people standing on the pavement at the far end. At first Mia thought they were waiting for a coach but as she drew nearer she saw billboards and realised they were demonstrators picketing outside the clinic. A couple of women spotted Mia and Vicky and moved forward to meet them.

Mia shrank back from the impending confrontation and slowed right down. Vicky tensed, pulled herself up and took hold of Mia's arm. "Come on" she demanded. "Just keep walking, don't stop!"

She forced Mia on towards the clinic; Mia kept her head down.

"You don't have to do this" one of the women told Mia ignoring Vicky "please take and read this pamphlet; that's all I ask you to do."

Mia took the paper unconsciously but didn't look up; she wondered why the lady hadn't picked on Vicky.

"It's a life you'll be taking!" the other lady said more forcibly. "Why won't you consider the alternatives? What about adoption? Surely you'd feel better giving your baby to a loving couple than killing it!"

The words sent a shiver down Mia's spine. She leaned into Vicky and wished Ralph was here; his broad shoulders would give much more protection than her tiny friend. Other demonstrators joined in, surrounding Mia and Vicky reducing their progress to a snail's pace. Comments were flung from all sides hitting Mia like stones. Vicky maintained her grip on Mia's arm and inched forward determinedly. Mia however wanted to justify herself to these strangers.

"You can't understand my circumstances!" she shrieked as loud as she could; her voice betraying her anxiety. "It's a very complicated situation."

Vicky cursed Mia and made an even more determined effort to move on but the comment had, as she knew it would, electrified the crowd. An onslaught of opinions showered down on Mia; whatever her problems they could be resolved without the need for a termination. The tone intensified. An edge of aggression was creeping in. The pair edged forward; the clinic door was so near yet so far. Then someone from the back of the crowd shouted "Murderer!"

That was too much for Vicky.

"You have no right to block our way!" she shouted. "Now let us pass or I'll call the Police!" She held up her phone to show she would carry through the threat. "Come on! Move away!"

Her authoritative attitude had the desired effect and reluctantly the group retreated enough to let them through to the clinic door; but not without several more jibes, some quite spiteful.

Inside Vicky breathed a sigh of relief and straightened herself up. She turned to Mia to exchange a comradely smile of victory but Mia had been severely shaken by the incident; she was trembling and had gone white. Vicky put her arm around Mia's shoulder.

"You mustn't take any notice of them" she said. "They're just a load of religious zealots! People with nothing better to do than poke their noses into other peoples' business! Don't let the likes of them upset you; what do they know?!"

"They accused me of being a murderer!" answered Mia distressed.

"They think you're a murderer if you practice birth control; they aren't in the modern world Mia and not worth getting upset over."

They waited a while in the hallway whilst Mia composed herself before proceeding to the reception area.

"You shouldn't allow those people to congregate out there!" Vicky told the receptionist. "Look how upset my friend is!"

"Did they actually touch you or physically obstruct you?" the receptionist asked.

"They stood in front of us and slowed us down almost to a stop. They also made nasty comments" answered Vicky. "It's just not good enough"

"We don't want them out there, obviously" the receptionist told Vicky "but we've made enquiries with the police and our solicitor and we're told they are within their rights to rally providing they don't actually accost or injure anyone. We don't like it but there's nothing we can do. Would your friend like a cup of tea?"

They were both given tea and drank it whilst sitting in the waiting area of the reception; then Mia was called in to see the counsellor.

"Don't forget what we agreed" Vicky whispered "it's best to say you were raped; they won't argue with that."

Whilst Mia was gone Vicky arranged for them to leave through the rear exit; she didn't want to go through the protesters again.

***

"How did it go?" Vicky asked as they left the clinic.

"Well, she was satisfied that I am aware of what I'm doing and have made an informed decision about having the abortion" answered Mia "but she was very thorough and probing. I got into difficulties when I told her I'd been raped and didn't want Ralph to know. She was adamant I should tell him. She was sure it would make me feel better and thought keeping it from him would be bad for our relationship."

"What did you say?"

"In the end I told her it was actually Ralph that had raped me! I told her I was divorcing him and didn't want his baby. That shut her up and she signed off the paperwork."

"Well done! That was quick thinking!"

"Maybe, but I do feel a louse saying those horrible things about Ralph. Supposing they tell the police or something gets put on his record. I wish I hadn't made it up now."

"Nobody here knows Ralph" Vicky consoled "and they wouldn't get police involved without asking you. Come on, cheer up, you've got what you wanted! Did they give you a date?"

"It's too late for the tablets so I've agreed to come in next Thursday for the procedure which I'll have without anaesthetic; she said it isn't too painful."

Vicky was up-beat but Mia was waning; she suddenly felt tired and wanted to go home. Ideally, she would be going home to Ralph; he was so supportive when she was finding things difficult. Thank goodness for Tony.

***

Vicky insisted on buying Mia a drink before they went home "to calm her nerves". They found a pub near Balham tube station and ordered two glasses of wine. Mia didn't really feel like going in the pub or having the wine but knew Tony wouldn't be home yet and it was preferable to the empty flat.

"Oh, that's what I was going to tell you!" said Vicky as she brought the wines over to Mia who had found a private table in the corner. "Guess who I saw at the gym yesterday?"

"Hmmm, let me see" answered Mia with mock puzzlement. "I know; Ralph."

"I don't mean Ralph. Obviously, he was there, we went together. No, I saw someone else."

She waited for Mia to guess but Mia was not in the mood and just mumbled "I don't know, who?"

"Bina!" Vicky smiled.

"Bina?" repeated Mia. "What was she doing at the gym? She hates exercise!"

"I don't know but you should have seen her! She looked ridiculous! She was wearing the most lurid pink joggers that displayed her disgustingly fat stomach; it was gross! Then on top she was wearing a bright purple tee-shirt and a headband with "I'm all yours" printed across it! What's more I'm sure she spent more time ear-wigging on Ralph and me than doing a work-out!"

"She does like bright colours and that may be all she had" Mia offered in defence of her manager. "She doesn't have much spare cash with two children at home. I think she's marvellous the way she manages everything."

"You think everyone's marvellous" said Vicky dismissively. "I think she's someone to watch."

"She's nice and very supportive" Mia stated trying to end the character assassination.

"You haven't told her about the abortion, have you?" asked Vicky ignoring Mia's reluctance to talk about her boss. "She's one of those disapproving types and she's bound to expect you to tell Ralph."

Mia went quiet and looked in her lap.

"You have told her! She did tell you to talk to Ralph didn't she!?" Vicky sounded patronising; Mia felt like a schoolgirl caught doing something wrong.

"I had to tell her" she justified limply. "I'll need time off."

"You should have taken leave and kept quiet!" Vicky spat. "Now there's a risk she'll spill the beans and tell Ralph. Podgy, nosey Mrs Do-gooder! I hate people like her! I thought she was spying on us yesterday; now I know she was. What a cheek! I bet she can't wait to tell you some cock and bull about what we were up to. Well bad luck Bina! I'm sorry to have disappointed you by not doing anything outrageous with Ralph. Nothing for you to report to Mia! Listen Mia, the best thing you can do is not tell her your business."

Mia was appalled by the venom in Vicky's tone. She was fond of Bina and trusted her. It was evident Vicky was afraid Ralph may find out about the pregnancy. Maybe he would try to resume their marriage and that wouldn't suit Vicky. It occurred to Mia that Vicky was getting obsessive over Ralph. She wondered what he thought of it all and whether he really was happy. "Sorry to have gone off like that" Vicky broke in on Mia's reflections. "I did find being spied on annoying. You must admit it is weird."

"If that was what she was doing" answered Mia.

"I think she's been listening to Alan's gossip, he does nothing but talk behind my back!" Vicky continued. "It gets me down sometimes." She stopped for a moment then added apologetically "sorry, Mia. You don't want to hear my woes; you've got enough of your own."

Mia softened. "No, that's OK" she said. "You're probably right, it's best not to tell Bina too much."

They finished their drinks and went their own ways. Mia had been grateful for Vicky's support, especially with those protesters, but now she was pleased to say goodbye. Vicky was far too intense, ranting on like that; it was like being at the end of a sand-blaster! Mia just needed some peace and calm. She knew Tony was getting dinner tonight and looked forward to a quiet evening in front of the telly.

As they parted Vicky breathed a sigh of relief; she had said enough to stop Mia confiding with Bina. She vindictively pondered on how she was going to get Bina out of her job and the hospital.

***

Ralph was in a lighter mood on the following Monday. He had taken leave to help his mother collect his father from hospital. David was well enough to be discharged but had not yet recovered full mobility. Ralph was looking forward to getting him settled back home and his mother was much brighter now she knew he was on the mend. At least something was turning out well.

Davina rang the hospital for confirmation of the discharge then packed some clean clothes and with Ralph as passenger drove to the hospital. She had a broad smile on her face and Ralph thought she looked several years younger than she had over the last few weeks.

"I've been invited to a retirement "do" tomorrow night" he told her in conversation. "Mia's friend Vicky has asked if I'd go with her but I'm not sure I fancy going out."

"She seems a nice enough person" answered Davina. "I think it'd be good for you to get out and have a change of scene."

"I know but the thought of being sociable; I'm not sure I'm up to it."

"That's why you should go, Ralph. It's no good you moping around. You've got to get on with your life whatever happens between you and Mia."

"Yes, I know" he conceded "but to be honest I find Vicky a bit strange. She always seems to be wherever I am; it's as if she's stalking me!"

As he said it he knew he sounded ridiculous and they exchanged a sideways glance; his mother looked bemused at the absurdity of the idea.

"It's just that she was at the hospital apparently visiting a friend that first Sunday Dad was in and I've seen her at the gym several times."

"Sunday is a popular day for hospital visits" Davina pointed out.

"That's true" he conceded. "But don't you think it's a bit of a co-incidence her friend being in the same hospital as Dad? When I bumped into her I had the feeling she'd been waiting for me. And why is it I haven't seen her at the gym before?"

"I didn't think you were getting to the gym much before you came to stay with me" Davina answered.

He felt foolish and regretted expressing his thoughts. His feelings about Vicky were intuitive; he might have known Davina wouldn't understand. His mind wandered on to his genetic father. He wondered how Mia had got on when she went to meet him. They hadn't had any time together since that fateful day.

He speculated about whether she had found him to be a sensitive man and what her impression had been. Suddenly he was curious. Maybe he'd been hard on Mia when she told him she was going. He'd been angered by her furtiveness but knew why she'd decided not to tell him. There was an irony about her having gone on the day his father had the heart attack.

Not speaking to Mia was ridiculous he realised now. Whatever the outcome of their marriage they should remain close; even if not man and wife they were brother and sister. He resolved to try to build bridges on a more distant but friendly basis. He had little hope of them returning to their former lives but wasn't prepared to let her go altogether. He'd rather have her as a sister than not at all.

Davina continued to drive without speaking leaving Ralph to his quiet contemplation. She was concerned for her son's sanity. An air of paranoia was creeping into his psyche. All that nonsense about Mia's friend was bizarre. After a short while she broke the silence.

"I really think you should go to that party, Ralph" she said imploringly and with conviction. "It will do you good."

"You're probably right" he agreed deciding he'd probably got Vicky wrong and it wouldn't do any harm to go out. "I'll send her a text. She'll be pleased to have a partner for the evening as those things can be a bit stuffy on your own."

"That's the spirit" Davina said relieved. "You never know, you may even enjoy yourself."

***

On Tuesday night he was all scrubbed up and dressed up in his dinner suit. He waved his parents good-bye and told his mother not to wait up for him. It felt like he was single all over again! He really must consider Vicky's offer of renting her spare room. He couldn't continue living with his parents at his age. She was offering an affordable alternative.

He'd agreed to meet Vicky at Covent Garden Underground Station as the function was in The Connaught Rooms just a short walk away. It was a posh event with many of the NHS upper echelons in attendance. The retiring consultant, Hamish Lamont, was well respected and had been awarded a Nobel Prize for his pioneering work and bestowed with an MBE. Vicky had explained she worked for the Professor before she came to Brentfield. She was one of the most junior people to be attending.

He waited outside the station, pleased he had worn his heavy overcoat as the April night was cold. He thrust his hands deep into his pockets. Soon he spotted Vicky as she came bounding up to him. He greeted her with a smile but no physical contact. She was a little breathless, not due to rushing but because she was bursting with excited anticipation for the evening. She wore a smart, fitted, black mohair coat and she had a carrier bag that she told him contained her evening shoes. She ignored his attempt to be distant, pushed her arm through his and pointed in the direction they had to go.

Inside they agreed a meeting place and went to their respective cloakrooms. Ralph got back to their rendezvous first and stood watching people arriving and greeting each other. He noticed some very classy suits and dresses. Soon Vicky came into sight and she looked fantastic. Her shoes had added at least three inches to her height and her black evening dress fitted perfectly, slinking its way around her breasts and hips, flaunting her ample cleavage. The flimsy material kissed her flesh as she walked; she was decent and indecent at the same time.

"You look great!" he told her.

"Thanks" she answered confidently. "Shall we get a drink?"

They made their way to a reception room where waiters and waitresses were circulating with trays of champagne and small savoury snacks. Neither of them recognised anyone and they stood with their glasses not speaking to each other or anyone else. Ralph felt a little nervous and conspicuous in his budget dinner suit. He wondered how Vicky would have coped if she'd come by herself; alone in a room of strangers. However, she showed no sign of any self-consciousness and stood boldly surveying the other guests. She then grabbed him by the arm and suggested they have a look at the dinner seating plan.

There were other people studying the plan so they waited politely until it was free. "Now" said Vicky quietly to Ralph as she studied the names. "I know my boss's boss, Robert, has been invited as he worked with the professor years ago. Where is he sitting and where are we? I need to be seated next to Robert. I've got to start making an impression if I'm going to make my way up the management ranks."

This was a revelation. Ralph thought they were finding their seats. Surely that was what the other guests were doing? What did Vicky have in mind? Her sharp, bright blue eyes flitted over the layout.

"Hmm, Don's manager Jeffrey is here; I wonder how he knows Hamish. Didn't you say Don was leaving and you were applying for his job?"

"Well yes" answered Ralph "so what?"

"We need to get into the dining hall" stated Vicky "so that we can move the place names around."

Ralph laughed "you can't do that!"

"Watch me" she dared as she stared into his eyes and pushed her chin forward.

"Seriously" he continued unmoved by her determination "don't you think it will look odd if we went into the dining hall and started messing about with the tables? And what do you think people will do when they come in to their places and find they've been moved?"

"Nothing!" stated Vicky. "It will be too late."

"You're mad!" he told her with a short laugh, amused by the absurdity of the idea. "I'm not getting involved with any skulduggery with the place names! If you want to make a fool of yourself go ahead but don't expect me to come with you. Why don't you just talk to Robert now, he's over there, or you could catch him after the dinner?"

"It's not the same as getting his attention throughout the whole meal" she said, then added curtly "you're just as much a wimp as that ex-wife of yours! Honestly, don't you want the promotion?"

"I do but not this way" he told her becoming serious "and I'd thank you not to be rude about Mia."

"You want to get the job all fair and square, do you?" she said mockingly and ignoring his protest about Mia. "Wake up Ralph! How do you think people get promotions? It's not by what they know or how well they do their jobs; it's about who they matey up with!"

She looked at him with disdain for his naivety.

"Are you with me or not?" she challenged.

"Leave me out of this" he said firmly.

She handed her glass to him and headed off towards the dining room. He moved away from the seating plan as if by doing so he could distance himself from Vicky's antics. Although he had refused to be involved he was tense. If she got caught he would be implicated, especially if she moved him next to Don's manager, Jeffrey. He felt hot around his shirt collar and anxious at the thought of an upset. He wished Vicky would come back having given up the idea but he knew she would see it through; it was a challenge now.

Minutes later Vicky returned looking self-satisfied.

"That's done!" she said. "All we have to do now is make sure we get into the dining room first to bag our seats."

Ralph looked at her sceptically. "What are you going to say when the person whose place you've taken comes to the table and finds you sitting in his place?"

"What are *you* going to say when *you're* found in the wrong place!?" she answered impishly.

"I'll say I'm sitting where I found my place name but I don't mind moving" he answered straight-laced; he'd already considered the scenario.

Vicky let out a derisive guffaw.

"You'll look a complete fraud if you do that!" she told him.

"Well I didn't want anything to do with this" he told her irritated.

"Don't be such a prig, Ralph, it's hardly the crime of the century for God's sake! Don't worry your little England self over it, only idiots "play cricket". As I told you, you don't get promoted by being good at your job! Oh look!" she carried on seamlessly "there's our host, let me introduce you."

Standing a few metres away was a tall, broad-shouldered man flocked by a small group of people. Ralph looked at him and noticed from his demeanour he carried the quiet confidence often present in such esteemed professionals. There was also something comradely and approachable about his manner that Ralph immediately warmed to. He was speaking amicably and his audience were smiling adoringly; he was clearly liked as well as respected. It dawned on Ralph that he'd come to a retirement party and didn't know the first thing about the person retiring. All he knew was his name, Hamish Lamont, and that he'd received major accolades but he had no idea what for. He'd only decided to come yesterday and had been preoccupied about the wisdom of attending a function with Vicky. It hadn't crossed his mind to actually ask her anything about the retiree.

Before he had the chance to protest Vicky started yelling over to Mr Lamont and pulling Ralph towards the group. He was put through another embarrassing episode as Vicky pushed her way forcibly between two of the people talking to Hamish; brazenly ignoring their indignation and making no apology for interrupting the conversation. There was no alternative than to lamely follow; it would look worse if he made a scene about not wanting to meet the host.

"Hello Hamish!" she said in a bold, familiar tone.

Hamish turned to the sound of her voice and, scanning the crowd, his eyes rested upon the face from which it had come. He momentarily took in a breath. He appeared to need to adjust to the image of Vicky standing in front of him.

"Don't you remember me?" she went on. "Vicky Dolosa; I worked with you when you first came to London."

"Oh, I remember *you*!" he answered emphasising the "you" a dark expression having spread across his face. It was clear to everyone except Vicky he was not pleased to see her.

"I wanted to introduce you to my friend" she went on unperturbed and turned to Ralph. "This is Ralph Davenport" she announced.

Hamish gave the remotest hint of a reaction to Ralph's name.

"Pleased to meet you" he said as he shook hands with Ralph and looked him in the eye for just a fraction longer than would be considered normal. "Do you work with Vicky?"

"No, we both work at Brentfield but I work in the IT department. I'm afraid I'm one of those computer nerds!" Ralph answered trying to sound casual but wishing he could disappear. He suspected Vicky was about to expose his ignorance about Hamish and make him look like a free-loader. He knew she would see it as good sport, she was already revelling in his discomfort.

"Don't apologise for that" Hamish answered kindly "we all rely on computer boffins. I for one would be lost without IT back-up."

Ralph couldn't think what to say next. He had no idea what field the Professor had worked in but any further conversation on computers would be inappropriate. He cursed Vicky for getting him into this humiliating situation. He was surrounded by a group of high-ranking NHS staff waiting expectantly, following Vicky's pushy introduction, for him to say something interesting. He felt worse because Hamish was studying him intensely as though waiting for pearls of wisdom. There was a pregnant pause; Vicky was gloating and made no attempt to help him out.

"Are you looking forward to retirement?" Ralph finally asked. He discerned a sense of anti-climax from the other guests.

"Yes and no" Hamish came out with his stock answer. "I'm hoping to keep my hand in. I could never give up altogether."

To Ralph's relief at this point Hamish was called away. He gave his apologies and left. The group broke up, participants moving on to find other conversations. The two were left by themselves; Vicky with a broad grin across her face.

"You cow! You knew I didn't know what field he was in!" Ralph said through clenched teeth.

"Your face was a picture!" she grinned.

"Very funny!" he said indignantly "I'll do the same for you one day."

They took another glass of champagne from a passing waitress and stood drinking in silence, Ralph seething and Vicky smirking. Her relaxed stance soon turned into a coiled spring, ready for action. A waitress she had paid earlier was giving the pre-agreed sign. She grabbed Ralph by the arm and started ushering him towards the dining hall; the guests were about to be asked to take their seats.

At this point Ralph was seriously considering going home; Vicky was really pissing him off! However, he reluctantly went with her towards the dining room and, like clockwork, the doors opened just as they arrived. They made their way in and Vicky pointed out his place name. They remained standing trying to look casual and inconspicuous, hovering around until a few other guests had ambled in and settled into their seats. Vicky then placed her small handbag over the chair back and sat down. Ralph continued to loiter; he felt really edgy. He would have liked to re-swop his place name back but knew it wouldn't be that simple. Vicky would have changed a number to get her and Ralph where she wanted. He was sure somebody would realise the place names had been swopped and he would be in the frame as the culprit, who else would want to sit next to Jeffrey? That would be enough to scupper his promotion. He wasn't like Vicky; he couldn't just blag his way out of a situation. He had been raised to put honesty above all other values and telling lies didn't come easily. Neither did he expect to be told lies; he expected people to tell the truth.

The guests continued to filter in and Ralph saw Jeffrey approaching. As Jeffrey reached the chair next to him, he introduced himself and they shook hands. Ralph then pointed out that the place names didn't appear to reflect the table plan so he hadn't sat down in case there'd been a mistake. He admitted he couldn't remember where exactly he should be sitting. Jeffrey told him not to worry and suggested he sit where his place name was. Ralph sat down feeling calmer.

Across the table he could see Vicky excitedly chatting with Robert who already looked charmed and was happily looking down her cleavage. The couple that should have been sat next to Robert finally arrived and looked perplexed when they realised their names were not where they had expected. The man wandered over to Vicky.

"I think you're in the wrong seat" he told her politely "you should be sitting down there." He pointed to two empty seats further down the table.

Vicky looked surprised but made no effort to move. "Really?" she said "I just sat where I saw my name; I can't say I made a study of the seating plan." She faced him out for a while then added "are you sure I'm in the wrong place? There isn't room for you and your wife here so I can't think this is where you were supposed to be."

Nearly everyone was seated by now. The man would have needed to ask several people to move to enable him to sit next to Robert.

"I'll move if you like" Vicky offered disingenuously.

"No" answered the man irritably. "That's alright, we'll go down there" and they made their way to the lower end of the table.

Vicky looked across to Ralph and gave a smirk that said "I told you it would work; what were you making all the fuss about?" He looked back at her with contempt.

***

Ralph didn't find out who was supposed to be sitting next to Jeffrey as nobody challenged him. Jeffrey was good company and they had a lot in common; both were rugby enthusiasts and both enjoyed playing the guitar. After the meal there was a short break before the speeches and guests took the time to stretch their legs and use the toilets.

Ralph wandered out to the reception area. He was still smart-ing and outraged by Vicky's behaviour. He was shocked by her scheming. To think he had considered her sexy and had contem-plated moving into her flat. He must have been mad; she was dangerous. He had an urge to speak to Mia and, having now had a good few glasses of wine, plucked up the courage to find a quiet corner and call.

"Hi Angel" he said when she answered. "How are you?"

It was an unexpected treat and she melted at the sound of his voice.

"Missing you" she answered honestly.

"Vicky told me you had company at the flat" he said immedi-ately off-loading what was foremost on his mind.

"Yes" she answered "Tony's staying; it's good to have him around."

"Tony? Did he go to the hospital with you?"

"Yes, did your dad tell you?"

"No, I saw you leaving but was too late to catch you. I wondered who you were with. I didn't recognise Tony or his car."

Ralph inwardly screamed. "You stupid, stupid bastard! You should have known she wouldn't have hooked up with some-body else. You let Vicky lead you right up the garden path."

"He's like a kid with that car" Mia was whispering into the phone so that Tony didn't hear. "Personally I think it's awful, not comfortable at all! Where are you? I can hear voices."

"I'm at a retirement party" answered Ralph deciding not to mention Vicky. "I'm going in for the speeches soon but I just thought I'd give you a ring."

"Who's retiring?"

"Eminent doctor called Hamish Lamont."

"How did you get invited to that?" she asked curious.

Ralph faltered; he didn't want to say he was with Vicky but didn't want to lie.

"Vicky invited me" he answered and winced, then added quickly to change the subject "I'm sitting next to Jeffrey Clark."

"Jeffrey! That's good!" exclaimed Mia secretly annoyed he was there with Vicky even though it was no surprise. "That won't be bad for your promotional prospects!"

"We'll see" he answered thinking of Vicky's manoeuvring. "Anyway that's not why I rang; I wanted to know how you are."

"I've felt better" she hedged.

He knew her well and sensed there was something she wanted to tell him.

"Are you ill?" he asked.

She took a breath. She had been adamant Ralph shouldn't know she was pregnant but at this moment telling him seemed the right thing to do.

"No but I'm p........." she started but a loud, high pitched voice drowned her out.

"Come on Ralphy my Love! The speeches are starting!"

"Go away!" Ralph demanded "I'm on the phone!"

"That's Vicky!" exclaimed Mia. "She sounds drunk!"

"Yes, I think you're right" he said.

"Come on my gorgeous Ralphy!" Vicky persisted right next to him. "We've got to get back!"

Ralph held the phone away from his mouth and turned to Vicky. "I'll be back as soon as I've finished. Now if you don't mind?" he indicated that he wanted to proceed with his call.

"OK," she said pouting "but don't be long my lovely!" and she wandered off towards the dining room.

Ralph breathed a sigh of relief and went back to the phone.

"Hello" he said but the line was dead; Mia had hung up.

Reluctantly he turned his phone off and made his way back for the speeches.

***

Mia was sad, frustrated and upset by the call. She told Tony and as usual he saw it from Ralph's point of view.

"He must be missing you to call even though he was with Vicky" he told her "and you've said you're happy they're together, so you can't complain that they are. I'm still convinced he'd rather be with you."

"I know" she said "you're not the only person to think that. Bina saw them at the gym last week and was sure there was nothing going on between them."

"What did she say?" he asked curious.

"Similar to what you have said, that there wasn't any intimacy about the way they spoke to each other and she was sure Vicky was waiting for Ralph to arrive; they didn't arrive together."

"Exactly!" he said. "Just because she wants to muscle in on Ralph doesn't mean he wants to be with her."

"I might be convinced but Vicky told me she spotted Bina at the gym and went on about how she'd been spying and was a nosey cow. I was surprised how hateful she was towards Bina. It was true, Bina did go there to spy and if they were aware of her it's likely they didn't behave as they might have otherwise. It's a bit over the top to go spying on your work colleague's husband isn't it?"

"I'm sure she was only trying to help you" Tony told her.

"Well, I did take Vicky's advice. Bina knows I'm having the abortion on Thursday but nothing else."

Tony was uneasy about Mia distancing herself from Bina. From what he'd heard she'd been kind to his sister.

"I felt so good talking to Ralph" Mia continued "then to hear Vicky's screeching voice butting in calling him "Ralphy" and sounding like she was all over him, I felt shut out and my good mood vanished. I know we can't get back together but it still hurts."

"Why don't you ring him back?" suggested Tony.

"What's the point?" she answered.

***

The speeches started with a tribute from a work colleague. Ralph was only half listening. He was still thinking of Mia. But then words started leaping out at him:

"Hamish Lamont, more fondly known as *Monty*"

"Pioneered the work on *artificial insemination* using a *non-paternal donor*"

"When he moved *to London from Manchester*"

The newspaper cutting "Monty's Mums Make History"! This man was Monty! What a coincidence! Or was it? Did Vicky know? He'd told her he'd been conceived through artificial insemination. Could she possibly have known Monty was the doctor that performed the procedure? How would she? Had she set Ralph up? Why would she? No reason he could think of. He concluded it was chance that brought him close to the person his parents had relied on all those years ago.

Monty was now standing to make a speech. Ralph studied him with interest and fascination. This was his creator. It would have been an exciting new area of work over thirty years ago and Ralph's parents had been progressive enough to try it. He felt suddenly proud of them and disappointed they felt they'd let him down.

As Ralph was mulling these things over he became aware that Monty was staring directly towards him. Ralph looked behind to see who Monty was addressing but there was nobody. Monty occasionally drifted to gaze at other people but he kept returning to Ralph. It was noticeable and other guests turned to look at Ralph. Jeffrey gave him a sideways glance.

"Why is Monty staring at me?" thought Ralph. "He must remember I'm one of his first test tube babies. Maybe he knows something about my genetic father. I wonder why he was so displeased to see Vicky? What the hell is Vicky up to?"

After the speeches Vicky wandered off to find somebody influential to impress. Ralph left her to it and went to find Monty's associates. He wanted to arrange a meeting with Monty to ask about Sandy Balls.

He'd seen a lady holding some papers for Monty and thought she would be a good place to start. She was speaking to two other individuals and he had to employ some of Vicky's boldness to gate-crash their conversation. The party was finishing and he didn't have time to mess about.

"Are you Monty's work colleagues?" he blurted out.

The three of them went quiet and looked at him, bemused. Then one of them, a man about the same age as Ralph answered "Yes, we are, is there something you wanted?"

"I just wondered when Monty was actually going; I mean this isn't his last day is it?"

"No" answered the man "he doesn't actually leave for another two weeks though he probably won't spend much of it in the office."

"Do you think he would be able to fit in an appointment to see me before he leaves?"

"That's Veronica's department" he told Ralph as he pointed. "The lady over there in the blue dress."

Ralph thanked him and made his way towards Veronica, a portly, middle-aged lady who was getting ready to leave.

"Excuse me!" he said as he rushed over to catch her. "Are you Veronica?"

"Who would be wanting to know?" she asked in an Irish accent with a twinkle in her eye as she boldly looked him up and down.

"A poor boy who needs your help to get an appointment with Monty before he leaves" answered Ralph in a jokingly melodramatic way. "It's very important."

"You've left it late if it's that important" she pointed out.

"I didn't realise he could help me until tonight. Do you think he'll remember much about his first test tube babies?"

"Now that was a long time ago, even before my time! What do you need to know?"

"I was one of Monty's babies" he told her. "There's something I need to ask him."

She looked at him with a renewed interest coupled with scepticism.

"How fascinating!" she said. "You are an actual product of his work! You know we're not allowed to divulge the details of the sperm donors, don't you?"

"Yes, of course, I realise that. I just wanted some information about my genetic father, not his name or anything."

He sounded vague. Veronica was looking doubtful and was starting to adopt a dismissive attitude.

"Can you just ask him?" he pleaded.

He looked so desperate she softened. "OK" she said "I'll ask him but don't be surprised if he doesn't entertain you; give me your name and a contact number."

***

Ralph was tempted to go home without bothering to find Vicky but he was too polite. He finally caught up with her talking to a man Ralph didn't recognise but who was evidently not very important because she dropped him like a hot potato when Ralph arrived.

"That bastard!" she breathed as they walked away "told me he was Chair of the Clinical Commissioning Group; turns out he only takes the minutes!"

"What a bastard!! Mr nobody wasting your precious time! How dare he!" Ralph mocked.

She flashed her bright blue eyes at him; they held an icy edge that could cut through steel but he didn't care. They walked together towards the tube.

"Tony" he said accusingly. "It's Tony staying with Mia."

"Tony?" she looked surprised. "Mia didn't tell me. Oh dear, sorry Ralph. I must have got the wrong end of the stick! It wasn't the impression Mia gave me."

They walked the rest of the way in silence.

"Thanks for coming with me" she said as they reached the station. "It's hard to cope with that sort of function on your own."

"We hardly spent any time with each other" Ralph answered "and you didn't appear to need any support as far as I could see!"

"We may have been separated for most of the evening but I felt more confident knowing you were there" she said in an uncharacteristic timid tone.

"So that you could swop name tags around" Ralph reminded her.

"Wasn't that a hoot!" she exclaimed. "Come on, you must admit it was great for you to spend the evening with Jeffrey, you must have that promotion in the bag now! What's the point in spending an evening like that making small talk with a load of people you're never going to see again? May as well take advantage of the invite to net-work with the right people."

"You're something else!" he commented.

She moved towards him and put her arms round his waist; he could feel her breasts through her coat.

"Are you going to see me home?" she asked coy and childlike.

"I'm sure you can manage on your own" he answered pushing her gently away.

"Don't be a spoil-sport" she toyed. "How would you feel if I got attacked on the way home?" She was playing to his chivalrous nature.

"I'm sure you travel alone most of the time and it's not that late. You'll be fine. I have to go in the opposite direction to get to Hillingdon."

"Stay with me!" she offered. "You don't want to travel all the way to Hillingdon when we could be at my flat within half an hour. You can go to work from there tomorrow. I can make us Irish coffees, I love them. The taste of rich cream followed by the kick of the whiskey, hmmm sumptuous!" There was a sexual connotation in the way she spoke.

Ralph hadn't had sex for a number of weeks and her invitation may have been appealing. But his eyes had been opened and he wasn't the least bit tempted.

"I'd prefer my Mum's cocoa!" he replied.

She didn't like the put down.

"Suit yourself!" she spat pulling away from him, the icy glint returning to her steel blue eyes. "I'll make my own way; thanks for nothing!"

She turned and stamped off into the station.

"Don't let the tube monsters get you" he called sarcastically to her back.

She didn't turn but waved her middle finger above her head.

"You won't look so clever after Thursday sweetie pie" she

thought vindictively "when I let it slip that your wife has killed your baby without telling you!"

He watched her disappear and breathed a sigh of relief. He didn't plan to spend any more time with Vicky. He'd had enough tonight to last him a lifetime!

***

Ralph received a call from Veronica the next afternoon.

"I don't know why but the man has agreed to see you!" she said. "There's one problem. He can only fit you in early tomorrow morning. Can you get here for eight?"

"Yes, that would be fine" he answered enthusiastically. "Thank you so much, you're a gem!"

"No problem" she told him boosted by his appreciation. "I admit I didn't hold much hope but he was actually keen to see you. He'll only be able to spare half an hour."

"I'm sure that will be more than enough time."

Ralph had no idea what may transpire from the meeting but if nothing else he hoped to confirm whether Sandy Balls was his genetic father. He recognised he was clutching at straws but his opinion of Vicky had plummeted enough for him to want confirmation of her test. It may be hard to get the information from Monty but Ralph was determined to try.

Chapter 11

To Grow Together in Love and Trust

It was more like May than April on Thursday morning. But the birdsong and sunshine failed to lift Mia's mood. She had hardly slept. Thoughts had churned round and round her head all night long. Vicky's bleak picture of what might be wrong with the baby contradicted her own research that there were not necessarily defects in offspring from incestuous relationships. She worried that she should have told Ralph about the pregnancy and wondered whether she should keep the baby. Would that rekindle Ralph's affection or make him feel trapped? Could she go back to him if she had the chance? These imponderables tumbled over in anxious agitation. She kept returning to the conclusion that, though unpalatable, termination was the only acceptable course of action.

Now she was racked with nerves and keen to get the day over with. Tony had arranged to work from home and Vicky had taken leave. The appointment was for ten with the procedure to be undertaken at eleven. They had agreed Vicky would come at nine and go to the clinic with Mia by tube and Tony would pick them up in his car at about one o'clock.

Tony watched his sister aimlessly pace about the flat, rubbing her hands together and scratching at her psoriasis. He turned the telly on. "Come and sit down My-mi" he pleaded. "You're setting my nerves on end."

"Sorry" she said and came to sit in front of the telly.

"Tony, I feel sick!" she told him. "Maybe I'm not well enough to go!"

"You don't *have* to go" he told her. "Maybe you should call it off and speak to Ralph."

"No, I've made the decision" she declared. "Talking to Ralph wouldn't change the situation; I'd only be giving him more to worry about."

"He may *want* to know" Tony persisted.

"No, I'm not going to involve him; I'll just have to face up to it alone."

They sat in front of the morning news, neither of them watching. Mia had scratched her throat so intensely large whelps had appeared. The time dragged on and at a minute past nine Tony thought she might burst. She stood by the window attacking her neck watching for Vicky. As soon as Vicky came into view Mia hurriedly put on her coat and started for the door. Tony gave her a huge hug and held her tight.

"Everything will be fine" he reassured her.

"Thank you so much Tony, I don't think I could have survived without you."

"Don't be silly" he responded. "Of course you would survive. Anyway, nothing's too much effort for you, My-mi."

He held her at arm's length and she gave him a brave, wilted smile.

"See you later" he told her as he held the door for her to leave.

He watched her walk heavily down the stairs to the front door where she turned to wave good-bye and left.

As soon as the door closed he charged back through the flat to look out of the front window and see his sister meet Vicky. He wanted to believe Mia was in safe hands but was suspicious of Vicky's motives. The pair made no physical contact. They spoke briefly then walked back up the road. He would have imagined, and liked, to see the friends hug each other on an occasion such as this. But there was no comfort in Vicky's manner.

In spite of his concerns he was relieved to see Mia go. He wanted this over with as much as she did. He hoped it would be her lowest ebb and he could start to build her up again. She had been fading since his arrival, like a dimming light, and he was scared. He needed to bring the life back into her. Their mother had wanted to visit but Tony had put her off. However, the weight of responsibility was too much to bear alone and he planned to enlist the help of the rest of the family as soon as this was over.

He went into the kitchen and prepared a beef casserole that he put in the slow cooker. Then he made himself a coffee and proceeded to work on his lap-top in the lounge. The time would soon pass and it wouldn't be long before he was collecting her.

***

Ralph was also up early that day. He arrived promptly for his appointment with Monty and Veronica showed him in. A row of loaded boxes lining one side of the office reminded him of the consultant's imminent retirement. He looked around the rest of the room and saw the walls hadn't yet been cleared of memorabilia. There were a number of framed certificates, awards and half a dozen or so photos. His eye was drawn to a picture he recognised. A framed copy of the newspaper article his mother had shown him with the heading "Monty's Mums Make History".

Monty saw him looking and smiled. He could hardly believe so many years had passed since those brave couples agreed to take part in his "experiment". Now the large lad standing in front of him was the very product of that exercise.

"Please, take a seat" Monty pointed to a chair in front of his desk "and excuse the mess. There are more than forty years of my life packed into these boxes!"

"It's very kind of you to see me, Mr Lamont" answered Ralph. "I appreciate you sparing the time."

"I was curious to meet you" answered the consultant "knowing you are the result of my early work. It's fitting you should come to see me just before I retire. Closes the circle as they say."

Ralph sat down and waited for Monty to settle into his large office chair on the other side of the desk.

"Right" said the consultant. "First of all please call me Monty, no need for formalities. Second, before you ask whatever you have on your mind I'd like to ask you a few questions."

"Of course" answered Ralph.

"I need to know what sort of relationship you have with Victoria Dolosa; are you two an item?"

"God no!" exclaimed Ralph surprised by the boldness of the question. "She's a friend of my wife. She asked me to accompany her to your retirement celebration as she doesn't have a partner at the moment."

"How good a friend of your wife is she?" he asked.

Ralph hesitated "Err good, I think. Well she seems to be my wife's closest friend at the moment."

"You don't seem very certain" the older man observed.

"No, you're right" admitted Ralph. "I'm not entirely comfortable with the friendship. She tends to constantly criticise my wife who has had enough of that from her mother. I've had to compensate by boosting my wife's ego. I don't think a good friend should be like that. But women are different, aren't they?"

"I think Ms Dolosa is very different from anybody else" Monty stated "and my advice is to get your wife away from her as soon as possible."

Ralph thought this was somewhat melodramatic. He chuckled. "My reservations aren't that strong! What do you imagine Vicky would do to my wife?"

"It's no joke" Monty answered poker faced. "I've experienced Ms Dolosa and can assure you she is poisonous, pure poison! I don't think it was coincidence she brought you to my retirement party. She knew I would recognise your name. I've been trying to work out what she's up to. I don't know how she wangled herself onto the guest list. Her name wasn't there when I sanctioned it! I believe she plans to discredit me and foul up my retirement; I just can't think how."

Ralph was no longer laughing. The doctor was deadly serious and the way this conversation was focusing on Vicky he feared he may not have time to get the information he had come for. But Monty was on a roll.

"She created hell for a very talented young doctor working in my team" he continued. "When I intervened she turned her attention to me. She nearly got me struck off! I believe she's driven by ambition and there are no limits to what she will do to realise her aspirations. Ms Dolosa has a brilliant mind but unfortunately only exercises it malevolently. She is a pathological liar, you can't believe *anything* she says, and she is manipulative and cruel. She has no remorse for the pain she inflicts on other people. You tell me she has criticised your wife. That's exactly what she did to my protégée. She constantly undermined her confidence until the poor girl became mentally ill. She spent several weeks in hospital. It was only the dedicated input of her family, me and other members of the team that saved her sanity. Unfortunately, she gave up medicine; a grave waste of talent."

Ralph was sceptical. "Surely this protégée, the young woman, must have already had problems" he reasoned. "It's hard to believe anyone could have that much influence over somebody else, especially an intelligent person. I accept Vicky is ambitious, I've witnessed some of her skulduggery myself, but you're suggesting she was able and nasty enough to purposely cause a colleague's mental breakdown. That sounds, well, excuse my frankness, it sounds absurd! I don't doubt she wangled herself an invitation to your party but only so that she could impress people that might help her get promoted; not to do anything to you personally."

"I appreciate you being candid, Ralph, and I accept I must sound like a ranting, paranoid old man! However, I implore you to believe me. Ask my colleagues; they will vouch for my judgment. Victoria Dolosa *did* have the ability to cause serious mental damage to that young lady and you *must* look out for your wife!"

"But why would she want to harm my wife?" Ralph asked.

"Because she is just plain evil" answered the consultant.

They faced each other, speechless. Monty saw cynicism and disbelief written all over Ralph's face. He took a different approach.

"How are you and your wife at the moment?" he asked.

Ralph reddened. "Not good" he answered. "In fact we're apart."

"So!" Monty exclaimed. "And was Ms Dolosa in some way instrumental in your separation?"

"Yes" answered Ralph, then added quickly "but only indirectly."

Monty grimaced. "Oh, so characteristic" he sighed "she never does anything directly! Look Ralph, maybe she's jealous of your wife or maybe she's just having a bit of fun. Whatever the reason I'm sure she's central to your problems. I can only repeat my warning and strongly advise you and your wife to have nothing to do with her."

Ralph reflected. Was Monty right or raving mad? Yes, Vicky could be annoying and she was certainly ambitious, but she had been kind too. It was outlandish to imagine her as "evil". On the other hand, Monty was a respected person. It was also hard to imagine he was completely wrong.

It was Monty that broke the silence.

"So" he asked "what did you want to talk to me about?"

"Well" answered Ralph turning his attention back to the original purpose of his visit. "As you know, I was one of your first test tube babies. It has become important for me to know whether a particular person is my genetic father. I know I'm not allowed to ask the name of my father" he added quickly "but I thought it may be possible to get a yes or no to a particular name."

"Ms Dolosa has put you up to this, hasn't she?!" Monty said accusingly.

Ralph felt like screaming. "Not back to her again!" he thought.

"No" he answered. "Well, not directly!"

Ralph faltered. Should he tell Monty about Vicky's test? It dawned on him that the illicit nature of the test had caused him not to talk to anyone professional about it. A large penny was finally beginning to drop. Had he been manipulated by Vicky? He decided to be completely open with Monty.

He took a deep breath. "As you probably know, Vicky, Ms Dolosa, is manager of the Diagnostic Genetics Department. She carried out a genetic test for my wife and me as a favour. It revealed we were half siblings. At first, we thought she'd got it wrong, it just wasn't possible! Then we discovered my mother-in-law had sex with a doctor up in Liverpool and I was a test tube baby from a procedure that took place in Manchester. We put two and two together and assumed the test result was correct. My wife had difficulty with the idea of us staying together as half siblings; it wasn't long before we had separated."

Ralph paused for breath; Monty stared at him earnestly.

"When I saw you on Tuesday" Ralph continued "I thought you may know who my father was and be able to confirm or deny whether he is the same person that my mother-in-law had sex with all those years ago. So, in a desperate attempt to prove the test result was wrong, I asked to see you."

There was silence as Monty weighed up Ralph's words.

"I'm sure there's something amiss with that test" he asserted. "You should get confirmation."

"I've suggested that to my wife but she can't see the point as she's convinced the test is correct. She thinks I'm burying my head in the sand. Now we're apart it's even harder."

A deep sadness spread across Monty's face as he reflected on this latest Dolosa mischief; she really was bad news.

"I feel an allegiance towards you" he admitted "being one of the first of my successes. However, it is completely against the code to reveal the identity of our donors."

"I don't want his identity; I just want to check a name."

"But obviously an affirmative would give you the name by default!"

"We believe he is the donor so what difference would it make?" Ralph pointed out desperately. "And as you know since 2006 donors haven't been allowed to remain anonymous; I found that out on line. I know in my case the donor has a right to anonymity, but morally don't I have the right to know?" he implored. "Besides I'm only seeking confirmation of what I already know!"

Monty went quiet again. "I'm worried you may be unwittingly playing a part in one of Ms Dolosa's plots" he said. "She nearly had me struck off before; I don't want my name sullied as I retire."

"What did she do?" Ralph asked.

"As I told you she's a very intelligent lady that should use her talents more constructively. Instead she uses her wits to cause hurt and destruction."

He seemed reluctant to carry on; the strain of the recollection showing on his face. Eventually he continued.

"She got into my computer" he explained "and over a number of weeks she searched for child pornography. When she'd done enough she reported a fault on my PC knowing the offensive material would be found. I correct that; she got someone else to report the fault. I was suspended. It took me months to clear my name. Even now I'm sure some colleagues regard me with suspicion. It was a shocking, terrible experience for me and my family."

Ralph felt goose pimples on the back of his neck; only last week James from Vicky's department had reported a fault on Alan Harpers' computer.

"Please help me" Ralph begged. "I won't ask for any other details, I promise. And I won't tell Vicky. I suspect she just wanted to give you a scare by turning up at your party and mar your retirement by making you worry."

Monty accepted Ralph may be right; Vicky had got him fretting like a child. He was being pathetic.

"Give me the name" he relented.

"Balls" said Ralph immediately "Sandy Balls."

"That doesn't sound like his true first name" Monty noted "but he isn't the donor."

"You know the donor, don't you?!" Ralph guessed.

"Yes" answered Monty. "You were one of the first and it wasn't easy to get donors. You are right in thinking I'd looked to medical schools for volunteers. As you can imagine most men were reluctant even though I promised anonymity. It wasn't me they distrusted but the system. They didn't want a stranger turning up on their doorstep years later. I've often wondered whether I gave enough thought to that aspect of the project. All I considered was the joy I could bring to couples that otherwise didn't have a chance of having children."

He paused momentarily in reflection then continued.

"There was also the problem of ensuring the donor sperm came from a decent source. We had to give assurance to the prospective parents; we couldn't just take somebody from the street. No, all things considered, getting donors was the hardest part of the exercise. I personally know your donor very well and he doesn't go by the name of Sandy Balls or anything similar!"

Monty walked to the framed article and took it from the wall.

"I remember your parents" he said "they were lovely people and very open-minded. All four couples were brilliant." He smiled as he remembered them. "You are lucky to have such a good father."

"Yes, I know" Ralph assured him. "I couldn't have asked for better; I love him very much. I am of course curious about my genetic background but as promised I won't press you for any further details."

"Thank you" said Monty.

"No, thank you!" answered Ralph "from what you tell me the donor is a good person and, more importantly, not related to my wife. I can't tell you how happy that makes me. Out of interest though, did you use the same donor for all four mothers?"

Monty shook his head and gave a half smile. "You don't expect me to answer that do you?"

"No" grinned Ralph "but I suspect I have three half siblings out there somewhere! Possibly more! But my wife is *not* one of them, that's the main thing. That's the best news I could have hoped for!"

The men silently appraised each other for a few moments.

Ralph slowly stood up and put his hand out to Monty who gripped it tightly.

"Thank you again" said Ralph. "It has been wonderful to meet you; I wish you all the very best for your retirement."

"Thank you" answered Monty. "I'm pleased to have met you too."

"Oh, one last thing" he added still gripping Ralph's hand. "I was talking to Veronica yesterday. She told me Ms Dolosa visited our offices several months ago. She has authority to see our files because her Department works across several hospitals. Veronica tells me she asked to see the file for Davenport. She's been here, Ralph, rooting about in your past. I don't know why, but she's up to something between you and your wife."

Ralph was flabbergasted; for a second time a shiver ran down his spine. His instinct about Vicky stalking him must have been right! Did she have some kind of obsession for him?

Monty interrupted his thoughts. "If you need any further help, for example, if your wife wants to speak to me directly, just contact Veronica. She'll be able to contact me after my retirement. I hope you manage to get back with your wife and away from Ms Dolosa!"

Ralph felt a warm affection for Monty who he strongly suspected was his genetic father. He thanked the consultant again and left the office keen to get back to work and find Mia.

Veronica took a coffee into Monty after Ralph had left.

"He was a very pleasant young man" she commented.

"Yes, wasn't he" Monty agreed and his chest swelled with pride.

***

Ralph reflected as he left the hospital. Vicky's test result was definitely wrong. But had she fabricated the results or made a genuine error? She'd been to Monty's Fertility Clinic to look up Ralph's record. Why would she think he'd been born through IVF? Was it possible she'd remembered Ralph's surname from seeing the photograph on Monty's wall when she worked there? She must have known he was conceived through IVF before she did the test. Maybe she assumed Ralph knew he was a test tube baby. If so she would have expected them to believe the test result more readily. But how would she have known about Mia's mother? Had Pam had told Vicky about the fling?

He concluded that whatever Vicky's agenda it made no difference; he and Mia were not siblings! He couldn't phone Mia from the tube and anyway he wanted to tell her face-to-face. He'd never been so excited to get to work! He was floating on air and desperate to see Mia. She'd be so happy. Everything would be as it was before this whole horrible experience started.

He got to Brentfield by nine thirty, made a short appearance in his office and rushed to the Physiotherapy Department. He hoped Mia wouldn't have started her ward rounds.

The only person in the office was Bina.

"Is Mia around?" he asked.

"No" she answered. "She's off sick."

"Sick?" he repeated. "What's wrong with her?"

Bina faltered. She had always believed it was Ralph's right to know about the pregnancy. She couldn't tell Ralph against Mia's wishes, though she had been tempted, but she wasn't prepared to tell him lies now. She closed the office door and stood in front of it to stop anyone coming in.

She faced Ralph, held his gaze and spoke frankly.

"Mia didn't tell you because she thought you were happy with Vicky and didn't want to put you under pressure. The fact is, Ralph, Mia's pregnant but she's gone to terminate the pregnancy today."

The words smacked him into a shocked silence before stabbing him to the core.

"NO!" he shrieked. "Where? Where has she gone for it?"

"She wouldn't tell me which clinic" Bina told him apologetically. "I'm sorry to say she didn't trust me."

"But do you know what time she's due to ....." he couldn't bring himself to say the words "you know?" he asked.

"I believe some time this morning" she answered regretfully.

Ralph reached for his mobile and called Mia. The phone rang a few times then went dead. Mia had cut him off. He tried again but got voicemail. He left a frantic message begging her to ring him back. He was desperate to stop her going ahead with the abortion but how was he going to find her? He considered going through all the clinics he could find on-line but knew that would take too long; it was already nearly ten o'clock. He looked back at Bina.

"Do you know if anyone has gone with her?" he asked already guessing the answer.

"I believe Vicky is with her" Bina confirmed.

Ralph felt sick with panic.

"Don't you have any idea where she may have gone?" he pleaded.

"Sorry, Ralph" Bina answered sadly "but maybe you should go to the flat, she may have left some information about the clinic there."

"Yes, good idea" he said "thanks Bina" and he rushed out of the office.

***

Mia and Vicky arrived at the clinic without a hitch; much to their relief the protesters were nowhere to be seen. They were shown into room 4 which was small and contained just a couple of chairs and a small table on which there were some magazines. Before long a nurse came in to see Mia and carry out some routine checks. She brought Mia a gown to change into and told her everything was running on time so the procedure would be going ahead as planned at eleven, just over an hour to wait. The nurse, Rowena, was an efficient, matronly type, in her fifties. She could see Mia was nervous and tried to be as friendly and light-hearted as possible.

Rowena had just started the blood pressure monitor when Mia's phone rang. Vicky picked it up and pressed the disconnect button.

"That was Ralph" she told Mia casually as she switched the phone off. "You obviously don't want to speak to him."

"No, I suppose not." Mia's head dropped, she would have loved to hear his voice.

"You can't go back to him" Vicky added for the nurse's benefit "he could rape you again!"

Mia winced. She'd shelved that ruse. Rowena continued unheeding and soon left instructing them to buzz if they needed her.

"Why did you say that?" Mia said after she'd gone.

"How would it have looked if you seemed fond of the person you've sited as responsible for having the termination?" Vicky explained calmly. "You've got to maintain the story now you've started it."

Mia sullenly picked up a magazine and flipped through the pages distractedly. The next hour was going to be one of the longest in her life. Vicky went to get a coffee. In her solitude Mia thought about Ralph and how unfair it was to pretend he'd done something so horrible. What if it went on his record? Did hospitals or clinics report violent behaviour to the police? Nobody at the clinic knew Ralph but even so it was terrible to imagine they could think of him as a rapist. She thought back to their sexual intimacy; how loving and gentle he was. The memories made her feel at once good and bad.

She looked at the time, three quarters of an hour to go. She considered ringing Ralph back but couldn't contemplate speaking to him now. She wondered how she would feel by the end of today. Would she, as Vicky had suggested, be able to put the whole experience behind her? She realised she'd been so focused on the actual termination she hadn't thought beyond it. What was to become of her? She felt wretched.

Vicky came back with her coffee and a newspaper which she proceeded to read. Then Rowena popped her head round the door to tell Mia her husband was on the phone and asked if she wanted to speak to him. Vicky went to answer but Rowena cut her short reminding her Mia was capable of speaking for herself. Mia reluctantly declined to speak to Ralph and Rowena left.

In the operating theatre Rowena started to prepare a few things for Mia's procedure. She then went into Dr Hussein's office.

"We've had Mr Davenport on the phone" she told him. "He sounded desperately unhappy about the abortion. I'm also concerned about Mrs Davenport; she seems to be completely dominated by her friend and she's unusually nervous."

"Hmmm, let me look through the notes" Dr Hussein said as he

typed in Mia's name. "Ah, it seems the husband is violent, that explains his aggression over the phone."

"He wasn't aggressive" corrected Rowena. "I'd say he was just desperate, very desperate."

"Well Mrs Davenport calls the tune on this occasion. Mr Davenport has no say in the matter, however desperate he is."

"I know but there's something I don't like about this case; it's just a feeling."

"Look, if she's the type of woman that ends up marrying a violent man it's likely she'll allow her friend to boss her about. It's just her nature. She's nervous because she's weak."

"Dr Hussein! You can't just dismiss her because you think she's weak! How do you know what her relationship with her husband is really like?"

"It's in the notes, nurse, I'm only repeating what she's told us herself!" he pointed out, then, seeing Rowena's hurt expression added "I'll have a chat with her before we go ahead. You may as well get her now, everything's ready isn't it?"

Doctor and nurse had formed a close relationship over several years of working together. They knew each other's idiosyncrasies but also had respect for each other, listening to the other's point of view. He liked to irritate her by being purposely controversial and she played along by being suitably outraged, both knowing it was all said in half-jest.

Rowena went to room 4 and holding the door open announced: "Ready for you now Mrs Davenport"

Mia looked at the nurse with resignation. She rose slowly. Her legs felt weak. She was light-headed. She turned to Vicky who gently but firmly pushed her towards the door and the nurse. She gave Mia a last encouraging pat on the back then watched her walk with the nurse slowly down the corridor until their echoing steps faded and they disappeared into a side room.

Vicky turned back into the room and closed the door with a long sigh of relief. She stood momentarily immobile then, with a sudden rush of energy, leapt and punched the air with one fist after the other. She repeated the exercise several times; jumping and thumping the air, biff, biff, buff! Biff, biff, buff!

"Yes! Yes!" she whooped in a whispered shout as she performed her weird victory dance in the empty room. "Fantastic!" She punched the air again. Her face was flushed, her blue eyes glistened. She felt SOOOOO, SOOOOO good! It was better than an orgasm! She felt high as a kite; a junkie after a fix!

It had taken years to reach this point, but it had all been worth it! She'd induced people into doing all sorts of damage to themselves, but getting someone to kill her own baby; that was a first! She relished the thought of Ralph's grief and disappointment when he found out about the abortion. He'd be gutted! There would be no chance of them getting back together after this! Mia was already fragile. Tipping her over the edge was just a matter of time and waiting was one of Vicky's many talents.

She mused over her fetish for destroying women like Mia. It was Annie's fault. Everything had been fine before she was born. But Annie had stolen all the love and attention. Her parents had made that clear by packing her off to boarding school. She remembered how she'd sat alone in her dingy dormitory resentful that the rest of her family were at home enjoying themselves. The only solace had been in thinking of how she would avenge Annie and her parents.

She'd been drawn to a girl in her junior class who reminded her of Annie. She was pretty, happy and popular. She thought of her as Annie 2 and became her best friend, sharing all her fears and doubts. Annie 2 trusted Vicky and didn't suspect Vicky was at the heart of things going wrong. Vicky felt cheated when Annie 2 left the school. She had been enjoying watching her suffer and wanted to carry on. Her appetite had been wetted.

By senior school she'd become well practised in manipulation and auto-suggestion. She felt no affinity to her peers who took pleasure in stupid things like pop stars and boring romantic books. However, she needed to be accepted as one of the crowd. If somebody experienced a misfortune everyone looked sympathetic; in the case of someone's good news they looked delighted. If she didn't make the right noises she found herself being criticised or ostracised. She did not genuinely have any regard for her classmates but over time she perfected a way of appearing to care.

She deviously influenced her contemporaries and was fascinated by what she could get them to do and say. She was never bothered by the consequences of her actions. Why should she have sympathy for people who were stupid enough to fall for her trickery? She considered her superior intellect absolved her from responsibility just as her parents had excused her bad behaviour as a child.

She chose Beverly to be Annie 3. Bev was good looking, sporty and adored by the other girls. It didn't take long to become Bev's best friend and discover her little weaknesses; convince her she was overweight. Other girls must have been jealous of Bev because Vicky had no problem getting them to make snide comments about the size of Bev's hips, legs or stomach. Vicky became Bev's defender, telling her to ignore what they said. She told Bev she wasn't overweight, she just had a healthy covering. By the time Bev was worryingly thin nobody could convince her she wasn't fat.

Vicky visited her in hospital just before she died. It was incredible to see the demise of such a healthy girl. The once robust body lay skeletal attached to a drip. It was most satisfying. Vicky had committed the perfect murder by getting the victim to do it herself.

At university Vicky befriended Annie 4. Everybody was fond of Hannah. She was witty, thoughtful and good looking. Vicky looked as stunned as everybody else when their tutor delivered the dreadful news. Nobody could believe that Hannah had committed suicide though she hadn't been her old cheerful self for some time. Vicky heroically soldiered on in the wake of her best friend's death and gratefully accepted the sympathy of her fellow students. They knew how close she was to Hannah and were concerned for her welfare. She basked in their attention. Some were more probing. "Didn't she say anything?" or "Didn't you know she was depressed?" were the sort of questions Vicky was asked. She pleaded complete ignorance and professed to be devastated her friend had not opened up; she could have helped. If the questions got too searching she'd feign distress and they'd feel guilty for asking.

She hadn't been completely successful with Annie 5. Liz, that bright young doctor, Lamont's protégée, had been easy enough to destabilize but that old bugger had interfered. If it hadn't been for him Vicky was sure Annie 5 was going the same way as Annie 4. She consoled herself with the memories of visiting Liz in that terrible institution. It had been very gratifying to see her, the once "so intelligent and going far" centre of attention, looking white and vacant, surrounded by a jumble of weirdoes.

She'd got her revenge on Monty. The silly old sod never locked his office or used a password on his PC which he left turned on whilst he was out; it was an open invitation! How easy it had been to enter paedophile sites from his computer and get someone to discover what he'd been up to. He suspected her but he couldn't prove anything. It took him months to defend himself. He could only deny any wrong doing. He wasn't struck off, the board accepted somebody else could have tampered with his computer, but that clod of mud would stay firmly stuck to him forever.

After that Vicky had needed to move away from Monty's department and obtained the position at Brentfield. She soon spotted Mia as an ideal Annie 6. The speed at which she had befriended Mia was impressive; only weeks after their meeting she had been invited to the hen party. What an opportunity that had been! Mia's Mum was a treasure chest of anti-Mia weaponry, spilling out all the fears she had for her daughter's weaknesses. It was easy to impress Pam and gain her confidence resulting in her off-loading that nugget of information Vicky just *knew* would be useful at some point; the admission of the "fling". Vicky was perplexed that Pam carried the guilt of one minor indiscretion for so many years. So what if she wasn't sure who Mia's father actually was!? It was hardly the crime of the century! But it certainly had paid dividends for Vicky to keep that little secret locked away.

Mia was her first married victim and she knew it was going to be a challenge. It proved to be more of a challenge than Vicky had imagined. Every time she successfully chipped away some of Mia's confidence, Ralph bolstered her up. It was very annoying. She knew the only way she could succeed would be to drive a wedge between them. It made her sick to see them so happy and lovey-dovey; she couldn't wait to smash them apart! She knew she would have to be patient and hoped that it may be easier after the first year of marriage. However, they grew closer than ever.

Finally, her patience was rewarded. She'd been thumbing through "The Lancet" and been drawn to an article about Monty's upcoming retirement. There was a picture of him sat at his desk in the office she knew only too well. Suddenly the image of an old newspaper article jumped into her head. He'd had an old cutting in a frame at the back of his office and she'd frequently looked at it. Now she remembered one of the women had been called Davenport and she was sure her first name began with D! Could she possibly have been lucky enough to discover Ralph was a test tube baby? She instantly recalled Pam's secret and saw the opportunity.

It was easy to find a reason to be checking records at the Fertilisation Clinic in her role as the Manager of the Diagnostics Genetics Department. She felt the most incredible elation when she confirmed it was Davina Davenport listed as a patient and the date of birth of the baby boy was Ralph's birthday. Bingo! They were the same!

She didn't act on her plan straight away. She wanted to ensure everything was fully prepared. She primed Mia by making comments over a number of weeks about the disastrous results of incestuous relationships. Her job meant she had an excuse, in the guise of talking shop, to regularly relate real and invented cases that demonstrated it was immoral and dangerous to have children with a half sibling. She sowed the seeds of abhorrence and disgust for any liaison with a half-brother.

When she thought the time was right she volunteered to give the test. She had thought Ralph would know about the insemination although Mia had never mentioned it. She guessed they might dismiss the results initially but was sure Mia would tell her mum; and Pam's guilty conscience ensured Mia would soon be furnished with the "fling" story.

Her plan started to falter when it became apparent Ralph's parents hadn't told him about his test tube origin. How was she going to ensure he found out without implicating herself? When he mentioned they were going to visit his parents that Sunday she knew they would visit his grandmother as they always did. It was a long shot but worth a try. She visited Audrey on the Saturday posing as a volunteer and taking the chance that Audrey wouldn't recognise her. After some time chatting she engineered the conversation to grandchildren and adoption. In no time Audrey was telling her about Ralph being a test tube baby.

Vicky convinced Audrey it was her duty to tell Ralph about his roots. She knew Audrey suffered from mild dementia but hoped she would remember until the next day. She wasn't worried about Audrey referring to her visit; any volunteer could have had the conversation.

Audrey did her bit excellently! It was so rewarding to watch the couple's wretchedness. They'd been so dismissive of the test. Treating her like an idiot. Now they had to eat their words! And the way it had all come to them. They didn't once think to question the results. Mia behaved exactly as Vicky had planned and was immediately repulsed by the thought of sex with Ralph.

Then there was a piece of very good fortune; David's illness. Ralph leaving his keys in the office was a gift! She had to take advantage of that opportunity. She got a warm glow remembering how Mia's euphoria had plunged into shocked despondency when she thought Ralph had given Vicky his key. There was a chance they'd rumble the deception but she'd been very careful with what she'd said to them. If challenged she could truthfully say she hadn't *actually* told Mia Ralph gave her the keys. She hadn't *actually* told Ralph Mia had packed the bag. She was thrilled by her daring, gratified and ecstatic over the success of her scheme.

All in all, this had been a fantastic achievement! The killing of the baby added a whole new dimension to previous conquests. She mused how she might influence her next Annie into killing somebody else. A nurse would be a good choice, maybe a geriatric one to start with, who she would influence into killing a patient for merciful reasons. She would start looking round the wards for likely candidates now that she had almost finished with Mia.

That brought her back to the present and she conceded there was one fly in the ointment as far as Mia was concerned; her annoying brother Tony. He was so caring and protective it made Vicky want to puke. He wasn't going to be a push over but she would have to think of how she was going to get him out of the way.

A noise rallied her out of her daydreaming. She turned and there, in the opened doorway, stood Tony.

Part 3

Reaffirming the Vows

Chapter 12

To Bring Comfort & Confidence to Each Other

Ralph fled from Bina's office, out of the hospital and down onto the tube platform. Two minutes to wait. "Come on, come on" he muttered as he paced up and down. On the train he pressed against the doors and at his stop squeezed through before they'd fully opened. He charged up the stairs into the shock of daylight and sprinted to the flat, the old familiar route flying by without registering. Time was racing and his chances of reaching Mia before she went ahead were slipping away.

He fumbled with the key to the main entrance, fingers like bananas, then galloped up the stairs two at a time. More fumbling with keys, an impatient shoulder against the front door and he was in their hall. He dashed down to the living room.

"Arrrrh!" his breath left him as he felt the full weight of somebody leap onto his back. His knees buckled but the adrenaline coursing through his veins held him upright. He grabbed hold of the thick muscled arms that were locked around his neck and, turning on the spot in a bent-legged spin, mustered all his strength to fling off his attacker. There was an almighty crash as the man landed on, and flattened, the coffee table.

Ralph breathlessly looked down at his assailant who, spread-eagled over the debris of the coffee table, stared back. They faced each other in mutual breathless astonishment.

"Tony!"

"Ralph!"

"What the fuck was that about?"

"I thought you were an intruder!"

"Since when did intruders use a key!?"

"It sounded like an army! I thought the door had been kicked in!"

Ralph realised they'd both been stupid.

"Sorry" he said offering his hand to help Tony up. "Are you alright?"

"No bones broken as far as I can tell" answered Tony rubbing his bum which had taken the brunt of his fall "but I don't think the coffee table will make it!" He looked at Ralph. "I guess you've heard about Mia."

"Yes. Tony, you've got to help me. There's been a terrible mistake and I don't have much time."

"She's determined to go through with it" Tony told him.

"Has she told you why we split?"

"You mean the whole sibling thing; yes."

"Well I discovered this morning that Vicky got it wrong! Mia and I aren't related! The baby is just the same as any other baby, it's our baby and I must save it! Please Tony, do you know where she is?"

Tony reached into his pocket and handed Ralph a card. "Here are the details" he said. "I've agreed to pick them up."

Ralph punched the number into his mobile. It was ten thirty. His mouth felt dry as he waited to be put through to the "nurse in charge".

"Could I speak to Mrs Davenport please?" he spluttered. "It's very urgent!"

"Who wants to speak to her?" Rowena asked calmly.

"I'm Mr Davenport, her husband" Ralph answered, assuming this would carry weight; he didn't expect her cool, non-committal response.

"I'll go and ask if she wants to talk to you."

"Please" he begged quickly into the phone before she left "tell her there's been a terrible mistake! I must talk to her before she goes ahead."

"I'm afraid we're not allowed to pass on messages" was the stony response. "Its Company policy."

"I'm her *husband*" he pointed out. "It's *my* baby she's having. I have a right to speak to her, don't I?" It was a statement more than a question.

"Actually, Mr Davenport, you don't have any rights at all" Rowena informed him officiously. "I *will* go and see if your wife wants to speak to you but I *won't* pass on any messages. The clinic can't get involved in family disputes or be seen to act for other parties. I'm sure you understand. Now, I'll put you on hold while I go and speak to her."

No, Ralph didn't understand. How was it he didn't have any rights to speak to his wife!? How was it he didn't have any rights over his own unborn child? The nurse was curt. Surely she recognised the seriousness of his request? He looked over at Tony and raised his brows; an electronic version of Green Sleeves played over and over. He willed Mia to speak to him. "Please come Mia, please come" he prayed silently.

The music was abruptly interrupted but not with Mia; the starchy nurse was back on the line.

"Sorry Mr Davenport" she said matter-of-factly. "Your wife doesn't want to speak to you" and in her head she thought "you raped her, what do you expect?"

"Please" he beseeched with every ounce of persuasion he could muster. "Can't you just pass on a message just this once?"

"No" Rowena was sharp; she had work to do and wanted to get on with it. "Now Mr Davenport I really must go."

"Wait!" he implored. "I *must* speak to her!"

"I'm sorry but I'm going to put the phone down" was her reply and the line went dead.

Tony saw the expression of bitter disappointment and frustration on Ralph's face and from hearing Ralph's end of the conversation knew he'd been unsuccessful. He wished he'd been more active in persuading Mia to tell Ralph. Now it was too late for self-recrimination. The baby couldn't be saved and that was that. But Ralph was far from giving up.

"I'm going to the clinic" he announced. "If Mia knows I'm there

I'm sure she'll speak to me and I can explain."

Tony's heart ached. This was desperate, oh so desperate. It was also likely to fail. If Mia wouldn't entertain Ralph over the phone why would the clinic allow him to see her? He couldn't let Ralph to go through the rejection alone.

"I'll drive you there" he said. "It'll be quicker now rush-hour is over. I said I'd pick them up anyway."

"OK" agreed Ralph. "Let's get going!"

On the way Ralph told Tony about his meeting with Monty that morning. Tony said Mia was convinced Ralph and Vicky were hitched.

"Why would she think that!?" exclaimed Ralph.

"It's what Vicky's told her" was the simple explanation "and it's a rumour that's all around Brentfield. That guy Alan was goading Mia about it the other day."

Ralph said nothing. His anger towards Alan for this latest attack on Mia was outweighed by a tremendous sense of foreboding; how had it gone so far so quickly?

"Do you think Vicky's got the hots for you Ralph?" Tony asked. "Why else would she scheme to get you and Mia to part? You'd better look out, mate, she's very strange if you ask me."

"I told my mother I thought she was stalking me but I can't believe she'd go as far as to allow Mia to terminate a pregnancy" answered Ralph.

"Mia having a baby could have brought you back together" Tony reasoned. "If Vicky is literally mad about you she couldn't allow Mia to keep the baby."

Monty's perception of Vicky was becoming more and more believable. Ralph became agitated.

"How much further is it?" he asked looking at his mobile and seeing it was quarter past eleven.

"Just down here" Tony said. "I'll drop you off and go look for somewhere to park. I'll see you in the clinic."

Ralph's first hurdle was to get past the reception desk on the ground floor. He told the efficient looking lady he'd come to visit his wife. She wouldn't let him go any further and directed him to take a seat whilst she "made enquiries". He was too tense to sit down and instead paced up and down the small lobby in front of the reception desk; the lady kept a wary eye on him whilst she spoke over the telephone. His optimism started to fade. He had a nasty feeling that he was too late. What should he do now? How could he tell Mia they were not related when she'd just terminated the pregnancy? It would devastate her.

"Go up to the first floor" the receptionist told him at last, pleased to be moving him on. "There's a desk on the left at the top of the stairs; report there please."

"It was easy for her to be calm" Ralph thought resentfully and unfairly. "It's just a job for her." His nerves were frayed; a sense of dread had taken grip.

He found the desk with a nurse behind it engrossed in the computer screen. She ignored him, continuing her IT task without looking up. Ralph wanted to grab hold of her and demand he see Mia, but he held on to his temper. After a few minutes that seemed like hours she calmly looked up at Ralph.

"Mr Davenport" she said and Ralph realised she was the same person that spoke to him on the phone. "You're a very persistent man. I'll go and see if your wife will see you now."

She walked into a nearby room labelled "Recovery room 3". His heart sank to the pit of his stomach. The confirmation of his fears was a shattering blow. He suddenly felt drained and close to tears.

At that moment he heard footsteps on the stairs and turned to see Tony, red in the face from running.

"We're too late" Ralph told him. "She's in recovery."

Tony let out a sigh of bitter disappointment. Ralph's blatant agony and grief cut right through him. He yearned to be able to make everything better, make the nightmare disappear, but all he could do was put his hand on Ralph's fallen shoulder in consolation.

The nurse came back and addressed Ralph. "Your wife has agreed to see you, it's the door over there, Recovery room 3" she said. She turned to Tony. "Who are you?" she asked. "Why didn't you report to the reception?"

"I did" Tony answered turning on his most charming manner "and the lovely lady invited me to come up. I'm Tony Sayers, Mrs Davenport's brother" he gave her a broad winning smile; it usually worked.

She softened. "Well you can't both go in" she said but didn't turn Tony away.

"No problem" Tony answered holding Rowena with his large, light hazel eyes. "I'm sure my brother-in-law would prefer to see my sister on his own. Is Mrs Davenport's friend here? I'll go and wait with her."

"Yes, she's in Room 4, down the other end of the hallway" Rowena told him.

"I'll see you later" Tony addressed Ralph, then quietly so that the nurse couldn't hear, "I'll get Vicky out of the way; I think that'll be best."

"Thanks mate" Ralph answered gratefully. He couldn't face Vicky today and didn't want Mia to have anything else to do with her; ever.

***

Tony marched down the corridor to room 4; his body riveted with anger. Ralph's account of Vicky's devilment had wound his innards together like a knotted rope and he was haunted by the image of Ralph's tortured face. Vicky had subjected his sister and Ralph to an ordeal that was beyond meanness. It was evil! How could she be so selfish and go to such lengths to get her own way? His temper intensified when he opened the door and found Vicky staring out of the window with a huge grin over her face! She was laughing whilst his sister, her so-called best friend, was going through an unnecessary abortion!

"You look pleased with yourself" he said resentfully, not bothering with a salutation.

"Oh, hello Tony" she greeted him, apparently oblivious to his abruptness. "You're early; Mia's not back yet."

"I know" he told her "I've just seen the nurse. I brought Ralph with me. He wanted to see Mia."

"Where is he now?" she asked.

"With Mia in the recovery room; they're making up I hope."

"I don't think that's likely" Vicky said seriously. "She didn't tell him about the abortion so I imagine he'll be more than a little upset with her!"

"That would suit you wouldn't it?" Tony spat. "But actually it's you he's upset with! He had a meeting this morning with your previous boss, Monty, and ..."

"Really?" she interrupted surprised. "Why did he see Monty?"

"Why do you think?" Tony asked.

"No idea" she answered.

Tony shook his head as if to say "you have every idea".

"What were you up to?" he continued accusingly. "Getting Ralph to meet Monty on Tuesday night? Did you get some weird thrill out of Ralph unknowingly shaking hands with the person responsible for his existence? Did you like the irony of it?" His voice was harsh and he held her in a hostile gaze.

"Don't be ridiculous Tony" she answered calmly, unperturbed by his onslaught. "I didn't know Monty was the consultant involved with Ralph's conception, how would I?"

"Because you went and looked him up in their records, that's how!"

"What *are* you talking about?" she came back defensively. "Yes, I do often go and look up records over in Monty's Department as part of my research; but there's nothing unusual about that and I *did not* look up Ralph."

"Well Monty reckons you did and what's more he confirmed Ralph's father isn't the same as Mia's, meaning your test result was wrong!"

Vicky sighed at Tony, an expression of exasperation spread across her face.

"How on earth can he claim that?" she said dismissively. "He doesn't even know Mia so how can he be sure whether she and Ralph have the same father? And how would he know what I'd looked at when I visited the records? I'm afraid Ralph has been taken in by that old schemer! Monty doesn't like me. He's convinced I somehow got the IT Department to look at his computer. They found child porn on it. Did he tell Ralph that?! The pervert is a paedophile! He got caught and wants to take it out on me!"

She spoke with conviction, reliving her indignation and hurt over the injustice. Tony wavered; had Monty told the truth? His anger began to ebb, chased away by doubt. He studied her, looking for signs she might be lying. She held his gaze unflinching. The moments passed, neither moved or said anything.

Eventually Vicky broke the standoff.

"You know what, Tony?" she said. "I wish I'd never done that damned test. They seem to want to hold me responsible for the fact that they're related! I just did the test for God's sake! They've become obsessed with proving the results were wrong; going to ridiculous lengths. Meeting Monty for example; what did Ralph think he was going to find out? He knows the donor has anonymity. And Mia, chasing all the way up north; what did she imagine that man was going to say? No, it's all been a disaster. They can't accept the truth and I've become the villain of the piece! I've tried to be as helpful as possible but in return I've become the butt of all sorts of accusations. I'm a doctor and professional; I don't expect to be treated like a charlatan, especially by my so-called friends!"

Tony felt chastened but defensive of his sister and brother-in-law.

"You couldn't expect them to just accept your test result without question" he said "they're in love!"

"I know, but it's *not my fault!*" she repeated.

A few silent seconds passed between them. Tony weighed up Vicky's version of the situation.

"You have shown a lot of interest in Ralph since you gave them those results" he stated. "I'm not accusing you or anything but it could appear that you wanted to split them up."

"What do you mean an interest in Ralph?" she asked indignantly. "Now what am I supposed to have done?"

"Oh, come on! You tried dating him the minute they split up. I know for a fact you took him to the retirement party. And Mia tells me you're totally besotted with him."

"Mia's told you that?!" Vicky exclaimed with a derisive chuckle. "She must be joking! Look, I don't mean to be unkind but, how can I say it, well, I find Ralph a bit dull to be honest and I'm not attracted to him at all! I have bumped into him a couple of times and yes, I did ask him to accompany me to the party because I needed a partner and knew he was at a loose end. I don't know how Mia's concluded I'm dating Ralph or that I'm "besotted" with him! It's absurd! I guess Mia's so in love with him she thinks everyone else feels the same."

"But what about the keys?!" he protested.

"What keys?"

"Their door keys; the ones you said Ralph had given you when you packed his bag!"

"I didn't say that! I *told* Mia he'd left them at the office! Ralph and I had been trying to contact her all day; she'd turned her wretched phone off. I took the keys to the flat hoping to meet her there. After waiting outside for an age, I was frozen and decided to go in. I knew Ralph had gone off in a rush and didn't have anything with him. There were some ironed clothes in the lounge so I packed them in a bag whilst I was waiting. Mia didn't show up so I wrote her a note. As I was leaving she arrived and I told her what I've just told you."

She looked at Tony and saw cynicism in his face.

"Look I did tell her he'd left his keys and I'd put it in the note!" she said convincingly.

Tony faltered. Was Mia imagining Vicky and Ralph's flirtation? He'd never thought Ralph was interested. He'd told her so but she just wouldn't believe it. What evidence had there been that his sister's friend and Ralph were an item? Only what Mia had told him. Was she becoming paranoid? He thought it *was* odd for Vicky to have packed that bag, but on the other hand it *was* an emergency. She could have thought she was doing a good turn *and* she'd been up front with Mia. It seemed that Mia wanted to believe Ralph had rejected her. And what of Ralph's anger against Vicky and all the things he had said in the car? That stemmed from his meeting with Monty; who, it turns out, is a paedophile!

He didn't know what to say but Vicky was already testily slipping on her coat. She bent down to pick up her handbag, revealing a pleasing view of her cleavage that Tony soaked in.

"I love your sister to bits" she told him as she stood up "but right now I'm sick to the death of her needs and wishes! You know there are plenty of ways I'd rather be spending a sunny day's leave than sitting in an abortion clinic! I'm going! Maybe when Mia comes to her senses she'll contact me."

She moved towards Tony who was still by the door and stood in front of him.

"I'll leave you to play gooseberry!" she said mockingly "Good luck!"

The words struck deep. Tony knew Mia and Ralph would be miserable because of the abortion and at the same time extra loving towards each other. He *would* be "gooseberry". And what could he say to them? He didn't know what to believe any more. He also had better things to do on a sunny day; a pub lunch with Vicky was a far more attractive prospect!

"I'll come down with you" he told her.

She looked surprised.

"Maybe I'll run you home" he added.

"Wow! A ride in your posh car; that sounds great!" she exclaimed making him swell with pride. "But what about Mia?" she added with concern. "She and Ralph will need a lift."

"I'll come back for them" he stated "or maybe they can get a cab. I'll see Ralph as we leave. If not, I'll send him a text."

He moved aside and held the door for her then followed her down the corridor. As they neared the recovery room he decided not to disturb Ralph and Mia. He would look up some local cab companies and text the details. He picked up pace to catch up with Vicky unaware of the broad grin she wore as she skipped down the stairs in front of him.

***

"Ralph! It's good to see you!" Mia said when Ralph came into the recovery room. He was relieved to be greeted with a smile but felt stung at how wan and pale she looked and noted a large plaster over the top of her right eye.

He stood by the bed and picked up her hand.

"How are you doing?" he asked.

"I'm OK" she answered not withdrawing from his touch. "Ralph I'm so sorry I didn't speak to you when you rang earlier, or tell you before about being pregnant. I hope you understand why I wanted the abortion. I was thinking of you. I thought it would be better for both of us to make a clean break and have a fresh start. You do understand, don't you?"

She was washed out. An anxious furrow had planted itself on her brow.

"Don't worry about me Mia" was all he could find to say.

"Have you seen Vicky?" she asked. "She's waiting for me in room 4."

The name triggered a wave of rage.

"No, Mia" he answered through clenched teeth. "I haven't seen Vicky and I don't want to see her ever again! She's been telling you a load of rubbish that I want to clear up. I've *never* been in *any* relationship with Vicky other than that of her being a friend of yours."

Mia noted the anger in his voice but didn't believe him.

"Then why did you give her our flat key?" she asked accusingly.

"What? I never gave her our key! Why would I do that?"

"When your dad was taken ill; remember?" Mia stated "so that she could pack a bag for you? Hardly something an ordinary friend would do!"

Ralph cast his mind back to the day his father had been taken ill. He had been panicked and preoccupied. He'd left his keys at work. Vicky had picked them up. He recalled his anger towards Mia when Vicky told him about the packed bag. Now he realised she hadn't actually said Mia packed the bag. He would never have imagined Vicky had used his keys to go into the flat and pack his clothes. Naturally he had assumed Mia had done so. What a schemer Vicky was!

"I thought you'd packed my bag" he confessed. "I let Vicky lead me into thinking you couldn't be bothered to come to see me!"

It was Mia's turn to grasp at the truth. "I thought" she hesitated "that is Vicky told me you wanted to be on your own; just the Davenports, excluding me."

"You know I'd never think like that!" he protested.

"We'd hardly been talking" she exclaimed justifying herself. "You were disgruntled about me going to see Sandy Balls. I thought you were just completely fed up with me."

"It was *you* that was fed up with *me*!" he corrected her.

Mia tried to think back over all the conversations she'd had with Ralph and Vicky but she was tired and they span disjointedly in her head. She was certain Ralph had dated Vicky; it was a fact firmly embedded in her brain.

"How *did* she get your keys then?" she asked him cynically.

"I'd left them on my desk when I rushed out to go and see dad. She brought them back with the bag."

"But why would she purposely mislead us like that?" Mia asked bewildered.

"All I can suggest is that she wanted to make sure I didn't convince you to get back together in spite of our so-called sibling relationship; which leads me on to something I want to tell you."

He paused. She looked very tired.

"Well?" she prompted.

"Maybe we should wait until we get home" he answered.

"You want to come back home?" she said.

"I always did" he told her.

"I was always happy for you to live with me. I never banished you Ralph." She looked hurt at the thought he could imagine she did.

Ralph was ashamed that after being led to believe she'd practically thrown him out, he'd later been convinced she was seeing somebody else. He stood there awkwardly, undecided how to continue.

"So, what did you want to tell me?" she broke his silence. "You might as well say; I'll find out in the end."

He reached for a chair and settled next to her.

"This morning I went to meet the man that performed the artificial insemination on my mother."

"Oh? How did you find him?" she asked.

"It's a long story. You know I went to that retirement party on Tuesday."

A shadow of annoyance crossed Mia's face.

"I know what you're thinking" he stated "but Vicky asked me to go because she didn't have a partner. I agreed but knew it was a mistake as soon as I got there. She was awful, Mia. She connived to get herself next to one of the big cheeses. That's how I ended up next to Jeffrey. She made me feel, well, odd. That's why I rang you. I needed to hear your voice. Vicky had never previously spoken to me the way you heard her speak over the phone, I swear!"

Mia looked at him cynically.

"So, what happened at the party?" she asked.

"The consultant retiring was a Mr Lamont, otherwise known as Monty. He was responsible for the first babies to be created from donor sperm. Mum had shown me a newspaper clipping and I recognised his name. I cheekily asked for an appointment and thankfully he saw me this morning."

She pulled herself up in the bed; her interest roused. Ralph stopped to collect his thoughts.

"This morning" he continued "Monty told me that without any doubt, any doubt whatsoever, Sandy Balls is NOT my father!"

Mia took in a shocked breath.

"How can you be sure?" she asked disbelievingly.

"Why would he lie?"

"I don't know; I just can't believe we're not siblings!"

"You are pleased, aren't you?" he asked uneasily.

"Of course I am! If I can be sure it's true!"

"There are lots of things we need to talk about" he told her "but if you like we can have another test to prove we aren't related."

She went quiet and became distant.

"I'm so sorry Mia" he said sadly. "I did try to speak to you before the abortion."

"The abortion?" she repeated rallying. "They haven't told you? I didn't have it!"

Ralph was lost for words, his throat constricted. He looked towards her midriff.

"It's still there?" he asked.

"Yes, it is!" she smiled.

He was euphoric, he could hardly believe it. "That's fantastic!" he said. "What happened? Did you change your mind?"

"No" she said.

Although she was ashamed of her rape allegation there'd been so many lies she decided to tell Ralph the whole story.

***

Her knees felt like jelly as she walked with Rowena down the hallway and entered the office where a doctor was sitting behind his desk. The nurse showed her to a seat and stood to the side whilst he introduced himself as Dr Hussein. He started to ask a couple of routine questions but on impulse Mia interrupted.

"Before we go any further" she said "I'd like to put the record straight about my husband."

Dr Hussein inwardly rolled his eyes and groaned, why did women protect violent partners? He stopped his questioning and waited.

"He didn't rape me!" she stated.

"Why did you tell us he did?" the doctor asked.

Mia realised she had no answer to such an obvious question. Vicky was right; she had told the lie and should have stuck to it. She'd been so desperate to clear Ralph's name. Now she floundered and could see scepticism written over both their faces.

"I had my reasons" she answered dismissively.

"What were they?" he asked calmly.

What could she tell him? A test had shown she was related to her husband? There'd be so many complicated questions. She might get Vicky into trouble. She looked at her lap trying hard to think of something. She felt their eyes drilling into the top of her head. She wanted to be anywhere but here; just be gone from this horrible clinic. They remained silent, waiting patiently for her to speak. Seconds felt like hours. She became more and more uncomfortable in their tacit scrutiny and broke into a sweat; her cheeks burned. Then a familiar sensation passed through her body; for the third time she fainted in front of a doctor.

Rowena winced as Mia's head struck the edge of the desk and she slumped to the floor, knocking the chair aside with a crash. The nurse rushed to help Mia whilst Dr Hussein dashed into the operating theatre and collected some surgical roll which he gave to Rowena to help stem the blood flowing from Mia's crown. He then watched and waited for the nurse's evaluation. He was irritated by this idiot girl. She'd been babbling on wasting time and was now pouring blood all over his new carpet.

Rowena asked him to pass his cushion. He quickly grabbed the surgical roll and wrapped the cushion before handing it over. She looked at him exasperated, one hand holding Mia's head and the other waiting, poised mid-air. He made no apology. He didn't want his cushion covered in blood, it was a present brought from Pakistan.

Mia soon came round but they weren't sure whether she'd lost consciousness from the knock or whether she had simply fainted. When they thought she was well enough they helped her up and took her into the recovery room where Rowena cleaned and dressed the wound, a nasty gash. She told Mia to pull the emergency cord if she felt sick, dizzy or in any way unwell. They agreed to keep an eye on her for a couple of hours but it would not be possible to proceed with the abortion.

Rowena had just finished cleaning the office carpet when the internal phone sounded and the downstairs receptionist told her Mr Davenport had arrived!

"May as well send him up" she said resignedly. "It's chaotic here anyway and I'm interested to see what he's like!"

***

Ralph was extremely upset with Mia.

"No wonder that nurse wouldn't pass on my message" he said "she thinks I'm a monster!"

"I'm so sorry" Mia repeated for the umpteenth time.

"At least you tried to put the record straight" he conceded "and in the end that's what saved our baby!"

Mia nestled her head against Ralph's arm. It was comforting though she still felt uneasy. He lifted his arm and pulled her towards him. He was shocked at how thin she was; he could feel the bones prominent in her shoulders. He was overcome with relief that the nightmare of the last few months was behind them though he recognised it would take some time for them to recover from their ordeal.

Rowena came in and found Mia wrapped up in her husband's arms. They looked contented but she'd seen all sorts here at the clinic and knew appearances often betrayed reality. However, Mia was a different person to the nerve-racked lady that had arrived three hours ago.

"Can I go now?" Mia asked.

"Is there somebody that can be with you for the next twenty-four hours?" Rowena asked.

"I'll be with her" said Ralph and the couple smiled at each other.

"She needs to remain *calm*" the nurse pointed out.

"I'll look after her" he insisted, offended she doubted him but knowing why.

"OK" she directed her words to Mia. "If you have any symptoms as I've described you must go to your local A&E Department. Now if you feel well enough you can go back to Room 4 and get dressed. Dr Hussein wants you to be checked over by your GP before you make another appointment here."

"I won't be coming back" Mia told her boldly. "I'm keeping the baby."

Rowena said nothing; she was too long in the job to be drawn into commenting on any of the patients' decisions or remarks. She just kept to business.

"There will be a charge" she informed Mia. "You won't get all your money back."

"Oh, yes, I understand" answered Mia though it was something she hadn't considered.

"I'll leave you to it then" said Rowena and left the room.

Mia suddenly remembered Vicky was waiting in Room 4 but Ralph explained Tony had volunteered to "get her out of the way". Mia slowly eased herself off the bed and although Ralph insisted on holding her arm she really didn't need it as they walked down the corridor. They couldn't wait to tell Tony the good news about the abortion. But room 4 empty; there was no sign of Tony or Vicky.

Mia started to get dressed whilst Ralph went to find Rowena to ask after Tony.

"He left with your wife's friend about half an hour ago" she told him.

"Did he say when he'd be back?"

"No" she answered with her usual brevity.

"I'll have to call a cab" Ralph stated as though Rowena should be interested.

She gave him a withering look, nodded towards a notice board near the entrance and walked away. He wandered over to the board where there were a couple of cab company cards. He punched their telephone numbers into his mobile and went back to Mia.

"They left together" he told her.

"Hmm, I've tried calling Tony but he isn't answering" she said pensively.

"I'll call a cab" Ralph decided "and we'll let Tony know we're making our own way home."

"I'll text him" Mia said. "He can meet us back at the flat. Do you think he's OK?"

"Yes, of course he is" Ralph said reassuringly. "Unless Vicky's turned him into a frog!"

His flippant remark hid his own concern; what *had* happened to Tony?

Mia smiled at the joke. All the same it was unusual for Tony not to answer his phone or to have phoned to say he'd been delayed.

***

It felt good to be back in the flat. There was a delicious aroma emanating from the kitchen. Ralph was curious when he saw the new cooking equipment lined up across the work surface.

"What's been going on here?!" he exclaimed. "It looks like a laboratory!"

"Tony's been showing me simple ways to cook tasty food" she explained. "He bought all this equipment."

Ralph walked to the source of the mouth-watering smell; the slow cooker. Inside he saw some braised beef, onions and carrots. It looked delicious. Yet for some inexplicable reason it irked him; he felt momentarily jealous of his brother-in-law's relationship with his wife.

"He must have put it on before I arrived" Ralph surmised trying to overcome his raw emotions and be reasonable about Tony, who had after all been very kind to both of them "so that you'd come back to a nice hot dinner."

"He's been very thoughtful like that" she said. "I don't know how I would have survived without him."

Ralph considered what might have happened to Mia had Tony not stepped in. A chill ran down his spine.

"I should have listened to him" Mia went on. "He kept telling me you may not be interested in Vicky. He thought she was weird and had a thing about you. I didn't believe him."

"That crossed my mind. I told mum I thought she might be

stalking me! Mum thought I was being ridiculous."

"I hope Tony isn't too much longer" Mia said concerned.

"So do I" agreed Ralph feeling guilty for his earlier jealousy. "Now you should go and put your feet up and I'll make us a cup of tea."

He started to fill the kettle but heard a shriek from Mia. He dashed into the hall and met her half way.

"Something's happened to the coffee table!" she exclaimed.

Ralph let out a sigh of relief; he'd forgotten about that. He explained how it had been flattened during his "fight" with Tony. That seemed ages ago; this had been a very long day. They picked up the pieces of table and looked at each other; he holding the broken top and she the legs. They laughed. Nobody would come between them again.

Over tea they compared notes on what each had been led to believe and what was the truth. They couldn't fathom out how Vicky could be so manipulative, dishonest and cruel. They were prepared to believe she had actually made a mistake when she carried out the test. If not, she would have knowingly watched Mia have an unnecessary abortion. That was too much for either of them to imagine possible.

It was nearly six o'clock and they were wondering what had happened to Tony. Then to Mia's relief a text arrived. It read "Thanks for message hope u got cab ok. Dealt with V & going home for nite. Will c u tomorrow. T x"

The message was brief and Mia wondered why he hadn't called. Ralph was sure it was because he'd decided they needed time alone and undisturbed. Mia sent a reply text. "Look 4ward 2 c u tom. Lots to tell u. No abortion! Thanks for dinner we'll enjoy! M x"

Knowing he was OK they relaxed and savoured the tasty casserole. The long process of extracting the wedge had started. It would take some time to shift and part of it would remain forever.

Chapter 13

Let No Man Put Asunder

They ran from the clinic like a couple of school children playing hooky; breathless by the time they reached the car. Vicky put her hands flat on the bonnet and panted whilst Tony rested his back against the side. They looked at each other and smiled, invigorated by the activity and the touch of the fresh, mild air against their skin, a contrast to the stuffy centrally heated room and depressing scenario they'd left behind.

Tony opened the passenger door and Vicky excitedly sidled into the low slung bucket seat. Her enthusiasm for his car was completely contrary to Mia's reaction a few weeks ago. No white lipped starchiness from Vicky who eagerly poured over the car's multitude of gadgets and listened with interest as he explained their use. She was as keen as him to have the soft-top open and squealed with delight as he pulled away, her eyes bright and her cheeks pink. The car felt twice as powerful with her sitting next to him.

They queued their way through a plethora of traffic lights and junctions. She drank in the passing stares and basked in any glimpse of envy. They got to the A3 and Tony opened the throttle, accelerating down the outside lane. Her hair went wild as the car reached seventy in the fifty-mile-an-hour limit and she hooted ecstatically. Her joy was infectious. Tony grinned as he manoeuvred between lanes. He had suddenly become besotted with a woman he could have killed an hour ago. Mia and Ralph were tucked away in a remote region of his mind. What would they make of his behaviour?

He made for a country pub he knew in Surrey where they could have a late lunch and warm up. Vicky giggled when she looked in a wall mirror and saw her rough blown, tangled hair. He hadn't expected her to be so game; he'd thought of her as aloof and stuffy. She asked him to get her a white wine whilst she went to the toilet. He bought the drinks, found a table for two in a nice cosy nook and waited to catch her attention. He was excited at the prospect of her joining him in the intimate snug.

He remembered Mia and quickly got out his phone to call and apologise for not coming back to the clinic. He saw she'd sent a text and was thankful to see they'd got a cab home. She'd suggested he meet them at the flat later. He would have answered but there was no signal in the pub.

"Don't worry about them" Vicky told him when she returned and he expressed concern over the lack of signal. "I'm sure they can look after themselves! To be honest, Tony, it would do Mia good to stand on her own two feet for a change; you and Ralph smother her!"

"She's my little sis" he answered defensively, uncomfortable with her comment. "I'll always feel protective." Then to direct the conversation away from Mia he added "what about you, Vicky, do you have any brothers or sisters?"

Vicky went quiet. He waited.

"I did have a younger sister" she told him quietly. "She died."

"Oh, I'm sorry" he said shocked by the disclosure. "Was that long ago?"

"More than twenty years now" she answered "but it still upsets me; she was only nine."

"What happened to her?" he asked.

"She drowned. Death by misadventure."

"How dreadful" he said sympathetically "for you and for your parents."

"Yes it was" she admitted "but unfortunately in their grief my parents blamed me for the accident. My sister was nearly six years younger than me" she explained "they expected me to look after her, much as you've been made to feel you should look after Mia. In the end though, Tony, there's a limit to how much you can do to protect younger siblings."

The revelation explained a lot about Vicky and her relationship with Mia. He guessed Vicky was a few years older than his sister and now it was plain she saw Mia as a sister substitute.

They were quiet for a while but Tony was curious. He didn't want to upset her by probing into the accident, but wondered about her parents. Did they still blame her?

"So how are your mum and dad now?" he asked.

"I have no idea" she stated. "I haven't spoken to them for years." She looked sad and defeated; a side he'd not imagined her capable of.

"I believe" she continued pensively "it would have been harder for me to cope with their rejection had I not gone to boarding school. However, as they sent me away when I was ten I didn't have the close relationship some children have with their parents. Still, they covered the cost of my degree course; I have that at least to thank them for."

His heart went out to her. How terribly she'd been treated. He couldn't imagine the psychological impact such rejection and blame would have. He reflected on her behaviour and realised much of it was due to her desire to be loved and do the right thing for his sister. She must have genuinely thought she was protecting Mia by keeping Ralph away from the hospital. She must have thought the abortion was the right thing for Mia to do. Her poignant and vulnerable expression appealed to Tony's paternal nature. She was becoming more desirable by the minute.

The subject was dropped as neither wanted to turn their impromptu lunch into a depressing tête-à-tête. Instead Tony told her funny stories about people at work. That made her smile and reminded her of a few of her own anecdotes. They were back on track for a fun afternoon.

After lunch they headed back to Vicky's flat, filled with excited expectation. Tony closed the soft top and the car became loaded with pheromones, perfume, deodorant and an erotic tension.

At the flat Tony nosed around the lounge whilst Vicky made coffee. There were no photographs, personal knick-knacks or anything else to look at. Tony thought the room unwelcoming but to be expected given her background. They sipped their coffees and made some small talk, but their passion had been simmering for hours.

Before long they were kissing and grabbing at each other's clothes. Vicky took Tony by the arm and pulled him to the bedroom where they hungrily finished disrobing each other. Then, out of the blue, Vicky gave Tony a hard shove. He was caught off-guard and fell backwards across the bed. She jumped on top of him, one knee each side of his waist, and leaned forward on her outstretched arms. He felt the warmth of her vagina on his erect penis. Her firm, round breasts were inches from his face. He relished being pinned there for a moment but then grabbed hold of her arms and rolled her over. He was now on top with arms outstretched and knees between her legs. Her startled face soon gave way to an inviting smile. She half closed her eyes and pursed her lips. He bent down to kiss her but sprang back; she'd bitten his lip!

"Ow!" he exclaimed kneeling up and feeling his lip. "That hurt!"

"Sorry darling" she answered as she pulled herself up to study the injury. "I got carried away!"

They were facing each other; kneeling up on the bed.

"That's OK" he said ruefully "you don't seem to have drawn blood!"

"You'll live!" she said and pushed him over again.

They thrashed about, rolling back and forth across the bed, each trying to dominate, more like a wrestling match than foreplay. She dug her nails into his back. He called her a minx and roughly grabbed her arms. They tussled across the bed, the sound of flesh against flesh percussion for their grunts and groans.

Suddenly she freed herself and slid off the bed.

"I'm getting dressed" she announced standing beside the bed looking down at him, her cheeks ruddy, her hair dishevelled.

"Dressed?" he repeated bewildered.

"Stay there" she demanded with a glint in her eye. "I won't be a minute; you'll love it!"

He tried to protest but in a flash her white bottom disappeared behind the closed bedroom door followed by the click of the bathroom door.

He lay back on the bed and gave an exhausted sigh. He'd had many partners but none this pushy! His heart was racing, his face was burning and his lip was swollen. She was wild and scary. He should get dressed and leave. But the prospect of intense sex rooted him. He pictured her returning in silky, erotic underwear, or a French maid's outfit. He was full of excited anticipation and cocky enough to believe he could handle her.

After a while it was obvious she was going to be more than a minute. His ardour cooled. He perused his surroundings. It was a decent sized bedroom with mirrored wardrobes down one wall. Kinky he thought, rekindling some of his excitement. The mattress was soft but firm and behind him was a large, expensive-looking spoked brass headboard. He lay on a rich satin duvet cover, his head on a soft matching pillow case. There were plump scatter cushions on the bottom of the bed, a small attractive armchair next to an elegant chest of drawers; the curtains draped heavily across the windows. It was luxurious. Her perfume pervaded everything.

He casually picked up his phone. He looked for Mia's message but it had disappeared as had all his other messages. He went into his contact list. Nearly all his contacts had disappeared! The only name he recognised was Mia's. He realised he'd picked up Vicky's phone by mistake.

Curiously he flipped through her messages, listening for her as he did so; he didn't want to get caught. All was quiet. Still in the bathroom! Not much in the messages so switched to applications, not much there either. How about photos? He opened her store and jumped at the sight of Mia staring back at him. Vicky must have taken the picture earlier that day. Mia was in her clinic gown on the chair in room 4. She looked wretched. It reminded Tony how low and depressed she'd become. He scrolled to the previous photo; Mia looking very tired and anxious in what looked like a pub. The one before was also of Mia. He skipped back through at least a dozen photos. The further back, the better Mia looked. He finally got to a picture of Mia on her wedding day; she looked stunning! The disparity between the first and last picture was alarming. The hair on the back of his neck stood up as he recalled Ralph's story of the young doctor working for Monty. Had Vicky got pleasure from his sister's decline? Had she set out to injure Mia?

He thumbed back from the wedding photo. Not Mia but another young woman. She had the most poignant expression he'd ever seen. He studied the photo. She seemed to be in some sort of institution. It didn't look like a hospital but maybe some sort of clinic. He zoomed in. He could see scars on her arms. He remembered his fear when Mia had pulled up her sleeve to show him her rash. He had thought himself stupid for entertaining the thought that she might try to harm herself. Now he wondered how near the truth he had been.

He continued back through the pictures until he got to an attractive looking, bright-eyed young woman. It was hard to believe the girl in the first photo was the same as the one in the last. Could this have been Monty's protégé?

He froze at the next image. He'd expected another young female but was faced with a man cuffed to the headboard; the very one behind Tony now. The youth's white frightened face was chilling. There were marks on his body. Tony hesitantly zoomed in, dreading the detail, but too curious to resist. What were those marks and how had the injuries been inflicted?

He had become so absorbed he'd forgotten Vicky and jumped when he heard the bathroom door. He switched off the phone and threw it on the floor in one movement. He felt clammy but very alert. Vicky was insane, that was certain, and now he feared for his safety.

The door flew open.

"Oh fuck!" he thought.

She strode in and stood at the end of the bed, legs apart and hands on hips. She'd changed into a black, leather trouser suit with long-sleeves. The soft leather clung tightly to her body. A large bulky zip ran all the way up the front, open at the top to expose her bulging cleavage. Some handcuffs were hanging from a thick, black, studded belt. The piercing quality of her steel blue eyes was accentuated by the application of false eye lashes, eye-liner and a blue-green eye shadow. Her hair was flattened to her skull and off her face. It was theatrical; she was barely recognisable. She held a whip in her black, leather, gloved hand.

He felt vulnerable and very, very naked.

"Have you been a naughty boy?" she asked toying with the whip. "We all know what happens to naughty boys!"

"I'm not into this" Tony answered as he moved to the edge of the bed. "I'm going."

"Don't be silly" she told him moving round the bed to block his way. "You'll enjoy it! You'll see!"

"No, no I won't!" he told her firmly.

"Come on!" she smiled. "You gave all the signs earlier!"

"What signs?" he asked.

"Well, you didn't seem too upset over being bitten, did you? And you were definitely up for a fight!" she reminded him.

"That was different" he told her. "Really, I'm not interested in S&M sex."

"Honestly Tony, I thought you were more daring!" she taunted. "Surely you don't just want promotional sex!"

"Promotional sex?" he repeated.

She laughed. "The sort of sex I have to tolerate when I seduce one of my bosses!"

He remained silent.

"Tony" she sighed. "You're as bad as Ralph! You don't think I became manager without doing a few favours, do you?"

"I thought you were the best" he commented sarcastically.

"I am!" she told him. "I'm doing everyone a favour by making sure I get the job!"

She returned to the task in hand.

"Lay back on the bed!" she ordered.

He ignored her demand, scuttled to the opposite side of the bed, rolled off and scrambled on all fours along the foot looking for the clothes he'd so eagerly shed earlier.

Crack! He felt a rush of air as the whip smacked the floor next to him! Too close for comfort; he couldn't allow her to continue. He launched himself at her but she was too quick. She sprang out of his way and jumped onto the bed.

Crack! The whip thundered above his head making him duck and bow down to her again. He grabbed for her ankle but again she was too fast. She sprang back off the bed, landing sure footedly on the other side. She laughed manically as she ran round the bed, the whip raised ready for action.

"Stop!" he panted. "This is not what I call pleasure! Find somebody masochistic for your sadistic fetishes!"

"Not the same!" she hooted as she cracked the whip across his leg making him yelp with shock and pain. "This is much more fun!"

She had a wild look. She was out of control. Tony couldn't shake away the image of the horrified face of the man cuffed to her bed. A rush of adrenalin coursed through his veins. He sprang up and pinned her against the bedroom door before she had the chance to lift the whip again.

Now he'd cornered her, his fear turned to rage. He drew his arm back ready to throw an almighty punch straight into her ghoulish painted face; his biceps were tense, his breath short. She braced herself and closed her eyes. There was a loud thud, but he hadn't hit her. Instead he had punched to the side of her head, knocking a hole in the thin panelling of the door and making his knuckles and arm shudder with pain.

She slowly opened her eyes but instead of being relieved seemed irritated. He was cursing and holding one hand in the other; his fist was smarting.

"Satisfied?" he said bitterly.

She didn't answer.

He studied her face.

"You wanted me to hit you, didn't you?" he spat accusingly.

She still didn't say anything.

"Did you want to be hurt?" he continued. "Maybe you hoped to be able to report me to the police? A criminal record wouldn't do my job prospects much good, would it?"

He caught the most miniscule flicker in her eye and was sure he'd hit on the truth. She was prepared to subject herself to injury to get him into trouble. He couldn't understand it. The adrenalin had now drained away. He was spent. She still didn't move or speak.

He grabbed hold of the whip, she offered no resistance. He returned to his clothes, constantly keeping his eye on her. He retrieved his boxers and stepped into them one foot at a time, the other securely standing on the whip. He kept her in view as he climbed into his jeans. He was wary. It was like being caught in a cage with a tigress that could pounce at any time. He reached for his sweat-shirt and put his arms through the sleeves, maintaining his vigil as he did so. With a deep breath, he tried to quickly pull the shirt over his head. A sharp pain ran through his injured arm stopping him dead in his tracks. The shirt was stuck over his face. After seconds that seemed like minutes he managed to push his head through. His eyes darted in all directions as he emerged, expecting her to attack. However, she was standing against the door where he'd left her, bemused by his ungainly reverse strip-tease, a broad, mocking leer across her painted lips.

He put his socks in one of his trouser pockets, picked up his phone and the whip and made towards her and the door. She sneered at him contemptuously and, with a bolshie attitude, reluctantly moved aside to let him through. As he opened the door she made a sudden, mock start towards him. He jumped and dashed out of the room; her derisory laugher following behind him. He hurried to the lounge to retrieve his coat, checking the pocket for his car keys as he put it on. He verified mentally that he hadn't forgotten anything, threw the whip to the back of the living room, and headed for the front door where he'd left his shoes.

As he picked them up he saw Vicky coming down the hallway. On impulse he raised his mobile in his free hand and took a photo. She looked thunderous and started to rush towards him. He got out, slammed the door and leapt bare foot down the carpeted staircase. He heard the door open above him but he was already at street level; she wouldn't come out dressed in that gear and anyway she was too far behind to catch him. He stopped by the main entrance door to slip on his shoes, without socks, doing up the laces with one eye on the stairs. Then he opened the door to the fresh early evening air and walked free from the building. He'd never been so relieved to get out of a place or away from a person.

He felt chilled not only by the temperature but also by what he had just experienced. He was shaken and filled with horror, disbelief and above all insecurity. He was keen to get to his car and reach the sanctuary of his own, familiar space; like getting home. He crossed the road and eagerly made his way towards the car which was parked opposite the flat.

He started to relax; the nightmare was behind him. But as he reached the driver's door his heart sank. Running down the entire length of the car was a deep scratch. He felt sick at the sight of the damage, the result of wanton vandalism. In parts he could see the bright base metal. He hopelessly looked up and down the road in a futile attempt to find the perpetrator. He considered asking in the shops whether anyone had witnessed the damage; but what was the point even if they had?

Crest fallen he took out his car key but as he went to use the remote he saw something on the shaft of the key. Closer examination revealed tiny bits of black, red and silver paint embedded within the metal indents. He held the key against the car; his own key had been used to do the damage! He looked back across the road towards the shops and Vicky's flat, his eyes lifting to the second storey casement window. There she stood, waiting for him to see her, a shadow half covered by the curtain. Her middle finger appeared beyond the curtain, followed by a brief peek of her smirking face. She'd not spent all that time in the bathroom.

He got into the car and drove off. He decided not to go to Mia's flat; he couldn't face seeing her or Ralph. He felt foolish and utterly abused. He just wanted his own space. He'd text Mia from home and maybe he'd see her tomorrow.

Chapter 14

To Be United in Heart, Body and Mind

Mia and Ralph both rang in sick on Friday; they couldn't risk asking for leave and not being allowed to take it. Bina was delighted Mia hadn't gone through with the abortion and willingly accepted Mia's bump on the head as a reason for being off. Ralph's manager Don was less amenable. He'd been sympathetic when Ralph needed time off for his father's illness but yesterday Ralph had disappeared in the morning and not returned or phoned all day. Ralph told him he'd been too ill to ring and was still feeling sick today; he knew it didn't sound convincing. Don was leaving at the end of the month and Ralph hoped with only a few weeks to go he wouldn't bother to take any further action in the matter. If he said anything to Jeffrey Clark Ralph had probably messed up his chances of getting the promotion; Jeffrey was carrying out interviews next week. He couldn't worry about that at the moment; Mia was his priority.

They spent the day pottering around and readjusting to their reconciliation; constantly going over the events of the last three months and analysing what had happened to them; they were still in shock and disbelief. Tony phoned to say he had a lot to tell them and would visit that evening. Mia thought he sounded subdued. Ralph also spoke to his mum who was delighted they were back together. He agreed they'd visit tomorrow to pick up Ralph's clothes and see how David was doing. He didn't mention that Mia was pregnant as they wanted to give the good news in person and see David & Davina's delight. For the first time in her life Mia looked forward to seeing them. At least something good had come out of this horrible experience.

She was still minded to have another sibship test to be absolutely sure. Ralph was irritated that she still half believed Vicky. But as they prepared dinner for Tony they reached a point of understanding and were in good spirits by the time he arrived.

He gave Mia such a long hug she thought she would suffocate. Then he hugged Ralph just as enthusiastically. They saw his hand was bandaged.

"What happened to your hand?" Mia asked as they settled in the lounge.

"I'll come to that" he said evasively.

"How did it go with Vicky yesterday?" she continued eagerly. "I'm dying to know. I bet you gave her a piece of your mind!"

Tony cringed. How could he admit he'd done the opposite and gone to her flat for sex? He took a deep breath.

"The truth is" he stated "I behaved like a complete dick-head."

They looked at him and waited.

"I let her convince me that you, Ralph, had got it all wrong and been taken in by Monty. She was very persuasive and her version seemed more plausible."

He reddened and waited for their reaction but they didn't seem surprised. He saw them exchange looks and it was evident he'd touched on a subject they'd already discussed.

"I offered to take her home" he continued "and on the way she suggested we get something to eat. It didn't seem a bad idea so I agreed and we stopped for a pub lunch."

They looked perplexed.

"Why didn't you let us know?" asked Mia.

"I did try to contact you but couldn't get a signal" he answered apologetically.

"Couldn't get a signal!?" Mia exclaimed. "Where were you?"

Tony reddened. This was excruciating!

"We went for a ride" he admitted. "she was really impressed with my car."

He paused then added "she really did know how to butter me up, didn't she?!"

They could see by his embarrassment something had gone wrong.

"Don't worry Tony" Ralph assured him. "We've all been taken in by Vicky."

"I know, but I feel such an idiot!" he admitted. "After all my suspicions about her and thinking what a fool you were Mia, and I go and get completely sucked in myself!"

"So what happened, dare I ask?" said Mia.

"We went back to her place" he said "and, well, we, er."

"You had sex!" Mia was outraged; she couldn't help it.

"No! We didn't as it turns out!" he told her defensively. "The truth is she likes kinky stuff; that sado-masochistic malarkey. I told her it wasn't my sort of thing but she started attacking me!"

Mia and Ralph stared at Tony open-mouthed.

"So you were undressed?" Mia quizzed trying to picture the situation.

"Yes, I thought we were going to have *normal* sex" he explained as though that made everything better. "Then she told me to wait while she got changed. That was when I looked at the pictures on her mobile. I thought it was mine, you see, and as she was so long getting changed I decided to check for messages."

"So you were both undressed" Mia repeated still unable to get her head around it "but she went to get changed?"

"We don't need to know all about that" Ralph interjected, helping Tony to by-pass detail he clearly didn't want to go into. "What photos did she have?"

"It was awful!" Tony shuddered as he thought about the images. "She had a whole set of you Mia! They started with you in your wedding dress, all radiant and lovely, and gradually showed you looking less and less well, ending with you at the clinic yesterday."

Mia was dumbfounded. "I didn't see her take that!" she said "or any other pictures for that matter!"

"That's not all" he continued "before your photos there was another set of a young lady I think may have been the student Monty spoke of. The first of those showed a bright young woman but in the last she was barely recognisable in some hospital looking dreadful."

"So she keeps photos as mementoes" Ralph surmised disgusted. "Were there anymore?"

"I didn't have time to look because Vicky came back" Tony answered choosing not to tell them about the ones of the young man. "It was then I realised what I'd got myself into! Here" he reached into his pocket, pulled out his mobile and selected the photo of Vicky. "I managed to take this!"

They studied the photo; mesmerised.

"Bloody hell!" Ralph said.

"And she had a whip" Tony told them. "It was fucking scary; look." He pulled up his trousers to reveal the red whelp on his calf. They gasped in unison.

"How did you get away?" Ralph asked.

"I finally managed to pin her against the door" he answered getting agitated at the thought of it. "I was livid. What with her whipping me and those photos of you My-mi; I completely lost my cool."

"You didn't hit her!" said Mia fearing the consequences.

"No" he answered "But I think that's what she wanted me to do! Somehow I managed to stop myself and hit the door instead; hence the sprain to my fist!"

All three of them would have loved to see Vicky get a bloody nose but at the same time they knew Tony would have risked arrest if he assaulted her.

"I'm so pleased you managed not to hit her, Tony" Mia told him. "She probably would have gone to the Police and had you done for GBH."

"That's what I think" he agreed. "I've thought a lot about it. Remember, at that point she and I didn't know you hadn't had the abortion. She would have thought she'd done enough damage to separate you two completely. I've been a major support for you in Ralph's absence. An arrest would have preoccupied me and made you miserable. She would have given you her version of events to turn you against me. She was trying to isolate you, My-mi, and give you a mental break-down."

A shiver ran down Mia's back. She finally had to accept everything Ralph had told her about Vicky and it made her feel nauseous.

"Do you think she'll leave me alone now?" she asked alarmed.

"I think so" Tony answered consolingly. "She knows she's been rumbled. She left Monty's protégée alone in the end, didn't she?" They sat pensively for a few moments. Ralph held Mia's hand and squeezed it.

"There was something else" Tony told them. "She damaged my car."

"Damaged your car? What did she do to it?" asked Mia.

Tony went to his mobile again and showed them the picture of the side of his car he'd taken for the insurance company.

"The car's parked outside if you want to see the damage for yourself" he told them. "It's scratched through to the base metal."

"But how do you know she did it? Did you see her?" asked Ralph.

"No, but there were black and red specs of paint in my car key; she'd done the damage with my own key! When I looked back towards the window she made the finger gesture."

"We can go to the Police" said Mia, brightening.

"I can't prove she did it" Tony said. "And she'd say I did it myself."

"But when would she have been able to do it?" asked Ralph cynically, wondering if a touch of paranoia was creeping into Tony.

"I told you she was a long time getting changed; she must have sneaked out then. It was a form of retribution knowing how much I love that car. Why she wanted retribution I don't know but she is sick in the head; we can't judge her actions on anything we know."

There was general agreement on that point.

"Oh Tony I'm so sorry" said Mia. "It's all my fault you got mixed up with her."

"Please don't apologise" he answered. "It's me that owes you the apology for not doing more to help you when I suspected Vicky was not what she seemed. I thought she was after your husband not you. She told me she had a younger sister that died. Maybe that's what turned her mind."

"What can we do about her?" Ralph said. "We can't just let her get away with all this misery she's inflicted on us."

"Maybe we should go to the Police" Mia suggested again.

"What evidence have we got?" Tony answered. "She's happened to have two friends that became depressed. Where's the crime in that?"

They were quiet again.

"I have an idea" Tony stated. "How about putting my picture of her on the hospital website. At least that would cause her some discomfort and embarrassment. You'd be able to do that Ralph, wouldn't you?"

"No" Mia jumped in. "If Ralph got caught he'd be in trouble."

"Pin it on a notice board then" Tony proposed. "You could do that whilst nobody was looking, surely."

"Hardly anyone would see it" Mia told him negatively. "She'd remove it before they had the chance."

"What about admitting she did the test" Tony tried again. "You said use of hospital equipment was against the rules."

Ralph and Mia both dismissed that idea on the grounds that they would risk getting into trouble themselves.

"Let's just forget Vicky" Ralph stated seeing Mia was fearful of a battle. "She's caused us enough problems. We'll avoid her and with any luck she will stay out of our lives."

"I agree" jumped in Mia gratefully. "There's no point in trying to start a feud with her. We'll just have to put the whole horrible experience behind us."

"What about her next poor victim?" Tony asked. "She's obviously a serial killer!"

"She hasn't actually killed anyone" Mia told him scornfully, intimating he was being over dramatic.

"She could have" he scoffed. "She would have been very happy to see Monty's student kill herself; and you, My-mi! We don't know if there's been anyone else."

Mia was pensive. Was her brother right? Did Vicky have the potential to be a serial killer?

"Well I don't think there's anything we can do" said Ralph. "I'll be satisfied if she stays away from Mia. I can't take responsibility for any possible future victims."

"I agree" said Mia. "I don't want any more trouble. I've a baby to consider now." Tony was frustrated by their negativity. Surely Ralph could have circulated the picture without getting caught?

They agreed to think on it and if any ideas came to mind tell the others. Tony could see his sister and brother-in-law had no stomach for revenge. He'd just have to do something on his own.

***

With some unease the young couple went into work on Monday. They'd seen both sets of parents at the week-end and the general joy at the news of the pregnancy had pushed their bad experiences to the back of their minds. Now they had to act as though nothing had happened in the last few months and naturally Mia was worried about bumping into Vicky.

It was helpful to Mia that her manager was so pleased to see her; it was as though Mia had been absent for weeks not days. Bina was relieved and delighted that Ralph had reached her on time to prevent the abortion. She'd romanticised Ralph's part and Mia didn't admit the truth, that he'd actually been too late. It pleased Bina to think she'd played a part in the couple's reconciliation and Mia saw no reason to shatter the illusion. Mia's other colleagues congratulated her on being pregnant with varying degrees of sincerity; it would mean them being short-handed during her maternity leave. Most of them noticed a complete change in her and were pleased to see a return of the Mia they had known a few months before. Generally, Mia settled back into work with a far more positive attitude than she'd had for weeks.

Ralph also had an easier day than expected. Don made no mention of Thursday and evidently wasn't going to pursue it. Furthermore, he gave Ralph a few pointers about the upcoming interview.

The week went by and neither of them saw or heard of Vicky; she was evidently just as keen to avoid them as they were her. By the second week they had settled into a post-Victoria sort of normality. Mia no longer felt the need to be tested to confirm they weren't siblings, the only medical arrangement she made was with her GP to oversee her pregnancy.

The long days of June and Mia's expanding girth made them feel relaxed and contented. They were preoccupied with the pregnancy and started house hunting. Ralph was awarded the promotion; everything was going well for them.

But can somebody like Vicky be ignored or avoided? Would she leave them alone? Would her very existence constantly lay in wait?

It was a few weeks later that the application arrived in Ralph's section. Vicky herself had signed the request form asking for Alan's computer to be checked against excessive internet use. It was a manager's prerogative to ask for such information if they had reason to suspect a member of staff was abusing work time. Alan had rebuffed a previous claim that there was a problem with the internet and only James's computer had been checked. Ralph, now manager of the team, looked at the application and was filled with foreboding.

Ralph didn't like Alan. His nasty gossiping had upset Mia. However he was sure the investigation would reveal something damning on Alan's computer. He wanted no part in getting an innocent person into trouble. What also worried Ralph was that it was not only Alan that Vicky was gunning for. She would know Ralph would suspect her but be obliged to reveal the facts. She was, in effect, forcing Ralph to reveal dismissible conduct that he knew was likely to be false. She had cornered him. If he took no action or tried to fudge it she'd bring the establishment down on him like a ton of bricks.

He contacted Alan by phone on the pretext that there'd been a fault reported. Alan was miffed but agreed to give his password.

"So your password is today's date and your surname!" Ralph exclaimed.

"I change it every day" Alan told him proudly.

"It's good to change it frequently" Ralph agreed "but not when it's so easy to work out!"

"I know you people want us all to act like we're in a spy ring or something" Alan said flippantly "but it's hard to remember all these passwords and who's going to be hacking into my computer!"

"How little you know!" thought Ralph but answered "you'll need to be more careful in future."

That night he worked late and entered Alan's computer remotely. It didn't take long to find the illegal sites that had been accessed, supposedly by Alan, it was just too easy. Again he wondered whether he, not Alan, was being set up. Over the previous two months Alan had apparently accessed a lot of pornographic websites. If Ralph ignored it he would be in trouble for not following up a serious issue. But could it look as though he had set Alan up? Everyone knew how Alan had treated Mia and that Ralph was unhappy about it. Could he be accused of fabricating the evidence? Surely that would be unlikely? But when Vicky was involved anything was possible.

He decided to take the matter to his manager, Jeffery Clark. They got on very well and he was a friend of Monty so might be sympathetic to Ralph's concerns.

The next day he explained his theory to Jeffery.

"It's difficult" pondered Jeffery. "I know why you're suspicious of Dr. Dolosa, I heard about that incident with Monty, but why would she do such a thing to her subordinate?"

"I don't know" answered Ralph seeing this wasn't going well. "But if she has set this man up it would be terrible."

"That's true but it's also terrible if he *is* accessing porn on work computers and in work time" Jeffery pointed out, unconvinced by Ralph's argument. "Have you looked at times and dates to see if he has been in the office on the days the sites were accessed?"

"Yes, I have thought of that and his record does confirm he has been at work when the sites were accessed. However, like the rest of the team he works in the laboratory for large portions of the day and it's impossible to prove when he was at his desk."

They were silent for a while.

"Would you give permission for us to request security put CCTV in the office?" Ralph asked.

"Hmm, I'm not sure" Jeffery answered wondering if he'd made a mistake choosing Ralph to manage the section. "What grounds would we have?"

"Alan Harper doesn't have a secure password" Ralph told him. "I suspect most of his colleagues know it. His computer isn't private and I have found somebody has used it to access pornographic sites."

The reasoning was sound.

"Yes, OK" Jeffery grasped the nettle. "You arrange it; I'll sign it off."

***

It was eight-thirty on Saturday night and the offices were deserted when Ralph accompanied a young employee from Security, carrying a pair of steps, to the Diagnostic Genetics Department. Ralph was in casual clothes including an old hooded top. He had the hood up even though it was summer. They crept into the office like a pair of agents in a Bond film; checking neighbouring rooms to ensure nobody was around. Ralph found himself breaking into a mild sweat. He was not cut out for this type of caper and his nerves were on edge.

They surveyed the office to decide where best to place the camera to ensure it was hidden but could view Alan's computer. Nobody must see them or suspect a camera had been installed. It was weird taking part in such a clandestine undertaking. Ralph found himself constantly surveying the office and looking out into the corridor. He had a creepy feeling that Vicky would turn up. The incident of her catching him late at work and seeing straight through his lies played heavily on his mind. Was it possible to outwit her?

They agreed to position the camera between some boxes stored above a cabinet. The young man set up his step ladder near another camera at the entrance to the block, displaced one of the false ceiling panels and climbed into the void to attach some cabling. He then made his way down the corridor with the steps lifting panels and feeding the cable through until he was above the office cabinet where he again disappeared up into the void. Ralph felt redundant during all this activity which seemed to be taking ages. He kept surveying the area outside, now in semi-darkness, half expecting to see Vicky lurking out there. The cable to the camera was dropped through and the young man crawled back out of the false ceiling onto the ladder.

"That cable's too visible" Ralph told him anxiously. "It's obvious from down here."

"It's OK" the youth answered with incredible confidence for his age. "I'm going to fix it to the corner; you won't be able to see it." After some time fiddling around he asked Ralph if he was satisfied the camera and cabling were hidden from view. Having got Ralph's approval he rang his colleague in the central security hub and waved his hands in front of Alan's computer to confirm the camera was focusing on the right place.

"All done" he said with a broad grin.

"Thanks" answered Ralph. "This mustn't get out, you know that don't you."

"Of course" the youth answered tetchily. "I do work in security!"

"Yes, sorry" Ralph apologised. "It's just that some people mention things inadvertently, like when they're in the pub or something, and I don't want *anyone* to hear about it."

"Mum's the word" the young man said with an edge of sarcasm as he placed his finger vertically across his pursed lips. He could see a line of sweat on Ralph's brow and wondered why he was wearing a hoody on such a warm evening. Was he trying to look cool? He was a bit past it, wasn't he?

They doubly checked they'd put everything back where it was

when they arrived. To the younger man's bemusement Ralph crawled along the corridor picking up balls of dust that had fallen when the panels were disturbed. To humour his paranoia the young man made a big show of checking under the desk and round the sides of the cupboard to ensure nothing had been displaced or left behind. Their mission completed, they crept back down the corridor like a pair of cat burglars and with a huge sigh of relief Ralph bade goodbye to his young accomplice. He had decided not to tell Mia what was going on; he didn't want to worry her. Now it was down to security to inform him whether anybody else used Alan's computer.

***

Unaware of her husband's problems Mia was finding life without Vicky much more palatable than she could have imagined: she was gradually regaining her old sunny disposition. She had thought a lot about Vicky since the day of the aborted abortion. She had gone over and over the conversations they'd had in the last three years. She was trying to determine just how malevolent her friend had been. There were facts that pointed to deceit she couldn't pass over as accidental or unintentional but she still couldn't believe Vicky had planned *everything*, including the test result.

"Mum, I want to ask you something" Mia was on the phone to Pam one night.

"What's that?"

"Did you tell Vicky about your affair?"

A short pause.

"Yes."

"When was that?"

"At your hen party" Pam said then added by way of explanation. "We were exchanging secrets."

"All that time ago" Mia said reflectively. "I'd only just met her. It's surprising I invited her after such a short time but she seemed so nice."

"Yes she did" Pam agreed. "I was certainly taken in!"

"So what was the secret she gave you in exchange?" Mia asked.

"Well" Pam breathed down the phone. "She'd been married to a nasty man and after the divorce she changed her name to Dolosa by deed pole so that he could never find her."

"Really?" Mia suspected there was no truth in this revelation. "Did she say what her name was before?"

"Let me think, it was the name of one of those minority political parties, yes, I know, it was Veritas."

"Veritas?" Mia repeated. "Another Hispanic name. That's strange as she's blue-eyed and blond! Anyway, she probably made the whole story up to get your sympathy, Mum, and open up."

"Yes I feel like an idiot now but why would I have imagined she was telling lies?"

"I know" answered Mia pensively. "We've always been honest with each other but with Vicky it's hard to believe anything she said was true. She told me she'd had an abortion but I suspect she made that up as well."

"She's out of our lives now and I think we should stop beating ourselves up about her" said Pam. "You've got a baby on the way, thankfully, and we should just concentrate on that."

"You're right Mum, oh and that reminds me, Ralph and I have got the afternoon off not this Friday but next. He's coming with me for a scan; we're very excited!"

"Why don't you come over for dinner on that Saturday?" Pam suggested. "We can look at the scan images."

"OK Mum, that'll be nice, thanks."

"I'll see if Tony can come too."

"Great! We'll see you Saturday week then."

"Look forward to it."

"Bye then."

"Bye Love."

***

Ralph was getting very tetchy by the end of the week; no word from security. Had Vicky seen the camera? He was beginning to think he wasn't going to be able to prove his allegation about Vicky and feared how this would reflect on his own character. So far all security had given him were the times that Alan was on his PC; no other people were seen using it. Ralph checked and no porn sites had been accessed since the camera was installed. He was sure Vicky had guessed there was a trap.

On Friday Jeffery came to see Ralph who had to admit there was no progress. Jeffery however had now received a complaint from Dr Dolosa because her request to the IT department for investigation into serious misconduct hadn't been acted upon for over a week. She had expected it to be investigated immediately. Jeffery told Ralph they wouldn't be able to delay for too much longer; she had a legitimate complaint. He gave Ralph one more week after which he thought they'd have to act. However he also made the point that it was only necessary to check the computer history for the last couple of weeks so if there were no more incidents of porn sites being accessed Alan would be clear. If in the next week porn sites were accessed they'd know who was responsible. Ralph was very satisfied with this result.

As the next week went on Ralph became despondent and fatalistic. Vicky must have suspected something wasn't right or given up on her scheme for other reasons. Then, on Thursday morning he received the call from security he'd been hoping for. They'd seen somebody else on Alan's computer.

He and Jeffery went down to the security central office known as The Hub where they were shown CCTV footage of Alan working at his desk. Then he left with a couple of his colleagues and the office was empty. Although he'd expected it, Ralph was still shocked to see Vicky appear on the screen. The camera caught a part of her body near the door then her face came into full view as she sat in front of Alan's computer.

"She was at his desk for a good ten minutes" the head of security informed them, adding "would you be able to see what she did whilst she was there?"

"Yes" answered Ralph mesmerised by Vicky's imagew "If you give me the exact times I'll get onto it straight away."

He felt vindicated for arranging the CCTV.

"Fancy that" Jeffery commented looking at the screen also mesmerised. "Fancy that!" he kept repeating.

Back in the office Jeffery decided to stay with Ralph whilst he accessed Alan's computer record. Sure enough, Vicky had spent the time accessing porn sites. They had caught her red-handed!

Jeffery told Ralph he would take the evidence to Ken, Vicky's manager, to furnish him with the facts. It would be up to him to take whatever action he thought fit. They didn't speculate on what might happen to Vicky. Ralph was relieved he'd extricated himself from a very difficult situation and at the same time very pleased with himself for catching Vicky.

***

On Friday morning Jeffery came to see Ralph with some news.

"I went to see Ken" he said "and he told me this was the second report he'd received alleging wrong-doing by Vicky. It seems an anonymous complaint has been made that she is carrying out private testing work with NHS equipment."

Ralph's stomach turned; was he going to be implicated after all? How ironic!

"Have they been able to prove anything?" he enquired as nonchalantly as possible.

"The cheeky cow had placed an advert!" Jeffery exclaimed. "Her mobile number was on it!"

Ralph was stunned to silence. He knew Vicky would never do anything so obvious. Somebody was getting even with her; there were enough that would want to!

"What will happen to her?" he asked.

"Oh you know the NHS" Jeffery scoffed. "There'll be an enquiry; she'll muddy the waters; they won't want to dismiss a precious doctor after spending all that money training her; they'll make an excuse for her behaviour or say it wasn't actually proved and get her to move on."

"But we have provided definite proof" Ralph argued indignant that their investigation may not be given the credence it deserved.

"You're missing the point!" he said. "She's clever and good at her job. They won't want to lose that talent for some petty staff issue."

"Petty staff issue?" Ralph repeated outraged. "I don't think Alan would see it like that!"

"As I said" Jeffery continued calmly. "She'll muddy the waters and they'll be happy for her to do so. If it makes you feel better she's unlikely to be able to continue in a management position. She'll probably end up working on a ward somewhere, she won't be very happy with that."

Ralph was irritated by Jeffery's cynicism but conceded he was probably right. At least Vicky would be moving on and away from Mia. It wouldn't be the best outcome but would be enough.

***

It was Friday night and Vicky was in that end-of-the-working-week mood as she lounged back on her sofa with a large glass of red wine. She smiled as she thought of the anxiety she was giving Ralph. He'd be in a right state having to expose Alan's bad behaviour. He'd know she'd set up Alan but he wouldn't be able to do anything about it. Still his discomfort was small consolation for her failure to get Mia to kill herself. She had worked on that for years and it galled her to see Mia back at work more cheerful than ever. Not only that but it was evident that Mia hadn't gone through with the abortion! How was that? She'd watched Mia go with the nurse. At what point did she have the chance to change her mind? Now the whole project was lost. She'd never get to Mia now she was back with Ralph in marital bliss. It made Vicky feel sick. What also irked her was the realisation that the whole charade with Mia's brash, self-loving brother had been completely unnecessary! She had to admit she had underestimated him. He was shrewder than she'd expected. She shouldn't have let him get away with taking that photo. Now she wondered where and when that would turn up. Still, at least he hadn't hit her. She'd goaded him but looking at her broken door panel she was grateful she hadn't succeeded. She did get even with the car damage; he looked as though he might cry when he saw it!

Looking back the whole Mia venture had been maddening and upsetting. The only consolation was that she'd learnt from the experience. She'd been too ambitious choosing Mia who had so much support. Next time she would pick somebody more isolated. There were plenty of immigrant women working at the hospital whose families were miles away. She still liked the idea of inducing her victim to kill somebody else; the thought was more warming than the wine. She'd spotted a nurse in geriatrics as her possible next victim but she would need to get to know her. She wanted to get it right next time.

Meanwhile she was excited over a discovery James had made in the laboratory. He was a bright young man and this had the potential for Vicky to get a paper published in one of the medical journals; that would give her professional respect and enhance her promotional prospects. Of course she would mention James in the footnote but it was a manager's prerogative to take credit for their staff's work; she'd make sure he got a minor promotion out of it.

She had a good week in front of her. On Monday she'd start by complaining to Ralph's boss again, she looked forward to imagining the torture on poor Ralph's face. Later in the week she'd make some discreet enquiries about that nurse and "help" James write up his discovery.

She took another sip of wine and thought again resentfully about Mia and Ralph; stupid, pathetic pair of idiots! They deserved each other! They'd live a boring life at the bottom of the pile whilst she waved from the dizzy heights of upper management!

Suddenly she felt a strange cool breeze. She looked towards the open window but the air was sultry and still; the curtain remained straight. She had a distinct feeling there was somebody in the room but she couldn't see anyone. A cold chill encircled her. She tentatively got up from the chair. She thought she heard a faint sound. She listened carefully; it sounded like her dead sister! It *was* her sister! That annoying laugh! Now she was scared. She surveyed the room uncertainly; eyes wide. She slowly started to head for the door; she needed to get out of the flat. But the chilled air turned colder freezing her to the spot. In front of her she saw an image of Annie. It stayed for a few seconds staring, then waved goodbye and disappeared, the frosty atmosphere leaving with it.

She blinked and looked around the room. There was nothing to indicate anything untoward had taken place; she no longer felt cold. "I must be imagining things" she thought looking at her half-empty glass. "I must have had too much to drink. All the recent disappointments have upset me more than I realised. Never mind, everything will look better next week."

***

On Saturday afternoon Ralph and Mia sat on the train to Dorking looking over the pictures of the scan; it was so exciting to see actual proof of the baby and they stared at the picture in wonder pointing to bits of it trying to make out the detail.

John and Pam were delighted to see them and Mia could tell they were making a special effort not to argue. Tony welcomed them with a big grin. Ralph couldn't wait to tell them about Vicky.

"So she's *still* likely to carry on as a doctor" Tony confirmed after hearing about the misdemeanours, disappointment and outrage in his tone. "Surely being found out to be dishonest is dismissible!"

"I know what you mean and that's what I said to my boss" agreed Ralph. "He may be wrong, we'll just have to see what the board decide. Vicky will have a cloud hanging over her for some time. I know I can prove she was using Alan's computer to search porn sites, she can't argue with that. I'm not sure they can prove she put the advert in the paper."

"Who else would use her mobile number in an advert?" reasoned Tony.

Ralph faltered. He hadn't mentioned anything about the mobile number being in the advert. He decided to remain ignorant of any skulduggery Tony may have been up to.

"I don't care what they do" he said. "At least she'll be out of our hair!"

Everyone agreed that was a good thing and there was a general desire to move on from talking about Vicky.

Mia reached into her bag and delightedly took out the photos of the scan. They all made enthusiastic noises though Tony couldn't make out which bit of the fuzz was the baby.

"Can you tell the sex?" he asked.

"We couldn't" answered Ralph. "But they could. You can leave it as a surprise if you want but we agreed that we would like to know."

"Come on then, tell us!" exclaimed Pam.

"It's a girl" said Mia.

"Any ideas for names?" asked John.

"Not yet" answered Mia but then Ralph piped up.

"Annie" he said "we'll call her Annie!"

"Annie?" said Mia. "What made you think of that name?"

"I don't know" he answered. "It just came to me!"

Mia considered the unexpected suggestion.

"Actually" she said "I *do* like Annie, it's a lovely name. Why not? Annie it is then. She'll be the most loved and looked after child in the world!"

Postscript

SWINDON ARGUS

Thursday 19th September 1996

COUPLE FOUND DEAD IN SUICIDE PACT
AFTER LOSS OF "MIRACLE" DAUGHTER

A local couple have been found dead after colleagues raised the alarm when they didn't turn up for work. Police discovered Mr Antony Veritas and his wife Maria, who were both emploees at Honda UK in Swindon, after breaking into the couple's house last Friday. They were in the front seats of their car parked in the garage; a pipe had been run into the car from the exhaust. They died of asphyxiation.

Mr Veritas, who was 51, had been with Honda since 1981 and was Manager of the purchasing department. Mrs Veritas, aged 48, started working for the Company's accounts department 5 years ago. Neighbours told the Argus that the couple had been devastated by the death of their nine year old daughter, Annie, who drowned two years ago in a lake whilst the family were on holiday in Kent.

Mr & Mrs Veritas had been told they would never be able to have children and they adopted their first daughter Victoria as a baby. However, nearly six years later, against all odds, Mrs Veritas gave birth to their daughter Annie. They called her their miracle child.

Victoria Veritas, now seventeen, had been walking along the lakeside with Annie on the day she died but had felt unwell and

256

returned to the family's rented caravan alone. When Annie did not return her parents and some other holiday makers started a search. She was discovered by a young man who took a boat onto the lake and found her tangled in the reeds. An ambulance was called but the paramedics were unable to save her.

The Argus reported on the accident at the time and although it was not clear what had happened to Annie the police found no evidence of foul play. Mr & Mrs Veritas were never satisfied with the outcome of the investigation as they were sure Annie, who was a weak swimmer, would not have chosen to swim across the lake, especially fully clothed.

Victoria, the only remaining member of the family, is currently staying with a friend. She has just started a four year degree course in medicine at Imperial College London. She was not available for comment.

About The Author

Pippa Barnes

Pippa spent many years working as an Environmental Health Officer within various London Boroughs. She believes the best life experience can be had in the workplace where people rub shoulders with others they wouldn't necessarily have otherwise met and there is opportunity to witness ambition, stress and dogma.

Note from the Author

I wrote this book with the intension of entertaining you, the reader. I hope you enjoyed it and I should be grateful for any balanced feedback or review you can give me.

Printed in Great Britain
by Amazon

62727250R00153